ANNA, SOROR . . .
with
AN OBSCURE MAN and A LOVELY MORNING

Born in Brussels in 1903, Marguerite Yourcenar was
nurtured on the Classics of Greece and Rome and
could also read English, Spanish and Italian literature
fluently in the original. After the Second World War
she settled in the eastern United States. In 1981 she was
elected to the Académie Française, the first woman to
be so honoured. A writer all her life, she has seen her
books translated into some two dozen languages.
Among the novels for which she is best remembered is
Memoirs of Hadrian. Marguerite Yourcenar died in
1987.

The present volume, originally published in English
as *Two Lives and a Dream*, comprises, as the author
says, "the third panel of a triptych of which *Memoirs of
Hadrian* and *The Abyss* form the other two". *The Abyss*,
as well as *Alexis* and *Coup de Grâce* are to be published
in Harvill Paperbacks.

Marguerite Yourcenar

ANNA, SOROR . . .

WITH

AN OBSCURE MAN

AND

A LOVELY MORNING

Translated from the French by Walter Kaiser
in collaboration with the author

HARVILL
An Imprint of HarperCollins*Publishers*

First published in 1982 by Editions Gallimard
under the title *Comme l'eau qui coule*
First published in Great Britain in 1987
by Aidan Ellis
This edition published in 1992
by Harvill
an imprint of HarperCollins Publishers,
77/85 Fulham Palace Road,
Hammersmith, London W6 8JB

9 8 7 6 5 4 3 2 1

© 1982 Editions Gallimard
Translation © 1987 by Walter Kaiser

A CIP catalogue record for this book
is available from the British Library.

ISBN 0–00–271222–9

Printed and bound in Great Britain by
Hartnolls Limited, Bodmin, Cornwall

CONTENTS

AN
OBSCURE
MAN

for Jerry Wilson

When the news of Nathanaël's death on a small Frisian island reached Amsterdam, it caused little stir. His uncle Elie and his aunt Eva agreed that such an end had not been unexpected. What is more, two years before, Nathanaël had almost died in the Amsterdam hospital; his second death, as it were, hardly aroused any emotion. It was rumored that his wife Saraï (had she really been his wife?) had died before him—better not to ask just how. As for Lazarus, the child of the couple, Elie Adriansen could not see himself going to look for the orphan all the length of the Jodenstraat, in the home of an old woman whose eyes were too black and lively and who for better or worse passed for his grandmother.

Nathanaël's birth had also been inconspicuous; yet it must be admitted that in both cases that is standard, for it is without much ado that most people enter this world and without much ado that they leave it. The first of these two events, if indeed it could be called an event, had interested no more than half a dozen Dutch housewives living in Greenwich with their husbands, carpenters working for the Lord Admiral and well paid in good shillings and pence. This small group of foreigners, looked down upon as such but respected for their industry and their unshakable Protestantism, lived in a row of spotless little houses along the edge of the dry dock. Their maritime village, which was downstream from Greenwich, sloped in one direction toward the riverbank, where masts rose above the roofs and sheets were hung out to dry alongside the sails; in the other direction, the shanties of the town disappeared into a still-rural area of cottages and grazing land. The father of the newborn child was a red-faced man, fat yet agile, forever perched on a ladder leaning against an unfinished hull. His mother, steeped in the Bible, scrubbed her children and simmered stews which her English neighbors wouldn't have touched any more than she would have been willing to taste their exceedingly rare roast beef.

Since little Nathanaël was weak-chested and afflicted with a slight lameness, he was not sent with his brothers to scrape the sides of ships in dry dock or to drive nails into the planks. He was put into the charge of a neighborhood schoolmaster who took an interest in the boy.

His upkeep wouldn't cost the family much. He could do small chores for the schoolmaster, such as filling the inkwells, sharpening the quills, and sweeping the classroom floor; he could help the schoolmaster's wife draw water from the well and hoe the garden. In time, they would make him into a preacher or a teacher like his master.

Nathanaël was happy at the schoolmaster's, despite the slaps and blows which rained down on the schoolboys. He was soon charged with teaching the alphabet to the youngest of his fellow students, but he did it badly, never managing to strike their fingers with the iron ferule in time. Nevertheless, for the boys of his own age, his attention to his lessons and his gentleness set a good example. In the evening, after the students had gone, the teacher allowed him to read, in summer as long as it was light in the garden, in winter by the light of the kitchen fire. The school possessed several large tomes which the teacher considered too valuable, and too hard to read, to be used by the unruly students, who would soon have torn them to shreds. There was a Cornelius Nepos, an odd volume of Virgil, another of Livy, an atlas in which one could see England and the four continents with the sea all around them decorated with dolphins, and a celestial planisphere about which the man was not always able to answer the boy's questions. Among the less serious books, there were a number of plays by a certain Shakespeare which had been a success in their day, and the tale of Perceval printed in Gothic letters which were difficult to decipher. The teacher had bought all of them cheap from the widow of a local vicar who, so far as books were concerned, valued only her dead husband's sermons. In this way, Nathanaël learned to speak correct English, which they slaughtered in his own home, as well as a little Latin, for which he had a certain talent. The teacher liked instructing him, since, no longer employed in a good London school, he rarely had the opportunity to use his own gifts. He was pitiless about grammar, and he scanned Virgil by tapping his finger on the desk.

When Nathanaël was fifteen, he began to keep company with a blond girl his age, somewhat saucy, somewhat shy, who was quite pretty. She was called Janet and was apprenticed to a tapestrymaker. On sunny days, they ate their bread and drank their cider together in a nearby meadow; later, they fell into the habit of walking in the woods, where Nathanaël gathered plants for his master's herbarium. Thus it was that they came to make love on a bed of bracken or grass; he took care of her as best he could, and it was tacitly understood between them that one day they would get married.

Once, she arrived at one of these rendezvous utterly terrified. A man from the town, a ship's chandler, who drank and was reputed to like young, adolescent bodies, had for some time been badgering her with propositions sprinkled with threats. On those evenings when they went out together, Nathanaël was henceforth careful to accompany her all the way back to the tapestrymaker's door and wait until it had closed behind her. One evening in May, as they were returning hand-in-hand, the drunkard blocked their way. He had apparently followed them and observed them on their bed of bracken, because he teased them about their lovemaking in a dirty, graphic way. More abruptly and deftly than a frightened fawn, Janet took flight. The man rushed after her in pursuit; luckily, he stumbled. He was so shaky on his feet that he grabbed hold of Nathanaël, putting his arm around his neck, whether to regain his balance or as the result of a sudden, foolish affection. His propositions were now addressed to the schoolboy. Nathanaël, overcome with fright and disgust (he couldn't have said which feeling was the stronger), pushed him away, grabbed a stone, and struck him full in the face.

When he saw the man lying on the ground, barely breathing, with a trickle of blood at the corner of his lips, he became panic-stricken. If someone had seen him from afar or if Janet were to recount the incident, he would be apprehended by order of the constable and made ready for hanging the next morning.

He in turn fled, but with the halting step of his lame leg; and in any case, he couldn't run, since that would have attracted the attention of passersby. Choosing the most deserted alleyways, circling around the dry dock where there was possibly a watchman still on guard at this late hour, he arrived at the place on the riverbank where he knew several large ships were to set sail at dawn. One of them appeared to be empty, with the hatchway in the middle of the deck wide open and a line from the winch hanging over it. The crew had no doubt gone ashore for one last drink. There was only a dog on board, but Nathanaël never failed to make friends with dogs. The boy slid down the line into the hold and concealed himself among some barrels.

All night long, paralyzed with fear, he listened to the footsteps of the men coming back on board, to the bang of the heavy hatch as it slammed shut, to the faint sounds of the wind and water against the hull, to the whine of the rigging, to the slapping of the slack sails. Finally, at dawn, he was aware that they were slipping downriver, but his fear did not abate. A calm could hold them moored near the coast, or, on the other hand, a storm could force them back into port. At the end of two days and three nights, dead with hunger, he feebly hailed some men who had come down with shovels to redistribute the ballast. At that point, the ship was already off the Scilly Isles. He soon realized that the boat was on its way to Jamaica.

The men dragged the trembling boy up onto the deck. Someone proposed throwing him into the water as a joke. But the cook, a half-breed, interceded for him; this young tramp could take care of the hens and the hog they had put on board and do the drudgery in the galley. The captain, who was not a bad man despite his fierce look, agreed. In the half-breed, Nathanaël found a protector on board. Surprisingly, he accepted from him without any repugnance the intimacies which had horrified him when proposed by the drunkard in Greenwich. Nathanaël felt an affection for this man with bronze skin who was good to him. He failed to appreciate the pleasure the other might take in protecting and caressing a young white boy.

·   ·   ·

7

At Jamaica, they made a long stop to unload the cargo brought from England and to take on a load of precious wood which would end up cut into panels and marquetry in the handsome mansions of London. The half-breed was a native of the island; he introduced Nathanaël to the fruit of his homeland and took him to shacks where there were girls much in demand just then, for several large vessels were in port. Nathanaël waited his turn with the others. These beauties pleased him because of the softness of their skin and the even greater softness of their eyes, which were shaded with long lashes, and because of their tranquil abandon. But these episodes of purchased love, reduced for lack of time to a brief embrace, and these men crowded about the doorway, all obsessed with the same desire, filled him with a vague loathing: it wasn't merely a question of fearing infection; he would have liked to have had one of these girls completely to himself for a long time, perhaps forever, as he had thought he would have Janet. But it wasn't good to dream about such things.

He pitied the blacks mounting the gangway, bent under heavy beams; perhaps they were no more miserable than the stevedores in the port of London, but at least the stevedores were not obliged to work under the lash. Despite their lacerated flesh, they often laughed, baring their white teeth. In the hottest hour of the day, when the overseers themselves stretched out in the shade, Nathanaël would laugh and chat with them.

They set sail for Barbados. The day before, the half-breed had been stabbed in the eye with a knife during a brawl. The wound became infected, and he died in great pain. They committed him to the sea after having recited a psalm over him; in truth, no one knew if he had been baptized or not. Nathanaël wept for him. He was given the job, now vacant, of cook; he did as well as he could, but in Santo Domingo he left the ship. He signed on as a sailor with an English frigate armed with four cannon which was getting ready to cruise the coasts of the Northeast to contest the encroachments of the French.

The sea that summer was almost always calm and, in certain latitudes, virtually empty. The farther north they went, the more the sultry humidity gave way to fresh breezes; the transparent sky became milky whenever a thin layer of mist covered it; on the banks of the mainland or of the islands (it was not always easy to tell one from the other), impenetrable forests descended to the seashore. Nathanaël vaguely remembered the virgin forests at the edge of sanctuaries that Virgil speaks of. But these places did not seem to contain either ancient gods or the fairies or sprites he sometimes thought he saw in the woods of England, only air and water, trees and rocks. Nevertheless, life stirred there in a multitude of forms. Thousands of marine birds floated on the swells or perched in the hollows of the cliffs; a handsome stag or a huge moose sometimes swam across the channel between two islands, lifting high its head encumbered with great antlers, then snorting as it clambered up onto the shore.

A number of times, Indians in canoes came up to the ship, proffering leather flasks of fresh water, berries, or still-bloody quarters of venison, and asking for rum in exchange. A few of them had retained several words of English, sometimes of French, as a result of this sort of bartering; on board ship, they always made sure that an officer or sailor was able to speak a bit of the jargon of at least one of the Indian dialects. Occasionally, they took one of these savages on board to act as pilot through a difficult passage.

One fine day, one of them imparted some news: a tiny band of white men of an especially serious and wise appearance, who spent their days in ceremonies honoring

9

their gods, had been abandoned on a nearby island by the mutinous crew of their ship; these men had lived there for a number of months now. The Indians of the mainland, who frequented that area in the fishing season, had sometimes given them food; the chief of the Abenaki, who had been confined to his camp by a long illness, had summoned them to demand a tribute of strong drink; they didn't have any, but they had poured some water on his head so that he would be favored by the Great Spirit; and since then, the chief had been better.

It wasn't the first time that the captain had heard tell of Jesuits come from France to convert the savages of Canada. Apart from the fact that these Catholic pretensions were insufferable, everyone was aware that the priests almost never settled anywhere without being supported by a rear guard of soldiers and merchants from their homeland. These men were the emissaries of the king who called himself *Très Chrétien*.

The island in question had only recently been indicated on maps. Steep and rocky, covered in its low areas with pines and oaks, its six or seven mountains could be seen from afar. Nothing valuable had been found there, but an arm of the sea reached far into the island from the south, forming a vast natural port marvelously sheltered from the wind. A small oval isle protected its entrance; on the left bank, at the foot of a large meadow, there was a spring of fresh water well known to navigators. Such advantages were enough for the King of England to fight over the place with the King of France. As one approached the shore, one could see, at the edge of the dark pines mixed with oaks already reddened by autumn, some huts made of pelts and boughs that the Indians must have helped the intruders to build. A great cross rose in the midst of them. The captain opened fire. Nathanaël had a horror of all violence, yet the exhilaration of the men working the cannons was infectious; the noise of the cannons echoed all along the low mountains. It was doubtless the first time those mountains had thrown back this human thunder, never having known until then anything but the rumble of lightning and, during the spring thaw, the cracking of blocks of ice as they broke away from the cliffs. From the distance at which the ship stood, they saw men in soutanes scatter into the tall grass. Two of them fell; the rest took refuge in the woods.

A longboat was sent out and made fast to the bank. When the huts were ripped open, the only booty they offered was a small pile of clothing and food, together with some books and a case of instruments, which the captain took possession of. Nathanaël noticed that one of the fathers had started a herbarium; its dried leaves rustled in the wind. There was also a notebook in which one of the Jesuits had begun a dictionary of the Indian language, with Latin equivalents in red ink. Nathanaël pocketed it, since no one else would have wanted it, but he later lost it.

He ran to see if he could help the two men who had fallen, aware that his comrades would give no thought to such a task. But the meadow was larger and contained more uneven ground than he had realized; he felt lost in this sea of grass. At all events, one of the two men was already dead. Nathanaël cautiously drew close to the second, who was still breathing. He gave little credence to the angry denunciations of the preachers he had gone to hear in the meetinghouse he attended with his parents during his childhood in Greenwich, and hatred for the Catholics, the enemies of the King of England, did not exist in him; nevertheless, he had been taught to fear Papists and Frenchmen. But this young man was not dangerous: he was dying. A portion of his thorax had been smashed in, and the blood, almost invisibly, was soaking his black soutane. Nathanaël lifted his head and spoke to him, first in English, then in Dutch, without being able to make himself understood. It occurred to him then to ask him in Latin what he could do to make him more comfortable. But the Latin of the Greenwich schoolmaster was doubtless somewhat different from that of a French Jesuit. Nevertheless, the dying man understood enough to say, with a weak smile of surprise: *"Loquerisne sermonem latinam?"*

"Paululum," replied Nathanaël shyly.

He took off his sailor's jacket to use it as a blanket for the dying man, who was no doubt chilled. The Frenchman begged him to take out of the pocket of his soutane a thick little book, which turned out to be a breviary, and to tear out the flyleaf, where several words were written. They were his name and the name of the town where his seminary was located.

"Amice," said the dying man, *"si aliquando epistulam superiori meo scribebis, mater et soror meae mortem meam certa fide dicerent . . ."*

Nathanaël carefully folded the paper and promised to write to the superior of Angelus Guertinus, *ex seminario Annecii,* so that his mother and his sister would not be left in uncertainty. Annecium meant nothing to him, and Annecy would not really have meant any more. The only thing that mattered was to console a man in his death agony. The young priest, lifting himself slightly on his elbow, asked him to open the book to a place he designated; Nathanaël recognized the psalms he had read in translation in his parents' Bible, but they sounded strange in this wilderness which knew nothing of the God of a kingdom called Israel nor of the Roman Church nor of those Luther and Calvin had founded. Yet some of the verses were beautiful—those about the sea, about the valleys and the mountains, and about the great affliction of man. His voice broke, as it used to when he read Virgil in school.

"*Summa voce, oro*," the young Jesuit whispered to him, either because he found it hard to understand the Latin words as Nathanaël pronounced them or else because his hearing was failing. He breathed now only with great difficulty. Nathanaël laid the breviary in the grass and ran to collect a handful of water from the stream which flowed only two steps away. The dying man painfully swallowed a mouthful.

"*Satis, amice,*" he said.

Even before the last drops had run down Nathanaël's fingers, the priest Ange Guertin, from the seminary at Annecy, was no more. It was time to reboard the ship. Nathanaël took back his jacket, now of no use to the dead man.

This instant later came back to him many times in dreams. But the person he gave the water to often changed as the years passed. Some nights it seemed to him that the person he attempted to help in this way was none other than himself.

The captain headed northeast. One of his orders was to check on what remained of a small English colony which had been established in recent memory farther to the north, on an island situated at the mouth of the Sainte-Croix River. It was rumored that this settlement was in danger. For several days there was heavy weather; the captain feared the enormous tides that broke on this coast during the equinox. He had just given the order to turn half-circle when a gust of wind threw them onto the dangerous island they were seeking. The vessel stuck between the rocks had not suffered great damage; but the gale redoubled in force as the tide rose, and the huge waves lifted the hull and left it high and dry. Its wooden backbone cracked. Nathanaël managed to jump onto a rock that was almost above the waterline, but an even bigger wave carried him away. He remembered hanging on to the end of a plank. Later, he learned that the undertow had dropped him unconscious at the end of a small sandy bight.

He came to on a pallet, lying between two or three large stones which had been heated and placed near him so that they could transmit their warmth to him. Under the low beams he perceived the faces of an old man and an old woman bent over him (or at least their appearance was so worn that one would have called them old), a very young girl with gaunt cheeks, and a child of perhaps twelve, who smiled continuously. There were also several other people squatting around a heap of objects that he recalled having seen on board ship. He was so exhausted that he fell back to sleep. But his constitution was good. At the end of several days, he felt practically no effects from his accident.

He soon realized that he was the only survivor of the crew. This disaster had caused mixed feelings in the small population of the island. Of the colony decimated by long winters, bad summers, smallpox, and French guns, there remained no more than seven or eight homesteads. For a long time these people had counted on the arrival of a ship which would replenish their provisions and perhaps take them back to their homeland. At least, they claimed to want such a return; in fact, notions of homeland and obedience to a master scarcely signified anything to them any longer; this poor island, whose name was not even to be found on maps, seemed to have returned to a time when it belonged to no one. Many of the cabins constructed some twenty years earlier had collapsed and were scarcely visible beneath the scrub growth and high grass.

A family of some ten people, suspected of causing ship-
wrecks with false signals when the occasion presented itself, lived alone farther north near a long sandbank; there
were also rumors about these people concerning stolen
sheep. To the east and south, a few cabins were hidden
in the trees; faint paths, indicated here and there by small
piles of stones, connected one to the other. In the winter,
they disappeared under the snow. A trapper, undoubtedly
chased out of Quebec for some ill deed, had settled in a
clearing with his wife Madeleine, of Abenaki blood, and
their straight-haired, dark-eyed children, and he did not
think of living anywhere else. Two brothers who had
settled on a small bay sold salt they produced by boiling
seawater in a great cauldron. They also used their prod-
uct, along with other stinking ingredients, to tan the hides
that were brought to them or those they skinned from
their prey; the other inhabitants relied on them to stitch
their boots and repair their snowshoes. The people there
had their own way of life; it is doubtful if they more than
barely remembered the Norfolk village where they had
grown up. A gentleman who, it was said, had fought in
Flanders and had been a member of the court of King
James, lived all alone at the foot of a cliff with his Indian
servant. Like Nathanaël, he perhaps had had reasons for
leaving England. The elderly pastor of the colony, having
been incapacitated by a stroke, no longer preached. With
his wife, his widowed daughter, and her sons, he scratched
out a living on a little farm. The family that had rescued
Nathanaël was comprised of the old man, who in his time
had also served on an English frigate; the old woman,
originally from La Rochelle, who had washed up there
after the wreck of a boat that was going to some French
outpost; their daughter named Foy; and a simpleminded
boy they hadn't bothered to name. These old people were
senselessly attached to this place where they had suffered

for twenty years, and they would have dreaded a long sea voyage. The children, ignorant of anything else, were unable to imagine that life might be better elsewhere.

But the wreck of the ship they had awaited so long had had its good aspects. Once the sea had calmed, these wretched people managed to bring ashore most of the cargo. No one lacked tin plates, tools, or blankets any longer, and they had even saved several cases of salted provisions almost intact. Nathanaël soon understood that it was not simply love for their fellow man that had caused the two old people to revive and heal him: even though they were still fairly strong, they realized that a sturdy twenty-year-old boy would be a considerable help to them in their labors, and Foy was of an age where she might take a husband.

As soon as he had recovered, Nathanaël assisted in the chores of the bad season, helping the old man attach a new handle to a scythe, caulking the canoe, and going every day to feed and water the horse, the cow, and several sheep stalled in the stable, which was also a grange. This shed was built against the cabin, so that the warmth from the animals' quarters passed into those of the family, and vice versa; a rope along the outside wall led from the door of the house to that of the stable; they held on to it when they went to the animals during snowstorms, for fear of turning in circles and dying where they were without finding the door to the house a few feet away. When the snow was hard, they transported dead wood or freshly cut timber. The little horse dragged the large trunks. When the water froze over, they went down to the bay and chopped holes in the ice to fish through.

The house had only one room, but a ladder led up to a garret. Only a short time elapsed before the old man and woman installed a pallet for two up there against the warmest wall, the one heated by the hearth below. There was no question of going to the minister, who lived the whole length of the island away, but the old people pronounced a benediction over this primitive sort of bed and its ragged counterpane. Every night, Nathanaël and Foy went up into their dark resting place, dark because both economy and fear of fire were sufficient reasons not to take a candle up there. Nathanaël loved this darkness. It felt good to sleep there or to caress each other until dawn, warmly lost in each other's arms. During their lovemaking, Foy trembled, uttered little cries, held Nathanaël prisoner in her smooth arms and legs; her hands and feet, which were always exposed to the inclement weather, were by contrast callused and covered with chilblains.

When spring came, they all went to work in the fields. They began working as the migratory birds were returning northward; the Indian children, who had great skill in shooting with the bow, came with wild geese killed in full flight, which they bartered for whatever grain was left. At other times, they brought rabbits they had clubbed to death or felled with slings: it was one of their favorite games. Since gunpowder was scarce, they generally killed the large animals of the woods by digging pits which they concealed with branches and in which the animal would slowly die, sometimes with its legs broken by its fall, sometimes impaled on stakes set into the bottom, until someone came to finish it off with a knife. Nathanaël undertook to do this once, but it made him so ill that he was not given the task again. In the water of the bay, which was almost always calm, they constructed a sort of labyrinth out of barriers of thorns and reeds in which the fish entrapped themselves; they were then dragged along the ground in a net, thrashing about and suffocating unless they were bludgeoned to death with blows of an oar. Instead of fishing, Nathanaël preferred gathering berries, so plentiful when they were in season that the color of the barrens was changed by them; Foy's hands and his were reddened by the juice of strawberries and turned blue by that of overripe blueberries. Although bears were rare on the island, where they hardly ever ventured except in winter when the ice supported them, Nathanaël came upon one, completely alone, gathering into his great paw all the raspberries from a bush and stuffing them into his mouth with such an exquisite pleasure that the boy practically experienced it himself. There was nothing to fear from these mighty beasts when they were gorged on fruit and honey, so long as they themselves did not feel threatened. He spoke to no one of this encounter, as if there had been some sort of pact between the animal and himself.

Nor did he speak of the fox cub he encountered in a clearing, who looked at him with an almost friendly curiosity, not moving, his ears erect like those of a dog. He kept secret that part of the woods where he had seen snakes, for fear that the old man would decide to kill what he called "them varmints." The lad was deeply attached even to trees; he felt sorry for them because, tall and majestic as they were, they were incapable of fleeing or defending themselves and were victims of the ax of the feeblest woodsman. He had no one, not even Foy, to confess these feelings to.

In spite of her cough and her slight shortness of breath, Foy worked like a man. She showed her young husband how to tie up sheaves and build ricks; she helped him pull out of the ground the big rocks which stuck up everywhere and impeded the tilling. Sometimes, when the old people were not within eyesight, she would lie down in the half-dry grass, which would make her laugh because she was ticklish, and, lifting her ragged skirts, she would entice Nathanaël to her. He liked that. Afterwards, he would think of Janet, not that he had loved her more, but because Janet and Foy seemed to him to be the same woman. Both of them liked to sing, in a small, high-pitched voice, bits of songs they never knew completely; both of them liked to stick flowers in their hair. But Foy's cheeks were always somewhat warm, as if she had a fever, and she was subject to heavy sweats, which would suddenly chill her.

When her illness worsened, they called in an Indian medicine man who exorcised sickness. He burned sprigs of herbs which filled the cabin with a strange, acrid odor, went into contortions, fell to the ground, and emitted hoarse cries which were at the same time chants; but Foy got neither better nor worse.

The Micmac and the Abenaki who came to the island in the fishing season bore no grudge against the few whites who painfully scraped a living out of the soil there. And anyway, the aged trapper and his Indian squaw acted as intermediaries between the bronze-colored men and those whose skin was more or less white. Nathanaël admired the physical endurance of these savages, the hardness of their dark, almost naked bodies, their care not to take more game than was strictly necessary to allay their hunger, and their almost complete disdain for all the man-made objects the whites had so bitterly fought over after the wreck of the *Tethys*. He observed, though, that these same Indians would willingly give all their catch for some old knife. Their habit of pissing straight in front of them, wherever they were, even inside the cabins, was a filthy one, but he thought that a horse or an ox, whose calm pride theirs resembled, would have done the same. Warfare often broke out among them; it was said they inflicted horrible tortures on their prisoners in order to honor them by giving them a chance to show how much courage they possessed; they would take the scalps back to their huts after having lifted them aloft five times on the point of their spears so as to liberate the soul. But Nathanaël remembered the heads of victims of torture hung from the gate of the Tower of London, and he realized that men are everywhere the same.

Each morning, he would seat Foy on a bench warmed by the autumn sun, but the old people always insisted that she do her part of the work. She could be heard coughing far off in the fields. They became solicitous of her only when she was no longer able to leave her pallet. The old woman boiled lichens for her that Nathanaël would collect from the rocks. At night, he slept on some sacks so that she might sleep more comfortably, but she would beg him to lie next to her, to comfort and warm her. Every time a trickle of blood came into her mouth, the fear of death shone in her eyes. Yet she passed away very quickly and almost without suffering at the beginning of October. It was at the time when the forests, scorched by the summer sun, produced great masses of reds, dark purples, and golden yellows. Nathanaël told himself that the queens for whom they draped the churches of London had far less beautiful obsequies than these. The old man took his mind off his grief by digging the grave: as he was digging, he saw a mole he had disturbed in its underground lair and brutally cut it in half with a blow of his shovel. Without knowing quite why, the memory of Foy and that of this slaughtered creature always remained linked in Nathanaël's mind.

He wanted to leave immediately. That would have been difficult, but not impossible. The Abenaki had informed him (for rumors spread through the woods) that the Jesuits of Mount Desert Island who had survived the guns of the *Tethys* had found refuge in an Indian encampment and that the Indians had taken them across the wide bay in a canoe and led them northward into the French sector. If the redskins were to stay a bit longer to take advantage of the days of calm sea for their fishing, he could perhaps persuade them to do the same for him before the bad weather set in; and one of the vessels bearing the fleur-de-lis which came from time to time to New France would surely have need of a sailor. He could disembark in some port in Normandy or Brittany and from there he could get either to Holland or to England, depending on the luck of the wind or on that of peace and war; if it turned out to be England, he could always conceal himself under an assumed name. He had no doubt he could find some school-teacher in a village far from London, and especially far from Greenwich, who would be in need of an assistant; that way, he could return to his studies. From this distance, his schoolboy years seemed to him marvelously peaceful and easy. Or else he could remain a sailor, could go back to the Caribbean, or might visit the ports of Asia. But the right moment never came along, and he felt sorry for the old man and woman, the one more surly than ever, the other more shrewish, who would have to spend the winter alone with the simpleminded child and the animals.

In the periods of intense cold, when he could not stand the smoke-filled atmosphere of the cabin (he had had a bit of a cough ever since he had caught a cold at Christmas-time), he would take refuge in the stable, where the animals exuded their comfortable warmth. Little redheaded birds, who had come in through the cracks, darted about high up in the straw. Deserters of even colder regions, they came only in the depths of winter. Nathanaël prevented the child from bothering them when he came with him into the barn. He had fashioned a flute for the boy on which he tried to teach him the few airs he knew, but the child could not manage to hold them in his memory. On the other hand, the boy did learn to make baskets; Nathanaël helped him weave these lovely, fragile receptacles. The Indians had left behind some bunches of sweet grass which they used for their basketwork, and it has the property of giving off again, whenever it rains, the odor it had months or even years earlier when it still grew green and fresh beside the streams. It seemed to Nathanaël that it was almost as if this grass had a memory: he himself needed very little—a pair of clogs tossed into a corner, a ray of sunlight under the door, a shower of rain beating on the roof—to bring back the sweetness of his first days with Foy. But except at such moments, preoccupied as he was with all his labors, he no longer thought about her.

Sometimes he would delouse the head of the child, who would hum to himself as he squatted before the fire. The boy would clap his hands every time one was caught. Foy had used to do the same.

Springtime returned, with its clouds of mosquitoes. Nathanaël had come to loathe the surroundings of the cabin, which were so trampled by feet that no grass would grow there anymore. The skins hanging from poles looked like scalps; the dried fish stank on trays. But the chance for flight didn't come until midsummer. One of the two brothers who made salt, a fellow named Joe, came by rowboat to trade his salt for a length of good wool the old woman had spun and woven during the long winter evenings. Nathanaël learned from him that an English ship had dropped anchor at the entrance to their bay, which a spur of rock hid from view. The vessel was going to stay there until some damage could be repaired. Nathanaël went down to the shore with the man to help him launch his boat. He leapt aboard, yelling to Joe to take him away. The old people standing in the doorway, stunned by this unexpected departure, waved their arms about like puppets; the little boy, not noticing anything, went on capering like a colt in the grass. They soon disappeared behind the spur of rock.

The ship had lost a man to scurvy; Nathanaël had no trouble getting taken aboard. The wind carried them toward Newfoundland, whence a spanking westerly took them in the direction of England. Nathanaël had learned seamanship during his first two voyages. Light and agile, with a good head for heights, he climbed nimbly from yardarm to yardarm, his weak leg scarcely hindering him at all. Sometimes he would linger up there, hanging by his hands and feet on to the rigging, intoxicated by the air and wind. Some nights the stars quivered and trembled in the sky; on other nights the moon would emerge from the clouds like some great white beast and then go back in as if to its den, or else, suspended high in space where nothing else could be seen, it would glisten on the heaving water. But what he liked best was when the completely black sky was indistinguishable from the completely black ocean. That immense darkness reminded him of the darkness that had filled the garret of the cabin, for that, too, had seemed to him immense. The only difference was that here he was alone. But all the same, he felt himself a living, breathing creature, placed at the very center of everything. He would expand his chest in order to breathe in as much of the pure air as possible, and then he would go back down to play dice with his mates belowdecks. Every roll of the dice that failed would cause a roar of oaths and elaborate blasphemies.

The vessel anchored at Gravesend; he started on foot toward Greenwich. Out of prudence, he went first to test the wind in that tavern where the crew of the *Fair Lady* had gone to drink when he had taken advantage of their absence to slip into the hold. No one knew him in that establishment, and anyway, after four years, he had changed. He said he was the mate of a sailor who came from Greenwich and who had asked him to go on an errand to his family. Yes, the tavernkeeper did indeed remember a master carpenter with bright red cheeks who had died the year before from a fall in the Admiralty dry docks; perhaps he was the man Nathanaël was asking about. The young man, feigning as best he could, turned the conversation to the subject of a fat ship's chandler for whom his mate had worked as a clerk. The tavernkeeper was well acquainted with that pious crook, who sold wormy hardtack to captains setting out on long voyages. He was a warden of his parish and more prosperous than ever.

"My mate thought he'd died," Nathanaël said cautiously, "from a fight with some passerby."

"Hell, no! Dead drunk maybe, 'cause the sanctimonious rogue really likes to bend the elbow. But if he'd been beaten to death, we'd sure have known. You don't get rid of a pig like that so easily!"

Nathanaël realized that the fat man had kept silent about the incident, which had been no credit to him. He must have told some story to whatever good samaritans had picked him up and taken care of him. Janet also must have held her tongue. No constable had ever gone looking for someone named Nathanaël. And so, his panic fear, his flight, his adventures in the New World had all been for nothing. They might as well never have happened; he might as well have stayed reading Latin in a schoolroom. Four years of his life fell away like one of those walls of ice that fall from an iceberg and drop as a single block into the sea.

Reassured as to his own safety, he didn't hide his name from the people, unknown to him, who lived in "Little Holland," the district where his house had been. They confirmed the death of Johan Adriansen, fallen from some scaffolding and killed on the spot. His two sons now worked in Southampton for the Admiralty. Their mother was said to be living in a Lutheran home for widows.

Ashamed at having left so suddenly and without saying goodbye, Nathanaël did not go to visit the schoolmaster. Janet, he learned from the wife of the tapestrymaker, was married to a draper in London. There was no point in going to bother her in her little sitting room at the rear of the shop.

Instead, he set off for the home in which his mother was living with other widows, all of them well enough off to pay a small rent to the community. Each of these worthy ladies had a little one-room house which looked out on a courtyard with trees. His mother's was astonishingly clean: the brass of the candlestick and the bed warmer glistened. It was mealtime; a bowl of gruel and a plate of smoked herring sat on the gleaming white tablecloth. His mother looked at him without emotion. Children took it into their heads to go off like that and see the world: there was nothing unusual in that. At first, they had assumed he was dead. But when they found neither his body nor his clothing, they said to themselves that in all probability he had set sail. The Adriansens had that sort of thing in their blood. All was well, so long as he had walked, or stood, in the ways of the Lord. Nathanaël vaguely recounted his adventures. The widow listened without a word, pursing her lips judiciously. But her attention was somewhat distracted by her cat, who stood up against her knees and pulled at her apron, attracted by the herring on the plate. In any case, she showed her usual practical common sense: what little the family possessed was taken care of by Uncle Elie, a printer in Amsterdam. The two older boys let him invest their funds against the time when they would go back to end their days in their homeland. If Nathanaël wanted his portion, he should go and claim it from his uncle, who was a just and honest man. What is more, they said that there was plenty of work in the ports of Holland, and life was cheaper there than here.

"May it please God to make you a worthy man, like your father and your uncle Elie."

Nathanaël wasn't quite sure what constituted a worthy man, nor what might be pleasing or displeasing to God.

The house in Amsterdam was a handsome one. The uncle ushered his nephew into the small room where he dealt with customers. Elie had bought the business from the printer-bookseller with whom he had done his apprenticeship; he was respected and earned a good living without being ostentatious about it. He had had to use the money from the sale of the family farm for this purchase; and for the moment, the capital involved could not be retrieved. But his nephews would eventually get it back tenfold. Nathanaël agreed in vague terms; he really understood nothing about such affairs. But Elie warmed up a bit when he realized that Nathanaël had the rudiments of a good education and a fine, legible hand. The uncle made his best profits from standard Greek and Latin authors carefully collated and edited by learned professors from Leyden or Utrecht, but the cost of correcting proofs was high, even when Elie assigned the work to starving scholars. In his shop, he had only two qualified proofreaders, who also took care of the page layouts, the indices, the marginalia, and the titles. Nathanaël would perhaps earn somewhat less than these workers with university degrees, but more than enough to live on. He should not expect to live and eat with the family; Elie himself would have liked nothing better, but his wife, who was wellborn and had a refined education, could not tolerate underlings around her. Nathanaël could doss down in a corner of the shop until he found lodgings for himself.

The young man thanked him: it was as good a place to learn as the school in Greenwich. Elie showed him around. The printshop was located in a courtyard sealed off from the street; the sounds of a fountain could be heard there. He saw the room with the handpresses, the room where the compositors bent over their cases, the storeroom with its bundles of paper, and the sales-and-shipping room from which volumes still smelling of ink left for Germany, England, and even France and Italy. On the wall hung a list of works that were proscribed in these various countries, since sending them there would have led to confiscations and financial losses. The great Latin and Greek tomes bound in vellum or hide, which were Elie's pride, covered the walls of a narrow parlor and were flanked by several worn-out volumes of genealogy and history, dictionaries and compendiums, in which the proofreaders were supposed to verify, in case of doubt, a proper name, a rare word, or an unusual turn of phrase. One of these word-pickers was a middle-aged man, exceedingly meticulous but embittered by bad luck; for it was said that he, not Elie Adriansen, was the man who should have bought the thriving bookstore of Johannes Jansseonius had he only known how to go about it. The other, a likable companion, had once occupied a chair in a college, from which, according to him, the envy of his colleagues had caused him to be evicted. As he worked, he softly sang some little verses of Anacreon in Greek, which he put to popular tunes of the day. Had it not been for his mornings-after, this prodigious scholar would have been capable of doing all the work by himself: the only thing was, his mornings-after often lasted for several days.

These two associates gladly taught him his job—such matters as how to read a text backwards in order not to be distracted by meaning or how to concentrate exclusively on finding errors of punctuation or syntax, on alignment or on capital letters. His schoolboy Latin, whose limitations he was well aware of, caused him to be both slower and more careful than these two experts, and they soon learned to give him the niggling tasks. Occasionally, plagued with some doubt and hoping to learn something, he would shyly put a question to the learned scholars who frequented the handsome showroom of the bookstore. These scholars would argue bitterly with Elie about the wages for their labors, then they would linger on to smoke a pipe. From one of them who was an expert in Roman antiquity, he asked the date of a consulate in order to put it in the margin of a page of Livy. The scholar took it into his head that this nobody was trying to catch him out in a point of ignorance, or at least of uncertainty, and he turned his back on him.

Elie had warned him never to speak of his days before the mast. People didn't need to know that he had once belonged to the swearing, drunken rabble of seamen. Accordingly, Nathanaël said nothing about it at the printing house. But nostalgia drew him back to the port in his time off. There, leaning against the narrow railing of a bridge, he could look down on the boats at the quayside, watch the bustle of arrivals and departures, and learn from the sailors, always at loose ends when ashore, the adventures of their voyages and how long they took. He rarely admitted that he had once been one of them, possibly because he was dismayed that he no longer was, nor did he confess to being a proofreader in a printing house, which would have set him apart from those simple men who signed their name with an X. When asked, he said he was a carpenter, as his father had been before him, a claim which seemed to be confirmed by his large hands. This professed skill enabled him to take possession, for nothing, of a shanty in an alleyway leading to the port, with the understanding that he fix it up. The windows were broken, the door smashed in, and broken bottles and other refuse thrown by passersby were the only things that grew in the little garden plot. He tidied everything up. Later he learned that all this disarray was not, as he had assumed, the result of the high spirits of the former tenants. The shanty wedged between two canals had served as a secret meeting place for the forbidden Catholic cult. Some policemen had broken in during a Mass and had carried everyone off to the watchhouse and from there doubtless to prison, where they were probably still languishing. Nathanaël felt sorry for them.

Elie and his wife said, and believed, that he would use this shanty as a place to drink and take girls. They couldn't have been more wrong. His head or his stomach—he wasn't sure which—could tolerate no more than one glass. As for girls, he feared he would be badgered by them if he let them know where he lived. But there was no lack of them, as many as he needed. Whores disgusted him with their cheap makeup and their secondhand clothing; he found they lacked the softness of the Jamaican girls. But all he had to do, in summer, was to sit on a bench in some out-of-the-way corner of the public promenade for girls to come and rub or snuggle against him: chambermaids or little shopgirls, or young ladies of the town clever enough to have got themselves a skeleton key or to have shaken off their chaperones. Their ardor amazed him: he had never taken the trouble to observe that he was handsome. But their desire awakened his. Sometimes he took them on the spot, or leaning against a tree on the promenade; the

late-night passersby were not offended by the rustling of
two bodies. Occasionally, well-dressed but furtive gentlemen approached him in the late hours of the night. He
pitied them that they felt themselves the object of God's
and man's wrath for a desire that was, after all, so simple.
Sometimes he agreed to follow them into some dark corner.
But the fact was, he really liked only small breasts, sweet
as butter, smooth lips, and tresses that shone like silk.

He was one of those people whom pleasure reassured
afterwards, rather than saddened, and who found in it a
renewed taste for life. Still, he could imagine the gossip of
those girls in their shop rooms or in the garrets of the
houses where they were servants, the joking, the compari-
sons, an abortion possibly, or an infanticide, as the result
of his or some other man's doings, or, even worse, one
more baby abandoned on the streets of the town. None of
that was right. Or else, awakened by a fit of coughing
(since he had had a touch of pleurisy in the spring, his
health had not been all that good), he reproached himself
for these occasional squanderings of strength and sub-
stance, for this insidious risk of disease. That was to pay
too dearly for a few spasms.

After having lived without thinking for four years (or
so he believed), he had regained the world of words em-
bedded in books. They interested him less than they had
formerly. He was given a Cicero to proofread, then a
Tacitus; but these wars and assassinations of rulers seemed
to him to belong to that heap of useless agitations (termed
glorious undertakings) that never end and that no one
takes the trouble to wonder at. The day before yesterday,
Julius Caesar; yesterday, in Flanders, Farnese or Don
John of Austria; today, Wallenstein or Gustavus Adol-
phus. The scholars, whose notes, explanations, and para-
phrases at the bottom of the page inflated the brief text of

the *Commentaries*, adopted the same obsequious tone in the presence of the great captain that they adopted in their epistles dedicatory to the notables of this world; from the latter they did indeed hope for a pension or a stipend, but one had to admit that it was really the sheer pleasure of flattering that mattered most to them. Or if, by chance, they disparaged Caesar, it was in order to praise Pompey —as if from this distance one could actually judge between them. From time to time, his elbows on the desk, his blond, practically white hair hanging down over his eyes, Nathanaël would pause in his reading.

Those tribes exterminated by the mighty Roman made him think of the savages slaughtered here or exploited there for the glory of a Philip, a Louis, or some James. Those legionnaires plunging through forests or marshes must have been like the men with muskets who scattered across the wastelands of the New World; the expanses of mud and water upon which Amsterdam, now swarming with people, was built must once have looked like the nameless estuaries he had seen on the other side of the ocean. But Caesar had imposed upon the Gauls only the authority of Rome; he had not had the effrontery to convert them to the only true God—a God who was not quite the same in England and Holland as he was in Spain and France, and whose faithful killed one another . . . The Batavian riffraff hurried to meet the ships returning from combat and bringing back booty from abroad. One saw precious woods and bales of spices; what one didn't see were the teeth ravaged with scurvy, the rats and vermin of the fo'c'sle, the stinking bilges, or that slave with his foot cut off Nathanaël had watched dying in Jamaica. Nor did one see the bag of gold of the merchant who had financed the launching of these great enterprises, and who sometimes sold adulterated provisions to the captains or cheated on the weight. He asked himself how much longer that same old refrain would go on.

He read the poets. The schoolmaster, who possessed only a Virgil, had warned his pupil against the lubricious elegies of Tibullus and Propertius, which weakened the will, and the obscene little poems of Catullus and Martial, which inflamed the senses. Nathanaël had to correct a small volume of Latin elegies and an edition of Ovid. He enjoyed them: sometimes, turning a page, he would come upon some verses that flowed like honey, an arrangement of syllables that left an aftertaste of happiness in his soul. As, for example, those birds of Venus: *Et Veneris dominae volucres, mea turba, columbae* . . . But all the same, they were only words, not so beautiful as the birds themselves with their smooth, iridescent throats . . . He had been in love with Janet; it seemed to him that he had been in love with Foy; yet the feelings he had had for them were much simpler and perhaps much stronger than those expressed by these poets streaming with tears, heaving with sighs, and burning with such fires.

He read Martial; he came across a Petronius. Some of their pages amused him. But those three rogues of Petronius pursuing their adventures like certain fellows he knew in the disreputable streets of Amsterdam, those jokes of Martial's, overlaid with the patina of centuries, those descriptions of bizarre sexual positions or groups, which so excited the hypocritical commentators—all that was only what he himself had done or seen done, said or heard said, at one time or another in the course of his life. Catullus's foul words reminded him of the cunts, pricks, and assholes with which his shipmates casually embellished their talk. That was what they were; nothing more.

The occasional theological treatises that Elie published were given to proofreaders more likely to be able to correct an error in a Biblical citation than he was. Yet the boss (for that is all his uncle was to Nathanaël) demanded that his employees attend church for the sake of propriety. After a quarter hour spent wondering if the sermon would be better or worse than last Sunday's, Nathanaël would have recourse to a technique he had developed as a child in Greenwich: he would go to sleep with his eyes open. Birds would chirp in the schoolmaster's garden; the sea would resound on the shores of the Île Perdue; the *Fair Lady* or the *Tethys* would flap her wings. Then, back once more on the bench of the meetinghouse, he would hear the pastor define the Holy Trinity yet one more time, or execrate the Socinians, the Anabaptists, or the Pope of Rome, or insist that the only salvation was in Jesus Christ. The parishioners sang or shouted hymns, relishing this communal vocal exercise; then they would go back to the steaming boiled beef and cabbage of their Sunday dinner, furnished with enough dogmas, admonitions, and promises for another week. Once, when Nathanaël had returned to the meetinghouse after the service to look for the mittens Elie's peevish wife had left behind on her seat, he found the preacher sitting alone, his head in his hands, in the middle of the empty pews. Perhaps the young man in clerical bands felt that his message hadn't got across; or was it that the truths he had enunciated seemed somewhat less true now than they had a few minutes before? Nathanaël would have liked to go up to him, as he once had to the dying Jesuit, but he didn't know how to go about it —and it could be, of course, that the pastor merely had a headache. He went out on tiptoes.

The next day, in the showroom, he looked up in a large Bible the only green and fresh pages he could recall from this forest of words—that is, some verses from the New Testament. Yes, those parables born in the fields or beside a lake were truly beautiful; a sweetness emanated from that Sermon on the Mount, whose every word is a lie in this world we inhabit, yet is doubtless true in some other realm, since it seems to come to us from the depths of some lost paradise. Yes, he would have liked that young agitator who lived amidst the poor and against whom Rome with its soldiers, the doctors with their Law, and the rabble with its cries had all been set. But that this young Jew, detached from the Trinity and descended into Palestine, came to save the race of Adam some four thousand years after the Fall, and that one could get to heaven only through Him—Nathanaël no more believed that than he did the other fables compiled by the learned. Everything was fine so long as these stories floated like clouds in men's imaginations; petrified into dogma, pressing with all their weight upon the earth, they were nothing more than baneful holy places frequented by the merchants of the Temple, with their slaughterhouses for victims and their courtyard for stonings. To be sure, Nathanaël's mother lived and died fortified by her Bible, with her copper bed warmer and her cat; but Foy, on the other hand, had innocently lived and ceased to live with no more religion than grass or fresh springwater has.

From time to time he would pass an hour with his comrade who was smitten with Greek, the carefree Jan de Velde, in some low dive that had singers. Jan drank heavily and ceaselessly told good stories, often dirty ones, that made him roar with laughter. Nathanaël would barely touch his glass of jenever, which the other man would then drain after he had finished his own. But he became inebriated nonetheless by the flickering lights, by the frenzied allemandes some of the couples would dance, their arms around each other's waist, and by the long pipes that breathed out hellish smoke like that in pictures of devils. The girls there were better tricked out than the whores in the streets, or at least, under the lamplight, their spangled galloons sparkled. Before long Jan would disappear in pursuit of someone who attracted him. Nathanaël would pay the bill for both of them and wander home full of dreams. But on this particular night a voice that was singing made him prick up his ears.

It was a girl somewhat past her youth, with a face as golden as a peach. Doubtless a Jewess, for only Jews had that warm hue and those dark eyes. She sang in English, for a table of sailors, tunes that were without any doubt already out of fashion in London: they were the same tunes Nathanaël had liked when he was an adolescent in Greenwich. Her rather hoarse voice was not unpleasant, but her lovely face sometimes grimaced when, during a plaintive ballad, she would try to express a tenderness she didn't really feel; her suggestive wink at the twist of a ribald refrain seemed more like a squint. But it would last only an instant, and there was something about the perfect oval of her face that was like a smooth pond which closes over again after the splash of a falling stone. When the girl was alone, he overcame his timidity and approached her.

She was called Saraï; she recounted her story in English, without any hesitation; when she was speaking rather than singing, the accent of the Amsterdam ghetto took over. In London she had worked in the houses of famous bawds, and then a certain lord had, according to her, given her a house and carriage. The scheming of her rivals had turned her patron against her; finding herself hard up, she had come back to her own country; this lousy tavern was only a temporary, makeshift engagement.

She ordered herself a beer. Even though the sailors of King James had left, Nathanaël and Saraï continued to speak to each other in English; using that language isolated them from the hubbub of the tavern and gave them the feeling of being alone and warm, as if behind the curtains of a bed. Her spirit was full of gaiety and vivacity; never having fully managed to believe that he was attractive to women, he was startled to realize that she was offering herself. At times, she stopped talking; her mouth and voice took a rest, as it were; her eyes became grave and seemed to Nathanaël like a night full of fires. He left the tavern with a promise to return.

He returned the following evenings, and she would sit next to him during the times when she wasn't working. One night, when the weather was bad, he was about to enter when he saw her outside, a shawl over her head, a bundle of old clothes on her hip. She pulled him away from the door, breathless. "They accused me of stealing," she said. "Me, a thief! Look where they beat me!"

She held out her arms, which were naked to the elbows. By the light of a ship's lantern he saw the dark bruises but refrained, out of shyness, from kissing them.

"Me, a thief! The boss told me to get out. Just because two Danish pigs lost their wallets. One of them lost the canions from his breeches, too. I don't give a fig for his lace canions!"

He realized she was talking about two foul, debauched ship's captains who were in the habit of sharing her.

"Where will you go?" he asked.

"I've no idea."

He offered to let her take refuge in his hut on the Groene Kade, some distance from the tavern. Scarcely accustomed to walking, she tottered awkwardly over the brick pavement, not managing to avoid the puddles and the holes. Tears of anger seemed to burn her eyes: instead of taking advantage of the lights from the shops that were still open, she plunged like a blind woman into every dark corner; he held her by the arm; she felt all rigid, and more angry than tearful. His heart was filled with pity for this victim.

"Quick!" she gasped. "Faster!"

But fear seemed to paralyze her: she could hardly walk.

He went first into the shanty, revived the fire, gave her the only stool, and sat on a log himself. He was as solicitous of her as he would have been of a queen. Restored by the bread and bits of food he gave her, she looked around with a rather disdainful glance. For the first time, he regretted that the windowpanes were broken and that a long crack ran down the wall on the north side. He would fix all that. Even so, now that she was there, everything seemed golden, as if lit by lamplight. The pots and pans lying on the floor were beautiful, and beautiful was the ragged counterpane on the bed; they laughed at the way it shuddered when they crawled under it. She wasn't niggardly with her charms. Her body, with its soft curves which melted one into the other, was sweeter than he had ever imagined a body could be. He held back from telling her that he had never enjoyed another woman so much, for fear she would treat him like a simpleton or a novice or that he would let her take advantage of him completely. And yet, the intimacy of pleasure seemed to him to establish an enormous trust between them, as if they had known each other all their lives.

He got to Elie's late the next morning and left early in order to buy the things that were needed at home. She had not yet got up. They ate mussels with vinegar and gingerbread sold in the open-air market. For several days or several weeks (he never did know quite how long), he felt as though he were living like a king or a god. This happiness suffused everything he saw, and it radiated in the gray streets: those men in their vests or their worn pea jackets, those ugly or plain women seen in the market-

place or the shops, they too perhaps had riches of passion
to give or to receive from someone. Under their threadbare
petticoats, their bodies were warm. Those unkempt cottages, so like his shanty, where the customs workers or the
dockers lived, perhaps they also contained a bed surrounded with an aureole like those that break through the
clouds in the frontispieces of books. That high-pitched
woman's voice pouring a silly song out the window was
perhaps, like Saraï's, balm for some tired heart. He went
home; he found her still in bed, mending her ragged clothing. As others seem to create order around them, she created disorder. But he didn't mind putting everything back
in its place. By the end of the week, she risked going out
a little into this neighborhood she didn't know in order to
buy bread at the bakery and milk from a neighbor who
had a cow, or to fill their ewer from a fountain whose
water was slightly cleaner than that of the canal. Once,
she even hung out their washing on the end of a long pole.
In the evening, when she turned her attention to warm-
ing up their dinner at the hearth, she would pause from
time to time to give him playful little kisses on the back
of his neck or to run her hands through his hair. Yet
sometimes it seemed to him that she really didn't love him
any more than some cat who rubs against its master.

One day, during one of Saraï's brief absences, he went
with a trowel and some mortar to repair the crack in the
wall, and he removed the rags that had been stuffed into
it. Something glittered in the light of the candle he had
stuck on the floor. It was a pouch full of gold pieces, silver
shoe buckles, and, folded into a handkerchief, some lace
canions. For a second, he could feel the rope around his
neck, just as he had in Greenwich when he thought he
had killed Janet's fat assailant. Convicted of receiving and
concealing stolen goods, he would have short reckoning.
But then he was filled with disgust at the thought of this

39

woman coming to hide in his shanty and making love with him as a means of paying the rent. Even in this remote quarter, where no one would think of looking for her, she had dared go out only after it was likely that the Danes had set sail. If they had in fact beaten her, and no doubt searched her, before her boss had thrown her out of the tavern, how could she have had these things on her or hidden them in the few rags she was allowed to take away? All this maltreatment she had told him about and which had horrified him, perhaps it was all a lie; she must have got out before the robbery was discovered. He put the evidence of the theft in the pocket of his old overcoat and carefully replastered the crack. When night came, he threw the stolen objects into the canal.

He didn't say anything to her about his discovery. For her part, she appeared not to notice that the crack had been plastered up. A few days later, however, the crack reappeared, and he realized that she had dug out the new plaster. He in turn acted as if he had noticed nothing. In thinking it over, he told himself that, after all, she had as much right to those pieces of gold as did two drunken Danes. In any case, the theft upset him less than the woman's hardness of heart: she had knowingly exposed him to shame and perhaps even to the gallows. At the same time, he owed his happiness to this unseemly episode. In a sense, he had taken advantage of her, too. Their nightly passion burned as brightly as ever, more than ever perhaps, since the language of their bodies was now the only one in which they were able to express themselves frankly. Yet he felt as if he were sleeping with a contaminated woman.

Everything got worse when she realized she was pregnant. She couldn't believe it, having always managed to avoid it up to then. When all her own resources had failed,

she spoke of going to an abortionist. Fearful of the fatal
effect of the powders and long needles, he dissuaded her.
She sulked for several days afterwards, sometimes in anger, sometimes in tears. She neglected herself; her old
dresses smelled of vomit. He had a new one made for her
out of good drugget, with a coif and a cotton apron, but
she refused to wear it. In order to put an end to the gossip
in the neighborhood, he decided to go through the formalities of marriage. That wasn't so easy to do, however; it
was necessary to find a broad-minded pastor who would
agree to officiate even though the husband was not entered
on the registers of any parish and who would accept Saraï
without making her undergo the awkwardness of cate-
chism and baptism. Nathanaël took his troubles to Jan de
Velde, who did in fact find among his numerous acquaintances an accommodating man of God. A little money
arranged everything. After the ceremony, which was
short, Jan de Velde invited them to dinner at an inn and
made the bride roar with laughter by imitating the half-
starved preacher pronouncing the verses of the Bible
through his nose in Dutch. Jan de Velde posed no danger
to women. But this marriage so quickly turned into a joke
by the bride herself, this wild celebration after that ab-
breviated ceremony—they were a source of bitterness to
Nathanaël: he felt as though he had somehow betrayed
something or deceived someone.

The marriage did nothing to sweeten the opinions of
the neighborhood: Nathanaël was patronized and treated
like an idiot. Nor did Saraï's black melancholy diminish.
Abruptly, and more than two months before her time, his
young wife announced that she was going back to her
mother's on the Jodenstraat. This unexpected mother
stunned Nathanaël.

He thought back over their days together since their
first meeting. Even if this mother was only a pretend

mother, why hadn't Saraï taken refuge there the night of
the episode in the tavern? Probably she had feared com-
promising the old woman. On the other hand, this desire
to return to her mother's, supposing she really had one,
was understandable: the shanty on the Groene Kade was
no more than a damp hovel; Nathanaël left early for
work and returned late. Not having managed to make any
friends in the neighborhood, she was, not unreasonably,
worried about having to give birth in his absence without
anyone to help her. Since she was already very big, he
had a sedan chair come to take her on the trip, which was
a fairly long one. The housewives of the neighborhood
laughed at her when they saw her get in.

Mevrouw Loubah, better known simply by the name of Leah, lived in a house with two doors, one giving onto the Jodenstraat, where she sold secondhand clothes; the other, with its carefully scrubbed and polished threshold, leading to her shop of French frills and furbelows located in a lane in the Christian quarter. The fashionable world was not above haggling there for its rhinegraves and Genoese mantuas. Leah was closed on Saturday, in observance of the Jewish law, as well as on Sunday, when the baptized customers didn't go shopping. Sunday was also the only day on which Nathanaël had some free time. Saraï had been put in a little room at the top of the house; either the Mevrouw or one of her nieces kept her company when they didn't have a customer. There was a sort of noisy, effervescent friendship between these women, full of laughter and hugs; their voices would suddenly rise to a diapason of anger or melt into tenderness. Either they hid their feelings or they shouted them to the rooftops. Leah and her alleged daughter spoke English, which was their secret language in the presence of the nieces or the maid; at certain moments, a Hebrew or Portuguese word

43

served to signal a danger spot, indicating that something other than what was said was meant or that one name had been substituted for another.

Nathanaël never knew whether they really were mother and daughter, but he learned from the jokes and recriminations exchanged in his presence that Leah had once operated an elegant brothel in London: it was no doubt she who had sold Saraï when she was very young to a certain Lord Osmond, and doubtless to others as well. Some scandal like that at the tavern had caused the young charmer to lose her position as *maîtresse en titre*; she had run off from London without her mother, who had beat her own retreat several months later. In any event, Mevrouw Loubah still went back and forth between Amsterdam and London in the employ of a diamond merchant. No doubt it was because of one of these absences that Saraï had pretended to take refuge on the Groene Kade.

Moreover, now that Nathanaël lived at home alone, his neighbors once again stopped to chat with him beside the canal. Thus he learned that, the summer before, Saraï often went out for long periods when he was absent, whether because Leah arranged some paid rendezvous for her or else because she was merely helping these women iron their laces or confect their pomades; but Saraï's silence about all this cast a shadow over her comings and goings. Perhaps his out-of-the-way shanty served as a convenient refuge for these receivers of stolen goods. Once he had discovered the parcel hidden in the crack, Nathanaël hadn't thought to search elsewhere. One evening he began to do so, but everything—the tattered thatch, the floor with its missing tiles, the pile of debris at the back of the garden —could have been a hiding place. In any case, Saraï had obviously taken everything with her when she left.

Although the women had promised to let him know when the child was born, in the excitement of the moment they forgot to do so. When he came as usual the Sunday after she had given birth, Saraï, radiant and rested, her hands lying upon the eiderdown, smiled at him; one of the nieces was brushing her hair for her. Looking about for the newborn child and not seeing him anywhere, Nathanaël concluded that he was dead. But in fact, that very morning, he had been put out to wet-nurse at a neighbor's who boarded children. Saraï did not have enough milk to nurse the baby.

He went to the house of the wet nurse. She was a dignified, middle-aged matron, a sort of Levantine Old-Woman-Who-Lived-in-a-Shoe, completely at her ease amongst the wailing and crying babies. Pious sayings studded her most casual remarks. The moment one opened her door, beside which hung a mezuzah, one felt far from the noisy street and equally far from the field full of traps that was Leah's house. The woman's husband was a ritual butcher, adept at killing animals slowly by draining away their blood. At home, he was a good man with a soft heart.

The wet nurse brought a lamp to show off the child. "Pretty, isn't he?"

Nathanaël found him quite ugly, but he knew that all newborn babies look pretty to women. He marveled that this tender blossom was the result of the violent pleasures he had known with Saraï, of their laughter and tears, of their lunging loins and voluptuous languors. The baby's skull with its scarcely closed sutures was covered with a dark down, inherited from his mother. Women, in any case, would dominate his little life, and if it should happen that Nathanaël were one day to take charge of him, what would he do with this urchin who would quickly be known as having come from a street in the ghetto? The baby had just been circumcised, which wounded Nathanaël to the depths of his own flesh, as if there were in this Biblical offering some offense to the body's integrity. Lazarus—

that was the name he had been given—would grow up with the usages and customs of the Jodenstraat, some of them better, some of them worse, but in any case different from those of the Groene Kade or of Kalverstraat, where Elie hung out his sign. He would no doubt go to school to rabbis, where what he learned would be no more true or false than what was taught in the meetinghouse. But it was more likely that the street itself would be his real school. He probably wouldn't get to know his father very well. But even about that paternity one might pose some questions.

Nathanaël had retreated a bit; he no longer insisted on taking Saraï back at once. It almost seemed a dream that she had ever lived on the Groene Kade. On the other hand, Saraï wouldn't object to going back there when the weather was good; but just now it was freezing in that hovel, as Nathanaël's cough bore witness. In the meantime, Mevrouw Loubah welcomed him, especially now that he was wearing some good new clothing, part workingman's, part bourgeois. He rarely failed to bring the women a little bauble or some sweetmeats. Saraï laughed and said that his new feathers must have come from some shady deal. That was practically the case.

A short time before the baby's birth, he had taken it upon himself to ask Elie for his small portion of the family fortune; he had even hinted he might set a lawyer or a bailiff on him. Elie paid up. It felt to Nathanaël as if he had tugged with all his might at a rotten stump, only to have it come out of the earth by itself. The contents of an old sack, four hundred and eighty florins in all, were poured out onto the table in the showroom, counted and recounted by the debtor, and finally poured back into the sack, which Elie tied up before handing it over to his nephew. Nathanaël put it on the floor, ashamed to have doubted the probity of this honorable man. A piece of parchment was there for the receipt.

"Sign!"

The young man signed without taking the precaution of reading it first. But, as he handed it back, his eye fell by chance upon one line. Nathanaël was signing not only for the sum Elie said was owed him but for all the money owed by his uncle to his family. Elie locked up the receipt.

"You should understand that we have lost some income and had some bankruptcies on the Amsterdam Exchange since your dead father gave me this portion to invest," the bookseller said acerbly.

"Are you talking about this mite, this pittance?"

"I don't consider myself wealthy enough to call four hundred and eighty florins a pittance," retorted the printer.

Nathanaël looked about him at the household furnishings of this well-to-do man.

"I hope you will manage your family's fortune as carefully as I have," his uncle said sarcastically. "Even though you probably have other, more pressing obligations."

Nathanaël put the sack back on the table.

"Whether you take it or not makes no difference to me, now that you've signed a receipt," the merchant remarked dryly; under some pretext or other, he had called Jan de Velde into the room, no doubt to make sure he had a witness. Nathanaël stuffed the money into his pocket.

He would have liked to leave at once and forever this house where he had worked for four years picking the lice line by line out of learned works. But his uncle pointed to some packets of proofs that needed to be taken away. He picked them up automatically. Elie's face was grim and melancholy.

"That's the sort of insult one has to put up with," he remarked, as if reluctantly, "when one increases the wealth of a family. The ingratitude . . ."

One would have said it was only his manly self-possession that kept him from weeping. Nathanaël spat as he went out.

He thought of writing to his brothers. Did they still work for the Admiralty in Southampton? His mother, living at the home (was she still alive?), knew how to read her Bible but not how to write. In any case, he would have had to confess the foolish embarrassment that had kept him from checking over the receipt for fear he might appear to be questioning his uncle. They would never have believed him.

He decided to go and ask the advice of old Cruyt, his senior at the printing house, whom a small inheritance had finally enabled to set up in business on his own. At his establishment, however, there were no handsome volumes bound in hide. With three presses and four workmen, whom in fact he tyrannized more than Elie did his, Niklaus Cruyt published on cheap paper collections of sermons brought to him by preachers puffed up with vanity or, conceivably, eager to spread the good word, shepherd's calendars, and little pamphlets on veterinary practice for farmers and farriers who could read. But his greatest profits came from coarse pamphlets and leaflets in crude French about scandals at the French court, which had been sent to him clandestinely at their authors' risk and peril. Business was reasonably good, and that day the old man was puffing contentedly on his pipe. He shrugged his shoulders when he heard about the trap Elie had set: that's how the old reprobate was.

"Listen," he said, sticking his head forward like a cautious turtle, "if you want to invest the three hundred florins you're setting aside for your brothers, I myself, Niklaus Cruyt, will gladly borrow them from you at twelve percent. I'll still make a profit, since the money-lenders are asking sixteen. Not that I'm short of money, thank God, but you've always got to take into account funds that are slow to come in."

Nathanaël, who detested usury, insisted on ten percent. They drew up a little contract and had a drink on it. As Nathanaël was going out, the old man called after him that he should see if he could get his hands on a certain splendid little dirty book on the love affairs between Mazarin and the Queen, since Elie would look down his nose at that sort of publication. Then he turned to yell at a man staggering under the weight of a bale for whom Nathanaël had stepped aside so that he could pass. It wasn't exactly the shop of comrades the young man had dreamed of, where each man would take what he needed out of the profits, and the surplus, considered as common property, would be reinvested in the business. Still, it was good that his two brothers' portion had been invested. His two brothers? Something told him that he would be unable to stop himself from taking their money for his own child, if necessary, or for Saraï, if she ever came back to him. His own honesty was not unimpeachable either.

He gave Lazarus's wet nurse fifty florins to use for the child in case of extreme necessity. The good woman respectfully put the Christian's money into a small coffer. Mevrouw Leah was paying the board and lodging, which did not cost much, but the wet nurse seemed to know a good deal about the ups and downs of such women. In any case, it was likely that this honest but gossipy woman would not remain silent about this deposit for very long and that Leah and Saraï would inveigle her into giving it over to them. This provision against the future was nothing more than a superstitious gesture, as if a way for Nathanaël to prove his paternity.

He had thought about leaving Elie for his rivals, the Blaus, but the shop of these brilliant publishers had no vacancy for the moment. In any case, the farce enacted in the showroom had improved rather than worsened Nathanaël's position at the printing house. Cruyt's departure had made him, in turn, one of the senior men, with privileges over the newcomers. But, above all, Elie, no doubt pleased at having gypped him, suddenly manifested an avuncular concern for him. Occasionally he would honor him with a tap on the shoulder, or sometimes he even congratulated him for having worked with special diligence on a day when there was pressing work. One Sunday, he asked him to dinner after the sermon. The meal passed in silence: the uncle and his nephew had nothing to say to each other. Nevertheless, Elie dropped a remark about Christians who get involved with the daughters of infidels. Jan de Velde must have talked. Mevrouw Eva, Elie's wife, who had formerly been so dour, now glanced from time to time in Nathanaël's direction with the curiosity of a prude about a lad of whom women are said to be enamored. Nathanaël looked away.

After such a dull meal, Leah's house seemed to him more cozy and pleasant than ever, the spicy dishes put on the table by the two laughing, shouting girls more succulent than ever, and the port and Madeira more heady. He spoke with enthusiasm of the improvements he had made in the house on the Groene Kade and of the trees along the quay that would soon be coming into leaf. Saraï enigmatically blinked her eyes. She was only slowly getting her strength back and still needed the attentions of the two nieces. Often they permitted him to sleep with her. But there was no longer that cloud of glory pierced with sunbeams, like those in the fabulous matings in Ovid, which had enveloped the bed in the shanty. Saraï no longer gave him any more than her prostitute's art; he no longer had any feeling for her but the banal appetite one has for any pretty girl, and the same sort of manners in bed which cause one, with guests, to eat rather more than one wants, or rather less. He knew he was the butt of the nieces' joking; they made fun of his game leg and rumpled his hair, calling him a thatched roof. He laughed with them about that. One evening, when Saraï was suffering from a migraine, she tried almost playfully to push him into the arms of one of the girls, who would have liked nothing better. He was less shocked than wounded.

He got his annual bronchitis; his neighbors took care of him. Three weeks later, well enough to do an errand Elie had sent him on, he went to deliver to a learned Jew named Leon Belmonte, who lived in Saraï's neighborhood, the proofs of his terribly abstruse *Prolegomena*. The scholar opened the door himself; he affably discussed with Nathanaël several marginal corrections concerning two or three Latin constructions. Nathanaël would have liked to linger on and ask about some of the author's ideas concerning the nature of the universe and of God, but he remembered the old adage which advises that a shoemaker, confronted with a portrait, should refrain from making judgments about the likeness or the beauty of the model and comment only on the rendering of the shoes. He was neither a theologian nor a philosopher, and Leon Belmonte had no need of his opinions.

Since night was falling, it occurred to him to stop by Mevrouw Leah's even though it wasn't one of his usual days. But he assumed Saraï might well have been worried by his prolonged absence.

The shop was dark, but the door was on the latch. A little light was coming from the small room in back through a slit in the curtain. Nathanaël held his breath: Saraï was in there with a man. It would be ignoble to spy on them;

all the same, he walked noiselessly up to the door of the little room, which was lit up like a stage set. The cavalier, still wearing his felt hat, was covering Saraï's mouth with mustachioed kisses, and she was returning them. The young woman's breasts had slipped out of her unfastened bodice, and the hand of the gallant was squeezing and pulling them mechanically, as if they were goatskin flasks. Saraï's hand slipped down her client's side with playful grace, hesitated lovingly on his thigh, and then slipped dexterously into the pocket of his coat. Nathanaël saw her take out something round and golden, probably a little sweetmeat box, which then disappeared into the ample folds of her skirt. As he silently withdrew, he heard behind him the cooing laughter she always used in his arms too. He found himself back in the street. He kept repeating to himself: "It's only her profession . . . It's only her profession . . ."

It didn't even make him sad, and it would have been silly to get angry. He felt sorry for the fellow, who would no doubt be finding himself in glory, as he had, and who had, like him, been tricked. But Saraï had been brought up to take advantage of men, just as men took advantage of her. It was that simple.

He returned to the Groene Kade, revived the peat fire lurking beneath the ashes, and by its light inspected the few new objects he had bought in anticipation of Saraï's return. Mechanically, he smashed the two plates and goblets of faïence, kicking the pieces into a corner; then he broke the slats of the crib he had had made for Lazarus. He thought of tearing up the almost new coverlet he had bought from a sailor, who unquestionably had stolen it from his captain's bedding, but in the end he pulled it over himself and slept. He took a long nap. The whole year of passion and disappointment fell into a void, like some object thrown overboard, in the same way that his panic fears of having killed the fat merchant enamored of young bodies, his long months of voyaging with the half-breed, and his two years of love and penury with Foy had all fallen away when he had returned to Greenwich. All that might just as well never have taken place.

He gave back the keys to the landlord, an old ship's captain with a jovial face, who, like everyone else, appeared to know all about his bad luck: "So, the bird has flown the nest, has she?"

The old sea wolf added that he had never had that sort of worry; women were for the taking or the leaving, and rather more for leaving than for taking. When he realized that Nathanaël was abandoning some furniture and a few utensils as payment of rent, since he had never finished all the repairs he had promised to do, the old man protested mildly and then shook hands goodbye. Nathanaël left some books and old clothes with a neighbor, who kindly offered him a pallet. But that entire family was crammed into only one room. In any case, the young man had had enough of this quay, these trees, and the faces of this neighborhood. But the need to talk with a friend, or someone like a friend, was great. For lack of anyone better, he went to see Cruyt, who would perhaps agree to let him stay in his shop for a small sum.

As he entered, he was taken aback. The presses had been smashed and crushed flat; broken crank handles and cut and twisted belts lay in a heap on the floor; a great pool of ink spread out over the counter and trickled off it in long streams. The shiny black puddle reminded him of the one Mevrouw Loubah used, behind closed doors, for telling the future. But strangest of all was the floor strewn with pieces of type fallen out of the gaping drawers; thousands and thousands of letters were all mixed up into a sort of senseless alphabet. Nathanaël slipped on this scrap metal.

"Did you come to see what you've accomplished?" The old man seated behind the counter, his head in his hands, one elbow in the ink, turned his angry face to him.

"You remember the little pamphlet on the French court you brought me from Elie's? Pardon me, from Mijnheer Adriansen's, the master printer," he corrected himself scornfully. "Oh, it sold well enough, especially in Paris, under the counter. Only me, I didn't have the time to read it first. That's how it was: your worship did me the favor of bringing me from his uncle's this little pamphlet unworthy of their presses, and, by chance, the Ambassador of France to the United Provinces happens to be mentioned in it. That whippersnapper who sleeps with the wife of the shipowner Troin. And since someone made sure to take him a copy fresh off the presses . . ."

"He sent round his lackeys?"

"And how! He got four hefty lads from the port, who arrived here this morning. They broke up everything . . ."

The old man's voice broke also. Nathanaël closed the door behind him; the draft was causing handfuls of torn paper ripped from their bales to flutter about. He went up to Cruyt to commiserate with him, but the old man pushed him away with a wide sweep of his arm, which sent flying what was left of the half-broken demijohn of ink. "Get out, you dirty dog! He connives with his uncle to ruin the small-time competitors . . . Get out, I tell you! Go find your Jewish whore! . . . And all your lies about money . . . You can take your money and . . ."

Nathanaël heard no more; he went out, mechanically wiping his sleeve, which had been splashed with ink. He felt sorry for the old man; but what was worse, he had considered him a friend. To be honest about it, though, their supposed friendship merely disguised a common dislike of Elie. And Saraï was a whore, of course, and she was a Jewess; yet those two words didn't manage to define

her. Neither the one nor the other meant quite what
Cruyt thought it did. In fact, they didn't mean much of
anything.

The simplest thing would have been to go to one of the
reputable landladies of the town and get a cold bed in
some waxed, glacial little room. He could afford it. But the
need for a bit of human warmth still obsessed him. Jan de
Velde lived a few steps away in the attic of an old ware-
house. You got up to his spacious apartment, well venti-
lated by drafts, through a series of trapdoors. Jan had
more than once begged him to come and stay at his place.
He decided to ask him for asylum for the night (as far as
a longer stay with him went, he'd see), if only for the
pleasure of hearing Jan's rather husky voice tell droll tales
or sing softly in Greek. After all, it had been Jan who had
found the minister who married him and Saraï: he could
speak to him frankly about her. Going up rung after rung
left him out of breath. Jan opened the door in his Sunday clothes—of course, it was a holiday. He was even
freshly shaven. Behind him, Nathanaël saw a table laden
as if for a feast: a pitcher of beer, some cheese, two pieces
of cake, a carafe of jenever.

He made his request in embarrassment. Jan blushed.
"What a shame, old man! You're out of luck. I have to
confess, this night I'm expecting the favors of Eros and the
smile of Celestial Aphrodite. But come back tomorrow at
suppertime . . ."

Nathanaël shook his head. Jan's rather colorless eyes
saddened; he didn't like to deny a friend hospitality. He
suggested: "A drop of jenever?"

But all he saw in the trapdoor were the shoulders of his
visitor, already commencing his descent. The favors of
Eros . . . The smile of Celestial Aphrodite . . . Jan had a
right to his own good fortune . . . Would Nathanaël have

urged him to stay at the Groene Kade on one of those nights when, all aflame, he could hardly wait for the door to close behind some importunate visitor and for Saraï to unfasten her chemise?

Rain, mixed with wet flakes of snow, had begun to fall. Nathanaël headed for the port basin where the ships from abroad anchored. From afar, their masts looked like wintry trees stripped of their leaves, waving in the wind. Here and there, a lantern shone; otherwise, one would not have guessed men lived in those black hulls. It seemed to him now that the happiest time of his life had been those voyages, those carefree anchorages in warm, languorous ports, or even those two years of hard life and innocent love on that island the inhabitants called the Île Perdue. But no captain would want as a member of his crew a former sailor who coughed and became short of breath at the slightest exertion.

He noticed that his jacket was all white. The rain had definitely turned to snow. It must be later then he had realized; the lights in the houses were all extinguished. But surely he would find somewhere in the neighborhood a hovel with a lighted candle. Without being aware of it, he was moving away from the center of town and walking in the direction of the open fields; but his attention was focused only on not coming too close to a canal or ditch, for he didn't like the idea of dying in dirty water or mud. Despite the melted snow that ran down his neck, he was very warm. He made an effort to walk in a straight line, lest people seeing him lurch along should think he was a drunk. But the streets were empty. Passing by a stall that had been set up for a fair, he noticed the recumbent shapes of two aged beggars, Tim and Minne, wrapped in rags and snuggled up against each other like a pair of homeless dogs at whom people threw garbage. Nathanaël drew from his pocket a handful of metal coins which were weighing

him down and threw them to them; at the clink of silver
and brass on the brick pavement, the two old beggars
scrambled after them, grumbling. His pay at Elie's was
not due for two days; his absence today and the three
weeks of bronchitis would be deducted, but it hardly mattered. He came out onto a handsome street, partially built
up with brand-new houses; their tall façades plastered
with snow looked like cliffs; fences or low walls separated
one from the other; the wind rushed through these brick
alleyways as if through crevasses. Nathanaël pulled down
his cap, but a gust of wind carried it off anyway, which
made him laugh. It seemed to him that the wind was continuously veering about, as it sometimes did at sea. In one
of the walls he discovered an indentation that seemed
somewhat sheltered, and he lay down there to sleep. The
snow quickly spread a thin coverlet over him.

He awoke in a large room with whitewashed walls, its windowpanes forming huge gray squares. Yesterday, today, and tomorrow dissolved into one long, feverish day, which also included the night. He thought he must have been involved in a brawl and been stabbed in the ribs: but that was only the sharp pains from his pleurisy. Several days later, he saw those same walls and windows, down which rain now streamed, more distinctly. The room was filled with human noises and smells. Someone, perhaps himself, was coughing. On his right, a man lay curled up in his bed moaning feebly; on his left, another man, more vigorous, kept pulling up and throwing back his covers, saying over and over again in the same monotone, "My damn leg . . ."

Farther off, an old man with a feverish complexion talked incessantly and with great rapidity, as inexhaustible as a thin trickle of water spilling out of some fountain. He was no doubt telling the story of his life. No one paid him any attention.

The doctor came by, wearing his felt hat and his starched collar and cuffs, accompanied by a group of students who were equally well dressed. The nurse's cold fingers stripped Nathanaël's shirt off (it was the same shirt he had been wearing when he entered the hospital, but someone must have washed and ironed it since then), exposing his thin ribs and his back, which bore the marks of leeches. Pointing with the thin stick he held in his elegant hand, the eloquent doctor uttered several Latin phrases on the course of this pulmonary illness. Thanks to his youthful strength, the subject would once again escape this time, but when the bad weather came, next winter . . .

Nathanaël thought of surprising him with a reply phrased in proper Latin. But what would be the point of startling that pedant? Anyway, he was too tired to talk; he closed his eyes.

When he opened them again, piercing screams were coming from the next room through closed doors. They belonged to his neighbor in the next bed; the surgeon was probably cutting off his damn leg. That patient never returned to the room; another man slept in his sheets.

Now the windows were framing the fading light of dusk. Feeling better, Nathanaël propped himself up on his pillow. Someone was passing a damp sponge over his body, the way they did over the corpses of the dead. He looked up. It was a tall woman, neither young nor old, with a white, cold face and an air of competence and concentration. She had brought a basket with some food, and she made him swallow several spoonfuls of thick, sweet cream. Then she went on to stop at other beds, but she spent less time at them. The nurses knew her; it was Mevrouw Clara, the housekeeper of Mijnheer van Herzog, the former burgomaster. Almost every day she came to visit the sick and the incarcerated.

As soon as Nathanaël was well enough to answer, she asked him his name, where he lived, and what he did. Several days later, she brought bad news. On Kalverstraat, where she had gone, the long absence of Nathanaël, preceded by his three-week bout of bronchitis at the beginning of the year, had persuaded Elie Adriansen to take on another proofreader, who now occupied his position. To be sure, there would be extra work which could be saved for the convalescent from time to time; he could also work in the shipping room. In addition to Elie, who had not had much to say, she had also seen a handsome man with frizzled hair named Jan de Velde, who sent him many greetings, as well as an old man who had gone on working without bothering to look up. That was no doubt Cruyt, content to go back among the employees now that he had known the tribulations of being an employer.

But it made no difference. Nathanaël had no intention of returning to work at Elie's; he could always find some sort of a job elsewhere. Then a wave of fear swept over him: when they had been young, Tim and Minne must also have said to themselves that they would always find something sometime. Still, the future he had to look forward to was probably not a very long one.

"We're the ones who found you at the entrance to our garden, sleeping in the snow," said Mevrouw Clara, who seemed to have guessed what he was thinking, "and we shall not abandon you. Several times before, they have permitted me to bring my sick and ailing back to our house."

She mentioned two of her protégés: an old man with a paralyzed right arm for whom they had nevertheless been able to find a job as caretaker at a little church near the Keizersgracht, and a man with dropsy for whom they had finally found a home in an almshouse. When she spoke of her employers, Mijnheer van Herzog and his daughter, Madame d'Ailly, she always used a vague plural. In moments of irritation, they became "the people upstairs."

Perhaps she thought of them only in vague terms, from a distance, or else perhaps she was trying to avoid sounding like an inferior servant, aware that her late husband, a master seed merchant, had been distantly related to the former burgomaster. Before leaving Nathanaël, she insisted on walking him the length of the corridor to exercise his legs.

The next day, she helped her convalescent put on his shoes and shaved off, with a barber's skill, the hair that had grown on his cheeks during his long stay in the hospital. Then she had him put on some carefully mended second-hand clothing, of which she seemed to possess a whole collection. Given the distance, she had borrowed the gardener's little skiff. They went slowly through the less crowded canals; the spring air was intoxicating to the young man lying under a rug. He leaned on his benefactress to climb the steps from the landing up to the bottom of the garden. But when he tried to thank her she told him to save his voice and his breath. This tall, taciturn woman, with her bulging forehead and her hair pulled back against her skull, made him think, much as he tried not to, of those allegories of Death he had seen in books. But that superstitious thought made him ashamed of himself; death, if it was anywhere, was in his lungs and had no need to disguise itself as the housekeeper of a great house.

He did not see her very often after that, even though he slept in one of the three rooms overlooking the coachhouse which were reserved for Mevrouw Clara's use. She herself was occupied every day with her duties in the opulent mansion; toward evening, she took her rest—that is, she went to take care of her sick and her prisoners. Her employers were accustomed to her habits and asked only that, when she came back, she hang out in the open air the voluminous cape and coif in which she would wrap herself for these visits, since they might have carried back bad air and fever in their folds. But in fact, no infection had ever touched her.

He encountered her only at meals, which at first they took together. Etiquette dictated that the housekeeper should not eat with subordinates, but Nathanaël, having been, as she put it, a student, was treated by her like a young gentleman.

Mevrouw Clara either chewed silently or else related what had taken place in the hospital or the prison. In this way he learned that whenever she visited the Central Jail she always carried with her a small tub to serve as a sitz bath, and a basin full of mutton fat for washing and oiling the wounds of the prisoners who had been interrogated and forced to sit, with weights on their feet, upon the sharp spine of a wooden horse which bit by bit sawed into their perineum. She also took along lint padding to slip between the heels and the irons of the condemned. Yet he never heard her express indignation at the barbarousness of the tortures or the brutality of the guards, any more than she blamed the doctors in the hospital for experimenting on the poor. The world was like that. If he voiced his admiration that she never turned away in disgust from any sores, she would answer, with the same simplicity, that that was how God had made her; Madame d'Ailly, who had once endeavored to accompany her, had, in contrast, been sick in the prison courtyard: not everyone has the temperament for enduring such sights. Without even noticing how much she had upset her tablemate, she calmly continued eating, gathering up the crumbs from under her plate with her fingertips. At the same time, she insisted that Nathanaël take a tisane of honey for his cough.

When the fine weather returned, she settled him in the garden while she was away. But the minute she went off

with her long, firm stride, her convalescent felt the need
to make himself useful and to try out his strength. He liked
plunging his hands into the rich, soft earth and planting
and weeding, which he hadn't done since the Île Perdue,
and the gardener was glad to acquire such a willing assistant. One rainy day, standing in the shelter of the coachhouse, Nathanaël polished the two sleighs they were about
to hang from the beams by their runners until the next
snowfall. Mijnheer van Herzog's was very simple, decorated with a thin gold stripe; Madame d'Ailly's, somewhat
smaller, had silver fittings and a swan's head. But the
smell of the polish made the young man sick to his stomach and aggravated his cough. At the same time, working
in the sun with spade and mattock—which the gardener,
laughing loudly, said was good for the health—soon left
him drenched with sweat and out of breath.

Madame d'Ailly must have seen him in this state and
have spoken to Mevrouw Clara about it when they were
doing the household accounts. One morning, the young
widow came up to him in the arbor and said shyly: "You
probably know that we have been obliged to dismiss my
father's valet, who was drinking and making a row in the
tavern. Mijnheer van Herzog needs an intelligent young
man like yourself with good will and some education.
Mevrouw Clara will inform you of your salary. You will
not be expected to wear livery."

He was about to say that it didn't matter to him whether
he wore livery or not. But it appeared that Madame d'Ailly
was making a great concession in that. So he had only to
thank her.

Up to that moment, he had scarcely known the servants
of the great house, except for the gardener and the groom,
whose wives did the laundry. He soon came to know the
cook, a big blond woman who ladled out food and beer in

heaping bowls and overflowing mugs and passed out as treats the leftovers from "the people upstairs." He became close to the husband of this powerful woman, a skinny henpecked man, who was something between a footman and a majordomo; he made friends with the floor polisher and the kitchen maid, lower-class employees who ate only after everyone else had left the table, with the errand boy who did the marketing, and with the linen mistress, who sometimes in the afternoon would ask him to help her balance a pile of linen and would lean against him perhaps a bit more than necessary while descending the stepladder. He even softened the heart of Madame d'Ailly's chambermaid, a haughty prude who did not mix with the other domestics and took her meals on a tray in her mistress's antechamber. He soon learned that the footmanmajordomo was given to bending the elbow late at night while Mijnheer van Herzog and his daughter were reposing in the arms of Morpheus; that the flirtatious linen mistress had a bastard child put out to nurse in her village of Muiden; that the scullery maid quietly gave the leftovers in the kitchen to a certain scissors grinder who was her very good friend; that Madame d'Ailly's chambermaid belonged to a little Mennonite conventicle and would from time to time receive in a downstairs room two or three venerable boobies dressed in black, who would take her money. At the apex of this pyramid, there was Mijnheer van Herzog, an old man with delicate features, a shrewd face, and fragile health, who had retired at an early age from public affairs and spent his time with his books and his physics apparatus, and Madame d'Ailly in her discreet widow's weeds.

Nathanaël found himself amazed that these people, who a month before he hadn't even known existed, now occupied such a large place in his life and would continue to do so until he left them, just as his family and neighbors in Greenwich had, as his shipmates, the inhabitants of the Île Perdue, Elie's clerks, and the women of the Jodenstraat had. But why these people and not others? Everything seemed to happen as if, on some road that led nowhere in particular, you met successive groups of travelers, themselves ignorant of their destination and encountered for only one brief moment. Others, in contrast, stayed with you a bit of the way, only to disappear without explanation at the next turn, fading out like ghosts. It was hard to understand how these people impressed themselves on your mind, occupied your imagination, and sometimes even consumed your heart, before they revealed themselves for what they were: phantoms. For their part, perhaps they thought the same of you, assuming they were able to think anything. All that seemed to belong to the domain of phantasmagoria and dreams.

For the first time in his life, he was living in the house of wealthy people. Elie was merely bourgeois, happy to own tin plates and two or three silver goblets; what cash he possessed was locked up in his safe. The wealth of Nathanaël's masters here was scattered amongst several dozen banks and businesses. The Cantonese porcelain off which Mijnheer van Herzog ate bore witness to the fact that his father had been one of the first to send merchant fleets to China, a voyage so hazardous that a third of the vessels and crew were discounted in advance from the profits and losses. Such an old fortune gave the former burgomaster the privileges and pastimes of a man born rich; the loss of human life, the extortions and tricks of the trade which are inseparable from the acquisition of all great wealth, dated from before his time, and other people had been responsible for them; his wealth and that of his daughter had acquired a sort of gentle patina.

When he had seen London again and then had discovered Amsterdam after two years spent on the Île Perdue,

Nathanaël had been amazed at the comforts of a large city, which exempt even the poorest from having to extract the necessities of life from the earth and the sea day after day. To bring land into cultivation, to work it, seed it, plant it, and harvest it; to dress the tree trunks used for building or tie up the fagots which serve for warmth; to shear the sheep, card, spin, and weave the wool; to kill the cattle and smoke or dry the fresh-caught fish; to grind and knead, cook and brew—each one of the inhabitants of the Île Perdue had performed more or less all these tasks upon which his life and that of his family depended. Here, the beer was found at the tavernkeeper's, the bread at the baker's, who blew a horn to announce when the baking was finished; carcasses ready to provide nourishment hung from the butcher's hooks; the tailor and the cobbler cut out the shapes of clothing from fabrics already woven and skins already cured and tanned. Yet the exhaustion of the man breaking his back to earn his Saturday night's pay was no less: one's daily bread took the form of a little copper coin, sometimes a silver one, which made it possible to acquire what was needed for living. The semi-rich worried over nonpayment of rents or leases; an unrecovered debt was for Elie the equivalent of a lost harvest. Insecurity had merely changed its form. Instead of being visibly subject to lightning, storms, drought, or frost, which were no longer experienced except at a remove, you now were dependent upon the publican, the minister of God who exacted his tithe, the usurer, the boss, or the landlord. Each man, even the poorest, twenty times a day made the gesture of giving or receiving a small disc of metal in order to buy or sell something. Of all human contacts, that was the most common, or at least the most visible. On Sunday, during the sermon Elie had obliged him to attend, Nathanaël always expected to hear: "Give us this day our daily penny, O Lord."

In this rich house, however, money seemed to renew and engender itself of its own accord: even its indiscreet clink was never heard. It masked itself as a marble frame for the fire in the tall fireplaces; it snored softly in the porcelain stoves; here, parquet; there, painted tiles; farther off, carpets which muffled footsteps. It greased the domestic machinery which took care of the little quotidian jobs and unpleasantnesses, sent first to Mijnheer van Herzog and then to Madame d'Ailly trays laden with fine food elegantly served and hot water for their morning ablutions, and brought back, morning and evening, the dirty water and the contents of the *chaises percées*. It was redolent in the flowers from the gardens and, at night, sparkling in the sconces and chandeliers with their white wax candles. Disguised as well-being, it was also present in leisure: it was money that permitted Mijnheer van Herzog to give himself to his studies and Madame d'Ailly to her harpsichord in the blue salon.

Yet, for all that, this man and woman sometimes seemed like captives to Nathanaël, and their servants, whose departure en masse would have left them as deprived as Tim and Minne, seemed virtually their jailers. Although they were good masters, they were not loved. Mijnheer van Herzog was treated as an old grouse when he criticized the upkeep of his flower beds; the learned men with whom he surrounded himself were considered ill-bred pedants by the young valets, fit to be rudely thrown out. His son-in-law, Monsieur d'Ailly, who had been killed ten years earlier in a duel, had been a tramp and a skirt-chaser— that is, a Frenchman. No one but Nathanaël seemed to notice that Madame d'Ailly was beautiful. Their claims that she was given to indiscreet liaisons did not accord with her grave, sweet expression. The footman-majordomo, bending forward to present the serving dishes, had seen her small breasts inside her modest décolleté; he never

stopped talking about a beauty spot there. The chambermaid, who accompanied Madame when she went out,
pursed her lips as if there were things she could tell if she
wished. Nathanaël would have liked to speak in defense of
the young widow they treated so impudently, but he would
only have been accused of being her gallant, or of wishing
to be. And anyway, these vulgar voices had no more sig-
nificance than belches or farts.

Since he had started serving as Mijnheer van Herzog's
valet de chambre, his feelings toward this stiff old man had
become more affectionate, indeed more filial than any he
had ever had for his own father, from whom as a child he
had never received much more than a slap or tuppence for
some barley sugar. Mijnheer van Herzog never had his bed
turned down, never called for his urinal, or never asked
the young man to climb the oak ladder to get a volume
from the top shelf without thanking him as if he were
an equal. Occasionally, he would ask Nathanaël to read
him a page printed in type too small for his own eyes.
The old man's brain seemed to the young servant like a
carefully furnished, correctly arranged chamber. There
was nothing in it either dirty or ugly, rare or unique,
which might disturb the fine symmetry of the rest. Sometimes, when Mijnheer van Herzog would turn his colorless gray eyes with their slightly pink lids toward him,
Nathanaël said to himself that his master, possessing as he
did such long experience, must have a well-ordered cupboard at the back of his memory in which things too precious or too frightful to be exposed were stored; yet that
wasn't completely certain, and it was possible that the
secret cupboard was in fact empty.

From time to time, the former burgomaster would receive some old friends, passionate, like him, about the
scientific or mechanical problems of the day; it would not
be long before they would pull from their pockets a small

microscope or phials full of some chemical mixture, or sometimes even an eviscerated frog; but such arcane studies often seemed to Nathanaël not much different from the experiments and games of the boys in Greenwich. These demonstrations sometimes left traces of acid on the tabletops which Nathanaël would do his best to polish away.

Once Mijnheer van Herzog had learned at least a few details about Nathanaël's past, he took pleasure in presenting to his learned friends this boy who had roamed about America and stopped in the Islands. The lad's voyages aroused their curiosity. Nathanaël would remind them in vain that he had known only the coast of a very small part of those recently discovered shores, and only a couple of islands out of hundreds; yet his enthusiasm and need to tell tales would carry him away. His own stories would be told back to him in the taverns as the result of the gossip of these gentlemen (those who were accustomed to frequenting taverns) or their valets (when by chance they had a valet): his accounts always resurfaced in unrecognizable and exaggerated forms. They attributed to him a long voyage down the Mississippi and through the Gulf of Mexico, neither of which he had ever seen, even in his dreams. At the little gatherings at Mijnheer van Herzog's, some of the guests would come up to him with a certain air of mystery and speak of Norumbega, the city of gold as rich as the ruined cities of Peru, which was still prospering in the mists and oak forests of the north, not far from that Mount Desert Island where he had landed. Some woodsmen had even drawn a map of it. He attempted unsuccessfully to persuade them that Norumbega was only a fable and that the sole gold in those forests was that of autumn. They took it for granted he was being devious and laughed in his face.

One evening, to his bitter regret, he alluded to his marriage of sorts with Foy, and soon it was assumed he had been married to an Indian princess. Others claimed that the Abenaki, "the tribe of the dawn" (he had translated the name for them), who lived at the extreme east of that newly explored land and several clans of whom he had confessed to having known, had taken him prisoner and would have eaten him had it not been for the supplications of his charming wife. These learned types had a boundless eagerness to know every detail concerning the length and width of the sexual organs of the savages and their squaws and in what positions they copulated. Nathanaël supposed that it was much the same as here.

Mijnheer van Herzog's curiosity was neither so crude nor so naïve as that of his guests. Yet, like them, this lover of exact sciences obviously lacked concentration: as soon as facts, for one reason or another, did not fit together, he no longer heard them, because he stopped listening. Simple facts hardly interested him at all; they had to be combined with something new or astonishing. Like his learned friends, he comprehended poorly and too quickly: if Nathanaël carefully described a plant from the New World, he immediately believed he recognized one of those in his herbarium, or, in contrast, he would rack his brains over some cutting of a plant which he could, in fact, have found in his own flower beds had he looked more carefully at his garden. The gentlemen who came in the evening amused themselves by turning a great globe which was placed beneath one of the chandeliers; they would move a lamp over the surface to show the changes of night and day; but if the young man, recalling what he knew about navigation, tried to correct their ideas about the time or the seasons on the other side of the world, they would get bored and send him back to the pantry. He asked for nothing better.

When he went to bed on those evenings, Mijnheer van Herzog would instruct his valet to air his clothes, which stank of stale tobacco smoke, without ever alluding by so much as a word or a smile to the carousing or the sharp, impassioned disputes of his guests. When one of the more gluttonous visitors would, upon leaving, take away a piece of pie in a greasy napkin, he would avert his eyes so as not to notice.

Nathanaël thought this little man had a good heart. But even so . . . It was possible that Mijnheer van Herzog took pleasure in surpassing his guests in politeness even as he unquestionably did in wealth. Rich and respected, he had much to offer the toadies who indulged his crazes. Nathanaël had heard him extol, as a quality special to the Low Countries, the spirit of equality which prevailed in their habits and customs, the sobriety of which rejected French gold braid and ribbons. All the same, there are many nuances of tone and quality in a simple suit of black. The equality which was not even conceivable between the former burgomaster and his valet likewise did not exist between the wealthy proprietor of the house and an unemployed chemist or a down-at-heels anatomist, even when they were invited to feast on the most splendid cuisine.

The receptions of Madame d'Ailly were rarer and less bibulous. She usually gave soirées or small cafés musicaux, which her father never attended, not having an ear for music. Young men dressed in the latest fashion appeared at them, or older men of austere aspect, all of them lovers of good music and beautiful voices; but it was especially women who came, mostly young, often pleasant, whose elegant dresses resembled those of Madame. The dowagers were dressed in a style that dated from the days of William of Orange. Occasionally, an Italian virtuoso could be recognized by his swarthy complexion, the bright colors of his clothing, and his excessive attention to the ladies. On the evenings when there was chamber music, Madame d'Ailly herself played the harpsichord. Nathanaël, in livery on those occasions, admitted the visitors, who seemed literally to glide across the carpets; the music imposed a silence before it had even begun.

In the pantry, listening through the door, the young valet tried to suppress as much as possible the clatter of the silver. Then, all of a sudden, *it* would rise up like an apparition, heard but not seen. Up to then, Nathanaël had known only tunes inseparable from the voices that sang them: the thin, small voice of Janet; the sweet, husky voice of Foy; the rich, dark voice of Saraï which shook your entrails; or the rowdy shanties of his shipmates, whose sound, sometimes accompanied by a guitar, shed a kind of warmth through the canteen and made you want to join hands and dance, despite the pitching of the ship. And often, in church, he had been transported by the organ into a world one was obliged to leave the moment one had set foot in it, because the discordant voices of the faithful brought you down to earth like so many broken rungs. But here it was something else.

Pure sounds rose up (Nathanaël now came to prefer those which have not undergone an incarnation, as it were, in the human throat), then subsided, only to mount higher and dance like flames of fire, but with a delicious freshness. They embraced each other and kissed like lovers—except that such a comparison was too corporeal. They might almost have seemed serpent-like, had that not suggested too sinister an image; like clematis or convolvulus, except that the delicate coils of sound did not seem that fragile. Yet they were fragile: a door carelessly slammed was enough to shatter them. As the questioning and answering between violin and cello, between viola da gamba

and harpsichord, took place, the image of golden balls
falling step by step down a marble staircase suggested
itself, or that of fountains melting into one another in the
basins of a garden like the ones Mijnheer van Herzog had
described having seen in Italy or in France. A point of
perfection was reached, as it never was in life, yet this
unequaled serenity was nonetheless ever-changing, formed
out of successive moments and impulses; the same miraculous harmonies occurred again and again; one longed for
their return with palpitating heart, as if it were some
long-awaited joy; each variation led like a caress from one
pleasure to an imperceptibly different one; the intensity
of sound swelled or diminished, or changed altogether, like
the colors of the sky. The very fact that this happiness
unfolded through time led you to believe that even there
it was not a question of pure perfection located, as God is
said to be, in some other sphere, but only a succession of
mirages for the ear, like mirages for the eye.

Then someone's cough would break that pervasive peace,
and that was enough to remind you that the miracle could
occur only in some privileged place, carefully protected
from noise. Outside, the carts continued to squeak; a mal-
treated donkey would bray; the cattle in the slaughter-
house would bellow or gasp in their death agony; under-
nourished babies, uncared for, would cry in their cribs.
Here and there men would die, as the half-breed had, with
an oath on their blood-moistened lips. On the marble table
of some hospital, a patient would scream. Perhaps a thousand leagues away, to the east or to the west, battles thun-
dered. It seemed outrageous that such an immense roar of
suffering, which would slay us if at any moment it were
to penetrate us completely, could coexist with this delicate
stream of pleasure.

During the musicians' pauses, Nathanaël would dis-
creetly circulate, offering coffee or ices. Madame d'Ailly,

seated at the harpsichord, would turn to take a cup or a glass, gently shifting her knees beneath the handsome folds of taffeta moiré. Conversations pierced with the sharp voices of women would start up at once; the expected praises would be lavished on the musicians; but the talk would quickly descend to the level of town gossip, to the merits of a milliner, to worries about health, or, behind a fan, to a furtive word with some gallant. Although people departed with the name of some Italian composition on their lips, they would heedlessly substitute for such melodious sounds their whisperings, their affected laughter, and their shouts for the coachman or the lantern bearer.

Worse yet, at the end of every sonata or quartet applause would burst out, unleashed so immediately that one would have thought these people were only waiting for this moment in order to make some noise of their own in turn. A dreadful din of clapping, which brought smiles to the musicians' lips and bent them double in satisfied bows, would then ensue, like a riot following some ultimate harmony which had been as sweet as a reconciliation. When the harp had been put back in its case and the violins carried off in theirs under their owners' arms, Madame, alone in the empty room, would dreamily go up to a mirror and adjust a buckle or rearrange her neckline; just before closing up the harpsichord, she would sometimes distractedly press a finger on one of the keys. That isolated note would fall like a pearl or a tear. Full, detached, utterly simple, as natural as a solitary drop of falling water, it was more beautiful than all the other sounds.

It was also in the great house that, for the first time, Nathanaël had the opportunity to look at paintings as he dusted them. When he was still a child, the woodcuts in his mother's Bible had shown him that an image more or less resembling visible and even invisible things could be put on paper: he remembered, above all, an eye within a triangle. Later, he had pored over the copperplate engravings in Elie's books, and whatever idea he had of the characters of fable came from them. But Mijnheer van Herzog had something better than that: a dozen canvases, large and small, covered with colors that showed here and there the marks of the paintbrush, framed in ebony or gilt. He had been instructed to be careful of them, because they were valuable. One day he looked at them closely.

The former burgomaster had two paintings of the port of Amsterdam in his study, which depicted galleons riding at anchor. The portraits of his parents, dressed in old-fashioned clothes, hung in his bedroom. It was said that in the blue salon of Madame d'Ailly (Nathanaël had never gone in there, since the chambermaid did that room herself every morning) there was a small picture which shocked the servants. The little he remembered from Ovid made him imagine a Diana at her bath. Madame also possessed a miniature of her late husband, a handsome cavalier with a trim black beard.

In the drawing room, two large paintings hung on opposite walls; Mijnheer had bought them in Rome when he was a young man. One of them, Nathanaël recognized immediately, was a Judith. It was, he was later told, a masterpiece of chiaroscuro—that is to say, a bit of day was intermingled in it with a great deal of night. A woman with sumptuous naked breasts, her belly barely veiled with gossamer, held in her hands the head of a decapitated man. The artist had unquestionably taken pleasure in contrasting the livid white of the bloody head with the golden white of the bosom. The headless corpse lay on the bed; it, too, was naked except for a few discreet folds of linen which, together with those of the rumpled bedclothes, offered yet another effect of whiteness to the beholder. The painter must have stepped back a pace in order to judge the contrast better. A little Negress was fastening a black cape about her mistress's neck. In the corner, a candle shed its light on a blade dripping with blood. A faint bit of dawn came in through an embrasure. The other painting, in contrast, depicted a scene in full daylight. In a square festooned with colonnades, a tearful young man, half naked but crowned with laurel, was portrayed leaving a swooning young woman. According to Mijnheer van Herzog, who was always ready to give his valet a lesson in Roman history, they were Berenice and Titus. But Nathanaël had read somewhere that Titus was short and fat, and Berenice an experienced woman in her fifties, who could hardly have resembled this delicate, fainting lady. For his own part, he doubted that a parvenu who wished to marry a queen and a queen who dreamed of becoming an empress could have been, as Mijnheer van Herzog claimed, noble examples of pure love, and he doubted even more that a lot of people strolling past in turbans and helmets would have witnessed their tender farewell.

Obviously, history did not have to be reproduced with complete accuracy on painted canvases framed in gold. Still, it seemed to him that the falsity of the gestures somehow corresponded to the falsity of the emotions.

The strangest thing, though, was the behavior of Mijnheer van Herzog and his guests in front of these pictures. In fact, almost no one looked at them. Nevertheless, the former burgomaster sometimes pointed them out as he spoke of his travels or recalled that he had purchased them at great price from a certain Prince Aldobrandini (which somehow seemed to increase their value). Neither he nor his friends were embarrassed or, so it seemed, aroused by the provocative breasts of Judith, and yet Madame would have created a scandal had she appeared in a more daring décolleté than the fashion authorized. Every one of them, and above all Mijnheer in his capacity as magistrate, would have grimaced with disgust had reality shown them that body lying obscenely on the unmade bed and that cadaverous head whose gaping mouth had probably, a moment earlier, been pulled away from that lovely breast. The Bible certainly contained a number of shocking stories. As for Titus and Berenice, Mijnheer, himself so restrained in his words and deeds, would certainly have found it in bad taste, except perhaps in the theater, that fainting imperial lovers should make their fond farewell in public like that.

But no doubt—and Nathanaël acknowledged it to himself in all humility—it was the skill of the painter and not the subjects which mattered to connoisseurs. He had learned that from having listened to the learned exposition of the French ambassador, the same ambassador who had had Cruyt's shop destroyed. This lord, who prided himself on his acquaintance with the arts, went into ecstasies over the diagonals in the composition of the *Judith* and the subtle proportions between the people and the columns in the *Titus*. And yet it seemed to Nathanaël that all those sophisticated appreciations failed to take into account the humble task of the artisan occupied with his brushes, his pencils, his oil paints, his colors which had to be ground. In such tasks as in all others, there must have been unforeseen detours and mistakes converted into opportunities. The wealthy lovers of art oversimplified or overcomplicated all that.

One morning, point-blank, as was his custom, Mijnheer said to Nathanaël: "Have you ever heard of a Mr. Leon Belmonte on Tinkers' Lane?"

"I once delivered some galley proofs to him there when I was working for a printer."

"Errand boy?"

"I was a proofreader," Nathanaël said modestly.

"Then you were one of the first to read those invaluable *Prolegomena?*"

"Hardly, Mijnheer. My job was limited to correcting a few mistakes and putting a checkmark here and there when a phrase wasn't clear, probably because some word or punctuation mark had been left out. But Mr. Belmonte didn't pay any attention to my queries."

"Were you able to speak with that great man?"

"For a few minutes, on his doorstep," said Nathanaël, who quickly got red in the face—a phenomenon for which Mijnheer found no explanation. Mention of his visit to Leon Belmonte reminded him that he had been in a hurry that day to get to the Jodenstraat and see Saraï, only to find her making love with a cavalier.

"That was a privilege," Mijnheer van Herzog said laconically.

Then, leaning forward stiffly: "Did they ever speak at the shop of an individual who assumed the costs of the printing? Everyone knows that Belmonte is a poor man, and no publisher would risk a penny on such a learned work."

"My employer did say something about some wealthy patron."

"I'm the man, I who am speaking to you now," said the former burgomaster with pride, but in a somewhat lowered voice. "But don't say anything about it."

Then why did he tell me, wondered Nathanaël. But he knew very well that, in the end, every secret is hard to keep.

"Sometimes I regret having done it," continued Mijnheer. "Certainly the *Prolegomena* have brought Leon Belmonte a good deal of fame. They say people write to him from England and Germany, and that even a Jesuit in China . . . On the other hand, he has been excommunicated by his own co-religionists and vilified in the pulpit by our preachers, who are for once in agreement with the sons of Israel. Like many other great men, he pays for his genius with adversity."

No answer was expected. Nathanaël foresaw that an order was about to follow.

"Those sublime *Prolegomena* are, as their title suggests, only the introduction to another book which it is my duty to make known to the world, even if it means that Belmonte has to suffer even greater persecution. But you understand that it's important for me to conceal the fact that a subversive book has been published with my help. Belmonte had promised me his finished manuscript by the Jewish Easter. That date has already passed. I want you to go to the philosopher's and ask him for the work on my behalf."

"If he'll trust me . . ." the valet dared to object.

"Here's a signed note, without the name of the addressee on it, asking for the promised papers."

Nathanaël put the note in his waistcoat pocket and went off.

"Try to determine as best you can how he is," continued Mijnheer van Herzog. "They say he is ill."

It was a beautiful summer day. Nathanaël took pleasure in this long errand. Avoiding the Jewish quarter, he reached Tinkers' Lane by way of the Christian side. Here and there, the alleyways were really quite filthy, but at least in those streets he wouldn't run into Lazarus playing with his top.

The back of the house gave onto a canal that stank rather badly in this hot weather, but there was a garden there where the landlady was taking the fresh air. Yes, Leon Belmonte still lived here. Turn right on the top floor. He was a tenant who always kept his door open.

Nathanaël climbed up, somewhat out of breath. The

dirty walls were covered with the usual obscene graffiti, but on one of the landings someone had drawn a Star of David and on another, no doubt out of some spirit of contradiction, a crude cross with Christ hanging on it. That must have been the work of some Catholic hiding out in this rooming house. On Belmonte's door an even cruder hand had written in chalk a Biblical imprecation against the godless, full of spelling errors. Belmonte obviously hadn't deigned to erase it. Whoever wrote it was no doubt an honest Calvinist, with a pew and a hymnbook in the meetinghouse. It was not impossible that he had also written some of the graffiti.

Nathanaël pushed the half-open door. After the cool, dark stairway, the room flooded with sunlight seemed boiling. The odor he smelled was that of the canal, mixed probably with the stink of a chamber pot the landlady had failed to empty. Flies buzzed about. A fully dressed man with swollen features, his hair and beard grown too long, was lying in bed on a pile of soiled pillows. His eyes were closed.

With a firm voice, he asked: "Who is there?"

"Messenger from Mijnheer van Herzog."

"Is that all?" said the sick man, as if disappointed.

He opened his eyes. His burning glance was as piercing as a tongue of flame. Nathanaël handed him the note.

"My glasses are somewhere on that table. What a humiliation . . . To be obliged to saddle your nose with a utensil in order to see some black on white a little better . . ."

When he had read it, he put the note down on his bed. "I'll think about it," he said. And then he added, in a peremptory tone: "I recall you. You're the boy I spoke with one winter evening here on the doorstep."

Nathanaël's eyes glanced at the note lying on the sheets. A hastily written postscript followed the signature. Mijnheer had probably reminded the suspicious sick man of the

previous visit from Elie's proofreader. This pretense of
having recognized him on his own and at first glance
seemed fraudulent to the young man. Or perhaps the ailing
man wanted to boast of a perfect memory for faces right
up to the end. Nathanaël's was in fact sufficiently striking
to be remembered, but the idea had never occurred to its
owner.

"*Deus sive Deitas aut Divinitas aut Nihil omnium ani-
mator et sponsor,*" said the sick man in a weaker voice.
"You criticized that phrase."

"The first three terms seemed redundant to me and the
fourth a contradiction," said Nathanaël. "But I'm no
scholar."

"You are like the others. In school they told you of a
simple *Deus*, and you quite reasonably forgot all about him
afterwards. *Deitas aut Divinitas* would possibly have stuck
longer. As for *Nihil* . . ." He brushed an insistent fly from
his face. "You're no idiot, and that's why your face stayed
in my memory," he said, as if to atone for his partial lie.
"You've read the *Prolegomena*, then?"

"Oh, hastily, and more than three years ago."

"Three years!" exclaimed the sick man. "You consume
your time and energy as if you were striving for eternity,
and a nobody, who has read you by chance, comes to tell
you he's forgot everything at the end of three years. So
much for fame . . ." He added a cruder word.

"I still have some idea of it, though," said the former
proofreader, trying as best he could to redeem himself and
oblige the man he was talking to, struggling to reach back
past Saraï and her mustachioed lover, the hospital and the
dead man with his damn leg, Mevrouw Clara and the insignificant sorrows and joys of the great house, to his last
scholarly reading. "Yes," he continued, "I remember it
like some beautiful, sharp-edged icicle that I held in my
hand by chance."

"A handsome comparison for a semi-illiterate," said the man on the bed. "But I know where you get such flashes of understanding. I've already heard you cough a number of times. You'll collapse like me in about two years."

Nathanaël agreed with an indifferent nod of his head.

"That wasn't meant to be a prophecy," the man said with an air of sarcasm. "It was an observation of fact. Please hand me that half-empty jug of beer, there, on the little table. My doctor forbids it, but you satisfy your desires as best you can."

"It's warm," said Nathanaël as he put his hands around it.

"That's all right."

Nathanaël emptied a bit of stagnant water from the bottom of a glass onto the floor and filled it with the warm liquid which made him think, grimacing, of urine. The man drank it as if it were nectar. Afraid he would choke, Nathanaël held him up on his pillows.

"Do you want some?" asked the philosopher with a toss of his chin, but Nathanaël said no with a gesture in turn. "Thank you," said Belmonte as he handed back the glass. "Gerrit van Herzog probably didn't expect me to treat you as an equal. But I have no equals. The stingy bastard didn't come himself, and anyway, it's thirty years now since we've had anything to say to each other. And all those learned men who praise or refute me in more pages than there are in my book wear me out. But, rather like a sick man stricken with impotence who still paws his nurse if he can, I take pleasure in talking about what I think I've accomplished to a young man who seems intelligent. You think well of my work, then . . ."

"I'm not exactly sure I thought well of it," said the young man in some embarrassment. "I believe I thought . . ."

"Well, I don't think anything of it anymore. Maybe I even think ill of it."

"It seems to me that Mijnheer manages to join together and link up things—and by that I mean both objects and human thoughts—with words that are subtler and stronger than the things themselves are. And when words are inadequate, with numbers, letters, and signs, as if with steel cables."

"They're called logic and algebra," said the philosopher with a smile of pride. "Perfectly clear equations, always precise, whatever thoughts or subjects one applies them to."

"With all due respect, Mijnheer, it seems to me that things linked up like that die on the spot and detach themselves from those symbols and words, like flesh that falls off . . ."

He was thinking of the group of black slaves, rotting in their chains, he had seen in Jamaica. The other man scowled.

"This time, your simile is revolting. Yet you're not wrong, young man. You are bringing grist to the mill of one of my favorite beliefs: I've always thought that the only gulf between the ignorant and the learned was one of vocabulary. Yes, there are things and ideas that are like rotting flesh"—he looked at the veins that stood out on his hands, frowning—"but the correspondences between them remain nonetheless unchanged. Other flesh and other ideas take the place of those which rot . . . Those myriad lines, those thousands, millions of curves along which, ever since man has existed, the mind has traveled to give at least the appearance of order to chaos . . . Those volitions, those forces, those levels of existence that become less and less corporealized, those times that become more and more eternal, those emanations and influxes of one spirit into another, what are they all but what those who don't know what they're talking about vulgarly call Angels? A world above or below, in any case elsewhere (and I don't need you to tell me that above, below, and elsewhere are empty terms), thrown like a net over this excessively constricting world which makes us so ill at ease . . . Those Sephiroth they taught us about in the synagogue . . . I've done those beasts the service of translating their outmoded notions into the language of deductions and numbers. They've thanked me by burning a few stinking candles in my dishonor."

"As for me," said Nathanaël, letting himself go as he had only four or five times in his life with Jan de Velde, who, sometimes at least, liked to cite a poet or talk about the delights of the bed, "it seems to me I said to myself that I was walking through your *Prolegomena* as if across drawbridges or footbridges with guardrails . . . At a height that made me dizzy. The earth lay so far beneath me I couldn't see it. But I felt uneasy on bridges elevated like that, bridges which swayed beneath me and only connected bare peaks where it was cold . . ."

"And don't you think there's something to be said for connecting such peaks? Doesn't this speculative trigonometry (do you understand what I mean?) tell you something important . . ."

"Perhaps . . . Yet I was never quite sure those peaks were anything more than clusters of clouds, like those you see on the open ocean. Or islands that are nothing more than fog banks."

"Ah, if you are going to take advantage of your former status as a sailor or of your knowledge of some Île Perdue . . ."

This time, Nathanaël thought he could smell a sorcerer. In his brief postscript, Mijnheer certainly had not recounted his valet's entire past, and the young man could not remember ever having mentioned in the presence of the guests in the great house the name of the Île Perdue.

"I agree with you on all these points," said the philosopher unexpectedly. "The guardrails of theorems and the drawbridges of syllogisms lead nowhere, and what they connect is perhaps Nothing. Still, it's beautiful."

Nathanaël thought of the quartets played at Madame d'Ailly's soirées. They, too, were beautiful, and in no way corresponded to the sounds of the world, which persisted quite apart from them.

"And," continued Belmonte, whose hoarseness seemed alleviated by the beer, "here is the explanation of the delay which Gerrit van Herzog objects to, the reason for which would elude him even if I deigned to give it to him. Having, according to some, ratified the universe, or, according to others (those nobodies are dismissible), proved the existence of God, or, on the contrary, His uselessness, here I am again, my bottom on the bare ground, with my perfect syllogisms and my incontrovertible demonstrations above my head, far too high for me to attempt to make the effort to lean on them. Logic and algebra having completed their masterpieces, there's nothing for me to do but scoop up a handful of this earth across which I have crawled ever since I was created . . . And of which I am made . . . And of which you are made . . . And of which the tiniest speck is more complex than all my formulations. I have considered going back to physiology, to chemistry, to all those sciences concerned with the inner nature of things. But in the first I found abysses and hidden contradictions in our bodies, for example, about which, in any case, physiology knows very little . . . In the second, I was thrown back on generalizations and numbers . . . If there were somewhere an axis on which, as on some greasy pole, one could climb toward what those people imagine are the heights . . . But the only one I see is the spinal column, which, as everyone knows, forms a curve . . . Or if I could find a hole through which I could descend toward I don't know what divine antipodes . . . Even so, that axis and that hole would have to be at the center, if there is a center . . . But the moment the world (*aut Deus*) becomes a sphere whose center is everywhere, as some clever thinkers affirm (even though I don't see why it can't equally well be an irregular poly-hedron), you could then dig anywhere to bring up God, just as, at the seashore, you bring up water when you dig into the sand. To dig with your hands, teeth, and groin down into those depths which are God . . . (*Aut Nihil, aut forte Ego*). For the secret is, it's myself I'm digging into, since at that moment I am at the center: my cough, this bubble of water and mud which rises and falls in my chest and asphyxiates me, the loosening of my bowels, we are at the center . . . This gob of spit streaked with blood that rolls inside me, these guts that torment me while another person's don't him, yet which are the same flesh as his, the same nothing, the same everything . . . And this fear of dying, when, for all that, I feel my life beat passionately down to the end of my big toe . . . When a breath of fresh air through the window is enough to swell me with joy like a bursting leather flask. Hand me those papers," he ordered Nathanaël, pointing to a bundle on the little table.

Nathanaël went to get it. It was comprised of sheets of different sizes and colors, many of them blackened and curled at the edges as if they had intentionally been brought close to the fire. All of them were covered with a tiny, nervous handwriting spreading out in every direction, but here and there the ink had yellowed. A string more or less held them together.

"You see all these crossings-out, and the others on top of them, and the scratched-out words that have been writ-ten in again? And Gerrit van Herzog is surprised that he's had to wait three years for my second volume . . . What has he done in those three years? Put his signature on con-tracts that have tripled or multiplied tenfold his ill-got gains? He assuages his conscience by advancing three

thousand florins to my publisher, who gives him back a
quarter of my profits . . . Such people praise my calm,
my coolness, the sureness of my demonstrations which
enrage my enemies; they are reassured to see me using
tools they think they possess and that, if necessary, they
could learn to use like me . . . They have no idea of the
black volcano into which I can descend . . . Ah, the *Prolegomena* . . . and to make the *Axioms* and the *Epilogues*
spout up after them . . . Chaos beneath order, and then
order beneath chaos, and then . . . I alone shall have
grappled with all that . . ."

"Mijnheer van Herzog would be grateful to have these
papers," said Nathanaël.

The sick man lifted his hands in anger. "Don't you see
it doesn't have a title yet? . . . And I have to go over some
of the pages once more. It's Tuesday today? Tell him I told
you to come back next Tuesday."

Nathanaël put the bundle of papers on the bed. Belmonte
put a handkerchief up to his lips, which the young messenger saw become stained with a bloody foam. Worried,
he said: "Would Mijnheer like me to stay for a while?"

"No," said Belmonte. "It's nothing. Don't forget to leave
the door ajar. I'm expecting the doctor."

Nathanaël went out into the dark stairway. On the landing below, he heard the rapid footsteps of someone coming
up. He flattened himself against the wall to let him pass.
It was a man in black, with a white collar and cuffs. In
the darkness, it was hard to discern his face, but he had
the vigor of someone still young. He was carrying a little
bag which he bumped against Nathanaël as he passed,
mumbling apologies. The local doctor, thought the domestic servant.

When he got back to Mijnheer van Herzog, he told him
what he had seen and heard, but without relating detail

by detail what Belmonte had said. He would, in any case, not have been capable of that. That torrent of words which at the time had overwhelmed him seemed to have disappeared underground. In any event, Nathanaël wondered if Belmonte had not really been talking to himself.

"Will he last until Tuesday?"

"He's still strong," the youth answered evasively.

In fact, it was painful for him to think that Belmonte might die. Something inside him hoped that the sick man might be immortal.

"Even when we were young," continued Gerrit van Herzog pensively, "he was always careful . . . Surely he will have told his landlady that in the event of his death his papers should be brought to me . . . But don't forget to go and see him next Tuesday morning. Bring me back the manuscript with or without a title."

But the following Tuesday, a sixteenth of August, Madame d'Ailly was giving a concert of chamber music. It was tacitly understood that on such occasions Nathanaël would don livery and be the waiter. Mijnheer resigned himself to ordering him to go early the next day to Tinkers' Lane.

That Wednesday was warmer and more humid, but less sunny, than the preceding Tuesday. The heat affected Nathanaël, who walked slowly toward the center of town through the Jewish quarter, but avoiding any streets which would take him near Mevrouw Loubah and her daughter. Tinkers' Lane was wedged between the Hebrew and the Christian quarters, like the fate of the philosopher who was rejected by the one group and disapproved of by the other. The wooden gate to the garden was open. The fat landlady was fanning herself with a dish towel. Without bothering to approach her this time, Nathanaël went directly up to the top floor.

Contrary to what he expected, the door was closed, but

merely with a simple latch. Inside, it was empty—empty
not merely of the man who had been lying on the bed,
but even of the furnishings. The windows, walls, and floor
were spotless, as if a full-scale cleaning had just been
done, but a pile of dust and debris had been carelessly
pushed by the broom into a corner. On the worn tiles of
the floor, you could discern four indentations made by the
legs of the bed.

Nathanaël went back downstairs slowly. In the garden,
the woman with the dish towel was still fanning herself.
Nathanaël sat down beside her on the bench.

"Oh!" she exclaimed. "You frightened me!"

"Has Mr. Belmonte been taken to the hospital?"

"To the Jewish cemetery," the woman said, without the
slightest inflection in her voice. "But apparently they
didn't want him."

"But his clothes, his papers?"

"His clothes weren't worth three farthings. I informed
his daughter right away."

"We didn't know he had a daughter," said Nathanaël,
including Mijnheer van Herzog in his response without
being aware of it.

"Yes. Illegitimate. That proper gentleman . . . But he
was young once, like the rest of us. She's a shopkeeper in
Haarlem. I got in touch with her right away so that no one
would accuse me of laying a finger on the belongings of a
tenant."

"What day was that?"

"A week ago . . . On Tuesday: the doctor always came
on Tuesday. He went up in the late afternoon and stayed
two hours with his patient. I know, because I saw him go
upstairs, and he only came down at nightfall. During that
time, the tenant died. It was the doctor who told me to get
in touch with his family. He seemed to be worried about
his fee. But he was paid."

A week. Nathanaël realized that he had been present at the doctor's last visit.

"His daughter's a good girl," said the landlady firmly. "She found a secondhand dealer who took the furniture."

"But his clothes . . . his papers?"

"The clothes were sold the next day to a ragman who was going by."

"But the papers?"

"The ragman didn't want them. So she brought them down and threw them in the canal. He'd had troubles with the people of his own faith, you know; she wasn't about to keep those scraps of paper."

Nathanaël stared at the leaden water. Many things had been thrown into that canal since it had been dug—garbage, fetuses, carcasses of animals, perhaps a cadaver or two. He thought about that hole which was Nothing or God.

He said farewell to the woman.

"I recall you," said the woman, speaking in the same way Belmonte had a week before. "You went upstairs that day too, didn't you? Or was it the day before? I've got eyes in my head, I have."

"I'm an errand boy."

"That's it. He always had his food and beer delivered from the local taverns. I hope he paid you on the spot?"

Nathanaël nodded yes. She wished him a good evening.

He made his way back to the great house more saddened than surprised. He thought of that handwriting blurred by the water and of all those sodden, limp pages sinking into the mud. Yet perhaps that was no worse a fate for them than Elie's printing house would have been.

Gerrit van Herzog did not agree. The old man paused a moment at his worktable, his mouth agape.

"So, he's gone . . ." And, strumming his thin fingers on the tabletop: "I shall never see him again."

"I wonder that Mijnheer did not go visit him."

"Me? Five flights?"

"Mijnheer could have sent his coach to fetch him," murmured Nathanaël.

"My position forbids me from keeping company with a man who has compromised himself," said Mijnheer van Herzog curtly. "But a masterpiece has probably slipped through our fingers. You should have kept the manuscript when he let you hold it."

"Mijnheer must pardon me. I would have been ashamed to argue with a sick man."

Mijnheer van Herzog gravely agreed. Then he added: "We shall never know what those pages contained, unless perhaps he gave you some idea."

"It was all too abstruse for a servant to understand."

Nathanaël's reply seemed to please him. After all, it was right and natural that the arguments of a philosopher should be inaccessible to a valet, however educated he might be.

"You may go," said the former burgomaster.

But at bedtime, after the drop of Madeira he took as he went to bed, he was more talkative.

"You knew him only when he was a ruin of a man," he said suddenly, tears in his eyes. "But I, I lived and traveled with him before we were thirty, when he still had money and respect, like me. I never knew a man more liberal, more lucid, more towering . . . His love of life embraced everything. We traveled together through Italy and Germany: he was always, as it were, one step ahead of me . . . But in Amsterdam . . . In the end, everyone goes back into the shell God has given him. I had my career . . . I married a woman of high birth . . . If only he had stayed with those Jews who are respected for their wealth and the rank they hold among their own people. But he chose to break with his people, to live in an attic, alone, as if one could be . . . Anyway, they say that his last associates . . . But maybe those were only rumors. As for me, I've always kept my place without wavering."

He stopped, aware that he was confiding in a valet. Lying flat beneath the covers, a lighted candle on his bedside table, he looked more dead than Belmonte had two hours before his end, and older by twenty years, even though the two men had certainly been of the same age. He could not refrain from murmuring, this time only for himself: "Yet I rendered him a magnificent service in having his book published. He never even thanked me."

That was all. Nathanaël thought he saw tears streak those hollow cheeks. But there was not much light in the room. He held it against the old man that he had made a distinction in that way between the friend of his youth and the ailing man who had struggled, covered with sweat, in his bedclothes. He was not a bighearted man. Mijnheer told him to blow out the candle.

Several months went by. When autumn came, Mevrouw Clara had to transmit through the hierarchic channel —that is to say, through Madame d'Ailly—the request that Nathanaël be spared going out in bad weather, since it aggravated his cough. Nevertheless, once in November he had to go out in a drizzle to Elie's shop in order to pick up some of Belmonte's unsold volumes which Mijnheer had bought back. The idea of seeing his former employer again didn't bother him. By now, all that seemed very distant from him.

But he did not see Elie again, since he was out, or said he was. As he was leaving the courtyard, he saw Jan de Velde coming down a side street, laughing loudly with a young man as he walked along. Good for him.

His way back led him along Kalverstraat. In an empty lot there were some old fair booths which were left there all year long. A few of them were temporarily rented to wandering mountebanks and showmen. One of them was lit up: in it you could, for half a florin, see a tiger brought from India. A small queue had formed. Nathanaël had money that day, and he had never seen a tiger. He was overcome with a desire to look at the handsome, ferocious animal, scarcely more carnivorous, he thought, than the race of man, and endowed with beautiful eyes in which a green flame burned. A small sign next to the doorway staggered him: entrance was free for anyone bringing a dog or any other healthy animal he wanted to get rid of. And, in fact, a middle-aged woman standing next to him, still attractive in her brown dress and white collar, was holding a small spaniel in her arms, a puppy hardly two or three months old.

The woman felt the reproach with which the young man stared at her. "My bitch had a litter. We found homes for most of the puppies. But this one, we don't know what to do with it."

Nathanaël held out his half florin. "Give him to me."

She handed him the small warm ball. Abandoning his plan to see the beast in the cage, he went back home— back, that is, to the little room he continued to occupy near Mevrouw Clara. Everyone was filled with pity at the story of the puppy. The cook said she would see to his food; Mevrouw Clara, not very pleased that the cleanliness of her little room was compromised by a dog that wasn't yet housebroken, nevertheless said nothing. Nathanaël combed, brushed, and bathed the little creature. In his time off, he never tired of taking it out into the garden. It filled him with joy to think that he had snatched this soft little body from the jaws of the tiger, even though he realized that, after all, it is in the very nature of a wild animal to devour living flesh. All the same, that woman who would so easily have sacrificed this poor, small creature filled him with horror. He felt as if all the hardness of the world were concentrated in her.

Mevrouw Clara grumbled, however, when she saw him walking Rescued (that's what he named the puppy) in the allées under trees dripping with rain. Now that he had committed himself to this innocent bit of life, it seemed to him that the essential thing was to make sure of its future, even if his own health were one day to cause him to leave the great house. He put Rescued in a basket and requested through the intermediary of her chambermaid the favor of an audience with Madame d'Ailly.

He knocked at her door. Madame was at her harpsichord in the blue salon. She already knew the story of the dog and would pat him gently whenever she encountered him in the garden. Nathanaël offered him to her as a gift, pointing out how handsome Rescued had become.

"But why are you giving him to me? You love him."

"It would please me if he were Madame's."

She took Rescued out of his basket and placed him on her knees to pet him. Nathanaël stroked him also, shyly, showing Madame his long ears and his thick, shiny flanks, which were mahogany-colored in contrast to his white paws. For a second, less than a second, his hand accidently grazed her bare arm inside her wide sleeve. Madame did not flinch: possibly she hadn't even felt so light a touch, which he held a second longer so as to appear not to have noticed it himself; possibly she considered the incident too slight to take offense at. But for him, the touch of that delicate skin felt like a gentle flame. No woman had ever seemed to him so soft or so pure.

The dog brought them together. When the weather was good, she had Nathanaël sent up and told him to take Rescued out for a walk.

In December, his pleurisy returned. He recovered quickly, but on Twelfth Night, as they were building a large fire in the drawing room in preparation for entertaining the children who would come to sing to the Star of Bethlehem and be treated to warm beer, he took it upon himself to bring up a basket of coal and collapsed, hemorrhaging. Mevrouw Clara put him back to bed with strict orders. Madame asked after him. Two or three times, she even went to the trouble of coming downstairs to bring him pastilles or syrup for his cough. She merely came in and went out, but she left the odor of verbena behind her. He was ashamed to have her see him in bed like that, not even freshly shaven, disheveled, with his scrawny neck sticking out of his white shirt. But Madame d'Ailly came out of pity and doubtless failed to notice such details.

As soon as he was better, he started once more to attend to his household duties. But now they gave him only light odd jobs to do. An aged chambermaid, recently hired, supervised, along with Mevrouw Clara, Mijnheer's preparations for bed. Given his chronic hoarseness, Nathanaël was no longer asked by Mijnheer to read aloud. But he retained his place in a corner of the former burgomaster's study; he would dust or clean the curiosities, sharpen the quills, and put Mijnheer's papers in order, which he would sometimes be asked to inventory because of his neat handwriting. Mijnheer, without making it evident, kept his distance from Nathanaël's cough. The servants did the same: in the evening, they laid his supper near the kitchen fireplace, away from the long table where the others sat, which constituted both a favor and a precaution. Aware that they were keeping him on only out of pity, Nathanaël would have left had he known where to go, but he was not ill enough to get himself admitted to the hospital.

The situation was resolved quite simply. One morning in March, Mijnheer, with his customary abruptness, asked him: "Do you know how to shoot?"

Nathanaël started, as if he had heard a gun go off. The question was so unexpected that it took him a moment to understand. Then he replied: "I practiced on board the *Tethys*. But I've never been a very good shot."

"So much the better, when all is said and done," Mijnheer van Herzog said cryptically.

The explanation was not long in coming. On one of the Frisian Islands, half of which was his property, Mijnheer owned a little house he had for many years now used during the hunting season. He himself no longer went there, but his nephew, Mijnheer Hendrik van Herzog, went almost every year. The last guardian, fed up with the lonely life, had abandoned the house the year before. The healthy sea air would give Nathanaël back his strength. A peasant who lived on the mainland would bring him provisions once a week, as he had for the former guardian. It would be Nathanaël's job to keep the few rooms clean in preparation for the arrival of young Hendrik and to show himself from time to time at the only landing with his musket in hand in order to frighten off any strangers who might take it into their heads to poach on this island full of birds.

"And what if they should be survivors of some shipwreck?" asked Nathanaël.

"You'll be able to tell from the way they look."

It was better, repeated Mijnheer, to frighten off such intruders without shooting too accurately: to put a bullet into the head of some farmer's son or some well-known Frisian would cause trouble. But such risks were rare, given how far out at sea the island was and the danger of running aground on the sandbanks unless you knew by heart where the channels were. In the winter, there were no problems at all, since the migrations emptied the island of birds and the stormy seas themselves protected its shores. Nathanaël would come back in October with young Hendrik and his wicker hampers filled with waterfowl.

The idea of such solitude made Nathanaël's pulse race. He thought of the Île Perdue and the good smell of wild vegetation rising from the barrens. Who was to say that a few months of such great calm would not suffice to cure him? After all, he was only twenty-seven. He immediately remembered, however, that Foy had been considerably younger than that when the same sickness had carried her off, and that the sea air had neither protected nor cured her. Yet Foy was a fragile little girl. Another thought, unexpressed even in the depths of his self, came to contradict this longing for solitude: for months he would not see Madame walk across the polished parquet floors accompanied by Rescued; he would no longer chance to encounter her smile. But he would have blushed to entertain such regrets for long: like everyone else, Madame was in favor of this plan.

She even had some private talks with Mevrouw Clara to decide what the new guardian would need by way of clothing, medicine, and dried foodstuffs in the event that his supplier from the mainland didn't arrive on the scheduled day. They stuffed these things into bags and packs.

The evening before his departure, Nathanaël went to say farewell to Mijnheer, who condescended to extend his rather cold hand and wished him good luck and told him to behave himself. It was his customary formula for such occasions.

Then he went to knock at the door of the blue salon. Madame opened it herself. The little dog was jumping and yapping around her. Nathanaël knelt down to pat Rescued. When he stood up again, she said: "We shall take good care of him. You'll see him again in the autumn."

These words warmed his heart, even though the time between now and when he would return had never seemed to him more forbidding. He wondered if Madame would also extend her hand and, if so, whether he would have the courage to kiss it. But kissing hands is not a form of politeness for a footman. Even as he was telling himself that, she came up and kissed him on the lips with a kiss so light and quick, and yet so firm, that he moved back a step, as if at the visitation of an angel. They stopped in the doorway. Madame, her beautiful eyes grave, said goodbye and closed the door.

The next morning, they loaded his baggage onto the flat barge tied up at the bottom of the garden. Mevrouw Clara accompanied him as far as the ship landing. People were moving about on the quay and blocking the gangplank, as they always do at moments of departure. Leaning against the railing, Nathanaël waved goodbye to the charitable housekeeper, who held herself, as always, a bit distant, kindly yet cold. Once more, this tall woman with her hair pulled back made him think of Death, and once more he told himself that was an absurd fantasy: death is within us.

The weather was beautiful. The Zuiderzee had not so much as a wrinkle on it. On the deck there was a large cabin with some tables and a counter where they served beer, cold meats, and fritters. Nathanaël had his food with him, but he went to stretch out on one of the benches along the outer wall of this canteen. He used one of his satchels for a pillow. The noise of the bundle of ropes thrown onto the quay and the scraping of the gangplank awakened him at each of the little way stations; all the tumult of Amsterdam was repeated there in miniature. People got off and on. The smell of fritters came through the open window of the cabin along with the sound of voices.

Nathanaël got up to look at some people who were laughing and talking very loudly. They were two couples: two rather vulgar-looking women, ornately and tastelessly dressed; you couldn't tell whether they were dealers in secondhand clothing or old prostitutes who had struck it rich; both, no doubt. One of them, short and stocky, had a large gold wedding ring on her finger. To Nathanaël, who was always given to seeking resemblances between animals and men, the two men with them looked like swine.

"The old girl wasn't implicated?"

"What do you think? They would have laid hands on her long before this if they could have."

"Still, she must miss her daughter."

"Daughter? No one ever witnessed that birth! All the same, she'll be hard put to find another so beautiful and with such well-trained fingers."

"So beautiful?" said the sour voice of one of the women. "Well, if you like: a beautiful Jewess."

"Beautiful any way you look at it," said the fatter of the two swine. "And I saw her close up, too. I was underneath her."

That admission caused the women to snicker.

"No matter: I'm damn glad I was at Nijmegen for the Tuesday horse market."

"What were you doing at Nijmegen?" asked the thinner of the swine suspiciously. "You're no horse dealer."

"Never mind: it's not your sort of work. The square was swarming with so many people my customer and I left the Golden Hound to see what was going on. It was worth the effort: a thousand thalers plucked right out of the britches of a captain from Hanover!"

"Was she working alone?"

"It appeared so . . ."

"Not long ago, she had a husband in Amsterdam, some sort of ninny," said the female who hadn't spoken until then. "He got out when he smelled the hemp. It's one thing to have a wife who brings home money; it's something else to risk the rope!"

"When she came out, you could have heard a fly," con-

tinued the pig with his mouth full. "As she climbed up the
ladder, she was singing."

"What, hymns?"

"Hell, no! Tavern songs! And when she got to the top,
she pushed away the man in red . . . you know . . . the
fellow it's unlucky to mention. One more push and he'd've
tumbled right off the ladder. All of a sudden, she jumped,
all by herself. The rope made her do a dance step or two in
the air, and everyone in the square saw what beautiful
legs she had."

"Only her legs?"

"It's a pity, but that's all I saw. Because of her skirts."

"Do they know what happened to the loot from Dort-
mund?"

"Loubah knows . . ."

And, leaning toward his chum, he whispered something.

"You blab too much," said the fatter of the females
scornfully.

Nathanaël had propped himself up on his elbow to hear
better. He put his head back down on his bundle. So Saraï
had died, after all, in the way he had always expected. As
for him, he was only a ninny who was afraid of the rope.

When those people got off at Hoorn, he went to the railing and threw up. The sailors who saw him laughed at the
passenger who got seasick in such calm weather.

At the next stop, the peasant who was to take him to
the island came for him with a cart. It was a long way to
the coastal hamlet where the old man lived. Seeing him in
some sort of trance he didn't know the reason for, the old
man spat from time to time and urged on his mare but
said nothing to his passenger. The smoke-filled shack had
only one bed. Nathanaël lay down next to the old man;
the old woman, who was skinny and cantakerous, slept on

the other side, next to the wall. Toward midnight, Nathan-aël, unable to remain there, went and sat next to the dead hearth, which reminded him of the peat fire in the little house on the Groene Kade—that fire which had cast rosy hues over Saraï's nakedness.

Yet it was good she sang as she mounted the ladder; it was good, too, that she had jumped off with a leap, as if to dance. He had heard that the necks of hanged people were stretched out of all proportion, pulled by the weight of their bodies, and that their congested faces caused their tongues to hang out all black. But her face was beneath the earth now. He didn't have to see her that way. He remembered everything: the lies, the ruses, the foul words, the insolent silences, the hardness underneath her softness; his memory, if not his heart, was pitiless. But there had also been the lovely, deep voice, which sang as if from beyond herself, her warm, somber eyes, her flesh, every inch of which he had known. Those legs flailing over the heads of the crowd had once wrapped themselves around his knees and thighs; they had rested, trembling, on his shoulders. That, too, mattered.

Toward dawn, overcome with bitter regret, he asked himself if someone who had known how to go about it better could have saved Saraï. He thought not. You could have saved her only by preventing her from being herself. In any case, he hadn't been the man.

They embarked very early. Since the wind was strong, the skiff with its square sail and its two pair of oars took only half an hour to go from the mainland to the island. Because the rowing tired Nathanaël, the old man put him at the rudder. The island was so flat that it was not even visible until you got quite close. Nevertheless, Nathanaël observed as he got off that the dunes along the shore formed ramparts and trenches of sand. As he sailed into a peaceful little bay, the old man jumped into the water up to his knees and tied his skiff to the pier of a small, worm-eaten jetty. It was hard for Nathanaël to climb up the dune dragging behind him his parcels at the end of a long rope. The little hut was below the level of the dunes; the old boatman opened the door with a kick and propped a big log against it. He crouched down to light the fire, but .he advised Nathanaël to use wood sparingly; there was practically none on the island except for some planks cast up by the sea. The rare trees here and there, which had been planted to hold down the sand, were too valuable to be touched. He could use peat, but that, too, had to come from the mainland.

Willem showed him the three rooms reserved for the owners, the kitchen, and a room off it where the newcomer would live. It was very small, but he could keep warmer that way.

Once he was alone, Nathanaël carefully arranged his clothes, the provisions he had had from the old man, and those the women had given him. Then he went out to look about. All the business of arriving had hardly given him time to see anything. Now, he was nothing but eyes.

Between the house and the sea, which could only be glimpsed, the dunes formed enormous waves, molded, it seemed, from the actual waves that had sculpted them. They were stable, if anything can be; yet it felt as if they moved invisibly, shrinking here and expanding there. A sort of mist of sand raced and scraped across them, chased by the same wind which scatters the mist from the waves. Tufts of isolated dune grass trembled gently in the strong wind. No: it wasn't the Île Perdue, which had been composed of rocks, shingle, barrens, and trees attached to the rock by their roots, as if with great clutching hands on which the veins stood out. On the contrary, here everything was undulating or flat, shifting or liquid, pale yellow or pale green. The clouds themselves heaved about like sails. He had never felt at the center of so much tremulousness.

After a moment, he bent his knees, as if he were about to fall, or else to pray, and ten or twenty times he cried out in a loud voice Saraï's name. The immense silence all about him did not even give back an echo. Then, in a softer voice, he repeated another name. The result was the same.

During the first days Nathanaël spent on the island, eight perhaps—unless it was seven, or nine (he hardly kept count anymore except by the quarters of the moon, which also marked the more or less weekly visits from Willem)—he dutifully kept his watchman's hours on the old jetty. On those days when the wind blew strongly, he soon learned to protect himself from the ceaseless whipping of the sand with a scarf worn like a mask. A few large and small boats pitched in the distance, but none of them gave any indication of coming to the island. Lying on his stomach with his head between his hands, as he used to when he was at sea during the free time given the crew in prolonged calms, he passed his time observing or dreaming. Recalling the bibelots of shell, ivory, and coral in Mijnheer van Herzog's study, he admired the encrustations of mussels and shellfish which formed curious designs in blue, pink, and mother-of-pearl on the struts of the old wooden scaffolding, now eaten away by sea worms. Those baubles, so prized in the great house, now seemed a bit less trifling, since they were not unlike the forms that time, wear, and the slow action of the elements give to things. Once, he picked up a sort of oblong biscuit made out of hardened, petrified sand, which had an indentation like a thumbprint, causing it to look like a painter's palette. Nature, like man, made some handsome, useless objects. Not once during his scrupulous guard duties did he observe a trace of human footprints on the beach, but birds left tracks there like stars and the rabbits left prints which seemed themselves to leap up. Occasionally, hoofprints made indentations in the sand: a herd of horses had been left in the interior of the island by one of Mijnheer van Herzog's farmers who had given up the venture after several years. These handsome creatures were too wild to let themselves be seen very often in the daylight, but occasionally, at dawn, they could be found licking the salt from puddles the sea had left.

After a time, Nathanaël left his useless musket hanging on its nail. He made do with watching the sea from the crest of the dunes.

When the wind blew hard, he sought refuge in the thin clumps of pines which also dated from the time of the farmer. In these compact copses, where the trees huddled against one another to protect themselves from the wind, there was no chance of getting lost as there was in a real forest: bare, empty space could be seen at the far end of the tunnels of branches. Yet it was as sheltered there as in a church. At first, silence seemed to reign, but if you listened carefully this silence was made up of solemn, soft sounds, so strong that they were like the roar of waves and as deep as those of a cathedral organ; they came as a sort of copious benediction. Each bough, each branch, each trunk moved with a different sound, from cracking, to murmur, to sigh. Beneath them, the world of mosses and ferns was still.

·   ·   ·

But best of all were the thousands of birds nesting on the island in this brooding season. The waders at the edge of the ponds looked frozen in the rising sun; every so often, at long intervals, you would see them advance with a cautious step, only to be disappointed by their fleeing prey. Nathanaël felt himself divided between the joy of the bird who finally snapped up its nourishment and the agony of the fish who was swallowed live. Wild geese formed clouds like banderoles and then, in a storm of cries, would swoop down to feed; ducks went before or came after them; swans formed their majestic white angle in the sky. Nathanaël understood that nothing about him was of any importance to these souls of a different species; they would not give him back love for love; he could have killed them had he possessed the slightest instinct of the hunter, but he could not succor their existence, which was exposed to the elements and to man. Nor were the rabbits in the short dune grass his friends; they were merely cautious, watchful visitors, who had issued forth from their holes as from some other world. Hidden beneath some bushes, he had once observed them dancing in the moonlight. At dawn, the plovers executed their nuptial flight across the sky, more ravishing than any choreography in the ballets of the King of France. At evening, the wader was there once more. One day, when he had arrived with his provisions, Willem abruptly disappeared behind a dune carrying an empty basket on his arm. He had gone to steal plovers' eggs for the table of Mijnheer van Herzog, to whom they would be sent on the next packetboat. He offered some to Nathanaël, who refused them.

When he arrived on the island, he had felt he was outside of the world. He was; yet nothing is so perfect as one thinks. The weekly arrival of Willem brought him back to what he imagined he had left behind. The old man brought news of the village: a cow or mare who had dropped a calf or foal, a fire in a hayrick, a battered wife or a cuckolded husband, a child who had been born or had died, the inexorable arrival of the tax collector. Sometimes there was even news of a town besieged or pillaged in Germany.

But above all, contrary to what Nathanaël had supposed, it turned out that the old man did not make these trips for him alone. Once he had deposited the rations on the doorstep, Willem, a sack over his shoulder, would walk two miles to an old farmhouse where no one lived except the farmer's half-crippled widow and her feeble-minded daughter, who was subject to fits that would leave her whole days on her pallet without speaking or eating. These women still had a cow, a few chickens, and a vegetable garden. But it was time something be done about them. One of Mijnheer van Herzog's agents had found a place for them in the almshouse at Hoorn as of midsummer. They would be taken there, by force if necessary.

Meanwhile, the old man proposed that Nathanaël accompany him to see the madwomen, as he called them. The two miles seemed long to the young man, who tried to conceal his shortness of breath and his exhaustion: it wouldn't be a good idea to show Willem that he was virtually an invalid. He even offered to do certain small jobs that were too hard for the women, such as repairing the low roof of the stable. For a few pennies he would buy some milk and two or three eggs from them; in that way they would lay by a bit for the almshouse. When the fifty-year-old daughter was having one of her bad days, he would milk the cow. He liked that task, not having had a chance to do it since the Île Perdue. The animal's flanks were warm and rough, russet-colored like a mountainside in sunlight. For the women, attached though they were to their old farmhouse crumbling beneath them, the almshouse would mean regular meals, a stove that would fend off the cold, the gossip of other women, and sometimes church on Sunday or a hot bath on Saturday. For the cow, on the other hand, who no longer had much milk, the change would mean nothing less than the butcher's block.

The day they left was almost festive. Several characters from the village had come with Willem. The peevish old woman was carried in a sort of sedan chair improvised out of a sheet made into a sling and carried by two young men. The mad daughter followed without understanding much of what was happening. The cow brought up the rear of the procession. In order to persuade the women to leave, the men took along a number of useless household utensils. Nathanaël persuaded Willem to keep the cow until autumn was over.

The departure of these quasi-neighbors deprived him of milk (since what the old man brought was quickly used up or turned sour) and of eggs when Willem's henhouse failed to provide them. But that was not what mattered. Now the island had two fewer human presences and one less domestic animal. Nathanaël's solitude had grown larger.

But the island as a whole was not without human beings. Willem stayed on one day to chat about a village of some twenty houses about nine leagues to the north, in the part that didn't belong to Mijnheer van Herzog. These low cottages were huddled together against the wind around a small port which was as round as a buckler. The people of Oudeschild, some of them fishermen, some of them farmers, had a little barley and some cattle. Willem lifted his elbow to indicate that they also had drink; some days the beer and jenever flowed in torrents. The community got along without a minister, and the girls there had the reputation of never saying no. Willem himself had never been there; the people traded with the mainland farther off, to the northeast of the Zuiderzee.

One day in August, Nathanaël saw two hearty, cheerful-looking lads come out of the interior, riding bareback. Their horses were from the abandoned herd; they had broken them as best they could; their manes and tails floated in the wind. Half naked, white, and blond, with those parts of their bodies not usually covered by their work clothes redder or more tanned, they seemed to Nathanaël like an apparition: it was as if life, in order to pay him a visit, had taken on their forms and those of their mounts. They made friends with one another. The two dismounted to drink springwater straight from the bunghole of the little barrel, refilled each week by Willem, in which there was not the slightest taste of the sea. They invited Nathanaël to go with them to the village at the other end of the island; they promised to bring him back the next day or the day after.

For a long time now, Nathanaël had refused any sort of festivity, for fear that a coughing fit or his spitting blood would spoil the occasion; he had been unwilling to go to the fairs with Mijnheer van Herzog's people. But the joyousness of the two lads tempted him. He got up on the croup of Markus's horse. Lukas dug his heels into his horse's sides to make him gallop. The horses flew noiselessly over the sand and the low grass. It felt good to put his arms around the solid torso of the rider and feel his warmth and strength. Even the odor of sweat that came from his healthy body smelled good. Nathanaël's arrival turned the night into a revel: there was a good deal of backslapping, embracing, and drinking; crêpes were tossed in the air and eaten; the plump girls who didn't say no but whom Nathanaël didn't give a chance to say yes danced in the arms of the boys to the rhythm of a

hurdy-gurdy; the old men who sat on the bench tapped
their heels on the dance floor of beaten earth in time to
the quadrille. Nathanaël participated in all this happiness
as if his weakness, his fever, and his cough had miracu-
lously left him; not thinking about the future and having,
as it were, dropped ten years from the past, he was once
again, for several hours, the eighteen-year-old sailor. But
the next morning, in the garret where he had slept with
Markus, he was seized with a coughing fit; he hid his
blood-stained handkerchief. Unaccustomed to sickness, the
lads thought it was only the result of yesterday's drinking.
Six leagues on horseback were out of the question, so they
made a sport out of taking him back by boat. For hours
they went along the most sheltered shore of the island,
avoiding the sandbanks; his comrades had a small barrel
of beer in tow; Nathanaël refused to drink any, but the
gaiety of his companions continued to intoxicate him. The
boys helped him get up the dune which protected the house
from the sea. They said goodbye with repeated promises
to return. But Nathanaël knew they would never see one
another again.

A few days later, he learned that Mijnheer Hendrik
van Herzog, called to Bremen on business, would not be
coming this year.

He had feared certain aspects of the visit. The idea of
stuffed game bags was repugnant to him. Yet this was like
the fall of some heavy curtain, isolating him in solitude.
He had seen himself as young Mijnheer Hendrik's valet,
getting on board the packetboat behind him; he did not see
himself getting on board all alone. The former burgomaster, however, had taken the trouble to add to his brief
note that he assumed Nathanaël was well again and would
be ready to resume his work in town at the beginning of
November. Nathanaël knew, however, that he would not
return in November.

And then, time ceased to exist. It was as if the numbers had been erased from a sundial and the sundial itself had grown pale, like the moon in the sky in full daylight. Without a clock (the one in the little house no longer worked), without a watch (he had never owned one), without a shepherd's calendar on the wall, time either passed like lightning or stretched out forever. The sun rose, then it set, in almost the same place it had yesterday, a bit earlier each evening, a bit later each morning. Dawn and dusk were the only events that mattered. Between them, something flowed past which wasn't so much time as life. The phases of the moon were no longer of any importance except that, when the moon was full, the sand shone white in the night. He no longer remembered very well the names and shapes of the constellations, which he had known by heart when the pilot of the *Tethys* had steered by Aldebaran or by the Pleïades; yet it hardly mattered: they were nothing more than incomprehensible fires burning in the sky. Clouds or banks of fog almost always concealed some of them; then they would reappear, like lost friends. Before his sickness, as it grew worse, took

from him bit by bit the strength to love anything passionately, he continued passionately to love the night. Here, it
seemed limitless, omnipotent; the night over the water
extended the night that was over the island in every direction. Sometimes he would come out of the house in the
dark of night, when only the soft masses of the dunes and,
beyond them, the white waves of the sea were dimly visible, and he would strip off his clothes to let the darkness
and the almost warm wind wash over him. At such moments, he was nothing more than one element of nature
amongst all the others. Although he couldn't have said
why, the contact of his skin with the darkness moved him
in the same way that, in former times, love had. At other
moments, the emptiness of the night was terrible.

The day subdivided itself more and more. The shadow
cast by the tufts of grass on the dunes became his sundial.
He would watch it turn. Or else, letting the loose soil flow
through his fingers, he made of his palm an hourglass
which did not count seconds, or minutes, or hours: it was
enough for him to flatten the tiny hillock of sand with his
hand to erase the evidence that a certain amount of time
had passed. In order not to lose all contact with the human
almanac, he cut notches in a beam with his knife to mark
the days between Willem's visits. But if he forgot for one
evening, it was enough to throw everything into confusion.
Willem, not having anyone else to provision on the island,
became less and less punctual. Whenever the expected
boat was late, Nathanaël was filled with an anguish which
had nothing to do with the bit of cheese, the coarse bread,
the vegetables already withered by the sea air, or even
with the fresh water, precious though it was, that Willem
brought him. It seemed as though he needed to see old
Willem's face to be sure that he had one himself.

Once, in order to prove to himself that he still possessed
a voice and a language, he uttered aloud, not a woman's

name this time, but his own. The sound of it frightened him. The raucous cry of the gull or the wail of the curlew contained a call or warning understood by other members of the winged, feathered race—or at least some assurance of existence. But that useless name seemed dead, as the words of a language are dead when no one speaks it any longer. Perhaps, to affirm his existence in the bosom of so vast a world, he should have sung, as the birds do. But, apart from the fact that his hoarse voice broke easily, he knew that he had lost forever the desire to sing.

Little by little, fear, insidious at first, then often whipped up into frenzy, settled into him. But it was not, as he had foreseen, fear of solitude, but rather fear of dying, as if death had become more ineluctable now that he was all alone. He must leave the island as quickly as possible. But where could he go? The visit from Willem, so longed for, became a danger; his almost continual cough, the fever you could feel if you touched his hand, they would not escape the old man's notice; they would contrive some scheme, as they had for the two women; they would find him, since they would consider it impossible to take him back to the great house, some final asylum in Willem's smoke-filled farmhouse or in the almshouse at Hoorn. Apart from anything else, Willem was surely eager to end his trips to the island before the bad weather set in.

His common sense told him that you always die alone. And he was not unaware that animals take themselves into solitude to die. Nevertheless, during his nocturnal cries of suffocation, it seemed to him that a human presence would have been some help, even if it had been only that of Tim and Minne, who would have stayed merely in order to strip him, still warm, of his last clothing. He thought once more of the doctor in the Amsterdam hospital, pontificating in Latin beside the beds of the dying; that wasn't what he wanted. He remembered the vigil he had kept at the side of the half-breed, who had lain on the deck in the shade of a bale of cloth; that man had coddled him and taken care of him as best he could; and yet the smell of infection and the sight of his eye half out of its socket had made him want to throw up; he had hoped the man would die, even as he was brushing away the flies which had settled on his wound. He had been able to offer the young Jesuit only a mouthful of water; he hadn't been able to comfort or reassure Foy. As for Saraï, she had breathed her last without his feeling anything, without his even wincing, during the last days he had spent in the great house in Amsterdam, perhaps at the very moment when Madame d'Ailly kissed him. High over the thronged square of the town, she had died alone.

He subsisted without books, having found in the little house only a Bible, which he burned by the handful one day when the stove was slow to catch fire. But it seemed to him now that the books he had managed to read (should one judge all books by them?) had given him very little, less perhaps than the enthusiasm or thought he had brought to them; in any case, he considered it would be wrong not to concentrate on the world he had in front of him, now and for so little time to come, and which had, as it were, fallen to him by chance. To read books was like swigging brandy: it was a way of numbing oneself into not being there. And anyway, what were books? He had worked too long at Elie's, amongst those rows of lead smeared with ink. The more painful the sensations of his body became, the more it seemed necessary to him to try instead, by focusing his attention, to follow if not to comprehend what was being done or undone inside him.

Once or twice he attempted, as he had heard men in clerical bands and long black sleeves counsel from the pulpit, to evaluate his own past as best he could. He failed. In the first place, it wasn't really *his* past, but that of the people and things he had encountered along the way; he saw them once more, or at least some of them; he failed to see himself. All the same, it seemed to him that men and circumstances had done him more good than ill, that, day by day, he had had more enjoyment than suffering, but no doubt from happiness most people wouldn't have cared about. He had known joys no one else seemed to pay any attention to, such as chewing on a piece of grass. He had never been rich or famous; he had never wanted to be one or the other. It also seemed to him that he hadn't done an evil deed, whether simply heaving a stone at a bird or uttering a cruel word which would suppurate in someone's memory. If that was true, it had been partly by chance. He might have killed the fat man in Greenwich; by pure chance, he hadn't. If Saraï had openly asked him to go and sell the gains from some theft for her, he might well have said yes out of cowardice and passion.

But, to begin with, who was this person he considered himself to be? Where did he come from? From the fat, jovial carpenter of the Admiralty dockyards, who liked to take snuff and deliver blows, and from his Puritan spouse? Not at all: he had only passed through them. He didn't feel himself to be, as so many people do, a man as opposed to beasts and trees; rather, a brother of one and a distant cousin of the other. Nor did he particularly consider himself male in contrast with the gentle order of women; he had passionately possessed certain women, but, out of bed, his cares, his needs, his constraints of money, sickness, and the daily tasks one performs to live hadn't seemed to him so different from theirs. He had, rarely it is true, known the carnal brotherhood other men had shared with him; he didn't feel less a man for that. People falsify everything, it seemed to him, in taking such little account of the flexibility and resources of the human being, so like the plant which seeks out the sun or water and nourishes itself fairly well from whatever earth the wind has sown it in. Custom more than nature seemed to him to dictate the differences we set up between classes of men, the habits and knowledge acquired from infancy, or the various ways of praying to what is called God. Ages, sexes, or even species seemed to him closer one to another than each generally assumed about the other: child or old man, man or woman, animal or biped who speaks and works with his hands, all come together in the misery and sweetness of existence. Despite their difference in color, he had got on well with the half-breed; despite her religion, which in any case she hardly practiced, Saraï had been a woman like any other; there were baptized thieves, too. In spite of the gulf that separates a servant from a burgomaster, he had felt affection for Mijnheer van Herzog, who probably had felt for his valet only a touch of benevolence; in spite of the bit of learning he had acquired at the schoolmaster's and, later, in the books he'd looked through at Elie's, he didn't have the impression that he knew any more than Markus, or than the half-breed, who had been only a cook. In spite of his soutane and the fact that he came from France, the young Jesuit had seemed to him like a brother.

Yet it wasn't for him to formulate general opinions; at most, he could speak only for himself. As his bodily deterioration increased, like that of a hut made of beaten earth or mud which is slaked with water, it was hard to say what it was that shone with increasing strength and brightness at the crest of his being, like a candle in the top room of a house about to collapse. He supposed that candle would be extinguished beneath the fallen hovel; yet he wasn't sure. Well, he would see—or, on the other hand, he wouldn't. Yet he preferred to opt for total darkness, which seemed to him the most desirable solution: no one needed a Nathanaël who was immortal. Or possibly the small bright flame would continue to burn, or be rekindled in other bodies of wax, without even knowing it or worrying that it had already had a name. In truth, he suspected that his spirit, or what the Jesuit would have called his soul, was nothing more than something which had briefly settled upon him. But, unlike Leon Belmonte, he wasn't about to worry all the way to the end of whatever axis or hole was God or himself. All about him there was the sea, the mist, the sun and rain, the beasts of air and water and land; he would live and die as those beasts do. That was enough. He would not be remembered any more than the insects of last summer.

With a sort of mania, he went on keeping the three rooms reserved for the owners in order, as if it had not already been decided that Mijnheer Hendrik was not coming. He became obsessed with cleanliness: to draw the brackish water for washing his few dishes and his meager laundry immediately exhausted him. The fire became a voracious beast which had to be fed incessantly with wood chips or lumps of peat. At the end, he nourished himself with cold boiled barley, white cheese, and bread. His bowels no longer retained food; he was often obliged to get up in haste and run to the door. The trail of liquid excrement left on the threshold appalled him; but in the morning it was nothing more than a few blackened spots over which he kicked a bit of sand.

The worse thing was his heaving cough, as though he carried within himself bogs in which he was engulfed. Every night, rolled up in one of Mijnheer van Herzog's handsome coverlets, which absorbed his feverish sweats better than a sheet, he thought he would not live until morning. Actually, it was very simple: how many animals in the woods would not live to see the dawn? He was suffused with an immense compassion for all living creatures, each of them different from the other, for whom living and dying is almost equally difficult. At daybreak, the

fresh, gentle air which came in from the ocean brought
him a sort of respite. For one instant his well-washed body
seemed to him intact, handsome even, participating with
every fiber of its being in the joy of morning.

Curiously, his impaired health, which he was most
strongly aware of in the middle of the night, had not destroyed the needs of love. For it was indeed love, since the
woman he possessed in his dreams always had the same
face. He had drunk with gratitude, practically with respect, the tisanes of borage and marshmallow that Madame
d'Ailly had sent him in a large cloth bag. He thought of
her with nothing but reverence. But at night, lying naked
in his shroud of brown wool, he avidly performed with her
the acts he had once performed with Foy, with Saraï, and
with a few others; he imagined her body in the positions
his other lovers had assumed, but sweeter than ever in its
total abandon. His memories, modified in this way, intoxicated him all over again. It was not rape, since he imagined it done with tenderness and received with gentleness.
Nonetheless, it was an abuse he was ashamed of . . .
Madeleine d'Ailly . . . Once he had loved to murmur her
name, but no name was necessary anymore, now that she
had come to represent all women for him. And, to be sure,
Madame d'Ailly had never done, said, or even suggested
anything which authorized him to use her in this way.
And then he thought how every human creature enters
without knowing it into the amorous dreams of those who
encounter him or live around him; and that despite the
obscurity or penury, the age or ugliness, of the person
who loves, on the one hand, and, on the other, the shyness
or embarrassment of the beloved or the fact that her own
desires are perhaps directed toward someone else, each of
us is, in this way, open and accessible to everyone. Even
were she dead, he could still have taken pleasure from her

in his dreams. But she was alive, and that thought made
him hope that he might continue to live a bit longer.

Those things passed, and returned only in rare moments. The equinoctial storms arrived on roughly the pre-
scribed date; their winds swept everything away. Willem
had warned Nathanaël that he wouldn't risk coming to
the island until they were over; it constituted a depriva-
tion, or a respite, of one week or perhaps two. It was no
longer possible to light the fire; the smoke driven back
down the low chimney would have filled the room. Yet it
wasn't cold. There was an atmosphere of wild festivity.
The gaping waves formed great hollows, all frothy with
foam, penetrated by other waves, yet that inert water was,
in actuality, furrowed by the wind. Only it and the sparse
grass that lay trembling on the surface of the dunes indicated the onrush of the invisible master who let his presence be discerned by nothing but the violence to which he
subjects things. Invisible, he was silent as well: once more,
the waves served as his spokesman; their thunder beating
heavily against the soft earth, their roar of runaway stal-
lions, came from him. All the rest was voiceless: the clumps
of trees were too far off for the grinding and screaming of
their branches and trunks to be heard.

For several days, Nathanaël did not go out at all: he did
little more than stick his head out the door from time to
time; immediately, it was lashed by the whipping sand.
He told himself that one more wave, one more gust, and
not only would the shaking cottage come down on him
but the whole island would disappear and become, under
the waters that closed over it, no more than another sandbank or another bit of flotsam endangering the living ships.
Yet at every autumnal equinox in the memory of man the
seas had risen and then subsided; the enormous fury had
calmed, and the winter storms had been followed by days

of respite, which in turn were followed by the floodtides of spring. This mass of sand which had emerged from the waters would be swallowed back up by them one day, but the hour, the day, and the year of that was unknown, like those of a man's death.

For now, birds trusted the island enough to take refuge there. Through the windows ceaselessly blurred with sand, Nathanaël watched them gather by the thousands in a hollow of the dunes, all of them aware that they must both endure and confront the storm, save their strength, and turn their heads into the wind so that its great force would not ruffle up their feathers, all of them silent and in formation like an encircled army. When the squall had diminished at least enough that he could attempt to go out, Nathanaël, crawling on his belly more than he walked, went in the direction of the birds. Most of them had taken to the air again, gliding high above, apparently delighting in the gymnastics of letting themselves be borne or tossed on the wind. The raucous gulls were already fishing, plunging their beaks into the thick, muddy soup which was filled with debris where the waves had scraped the depths. Thin, calm teals sat effortlessly on the shoulders of the heavy swells and then slid down into their hollows. Several more timorous groups of birds remained silently in place. Nathanaël's crawling over the sand did not bother them. On the far edge of the hollow in which they had taken refuge, he saw a gray gull beating its wings. Not yet completely an adult, to judge by its feathers, but dead. Its inert wings no longer obeyed the volition of its head or its feathered breast, but passively surrendered to the immense will of the wind. Nathanaël turned it over with the end of his stick. This object was nothing more than the form of a bird; this life that had existed was no more. That night, in the shelter of his room where he had lighted a candle in order to feel a bit less alone, as he leaned on his elbow during one of his coughing fits he distractedly watched a fly on the windowpane, which was no longer trembling in its frame; the fly was dying, but, deceived by this bit of warmth and light, it buzzed against the impassable glass.

The next day, the wind had fallen. Everything seemed amazingly calm. Well before dawn, he put on his shirt, trousers, and vest and pulled on his shoes, breathing heavily as he always did when he had to bend over. He closed the door tightly behind him so that it wouldn't bang in the wind. The blackness of the sky was turning gray, indicating the approach of morning.

He started toward the interior of the island. He knew fairly well the faint paths he himself had made in order to find the way to his favorite spot in the half-light; in his present state of weakness, he would have to count on walking for a good half hour. From time to time, he stopped to look about him. The storm which had torn up the coast had hardly touched the interior, except perhaps on the side where the copses were, where there must be some uprooted trees. Nathanaël hoped that those vigorous young brothers, huddled one against another, had mutually protected each other. But on this side there was only short grass and very low plants dragging on the ground, beneath which the sand was visible. In order to get where he wanted to, he was forced to cross a small natural canal which the rain had hollowed out and which probably rejoined the sea farther along. But this tiny stream wasn't deep. He understood, without feeling obliged to tell himself, that at that moment he was doing what sick or wounded animals do: he was seeking a place of refuge where he could achieve his end all alone—as if the little house of Mijnheer van Herzog weren't altogether solitude. At every step, he told himself that he could, if he wished, retrace his path and go eat his evening broth in the house.

But, at every step, exhaustion and lack of breath would also have made such a return more difficult. He fell, and had trouble getting up again; he had done that before.

Finally, he arrived at the hollow he had been looking for. Some arbutuses grew here and there, providing refuge for the birds and for their nests in the springtime. As he approached, he flushed out two pheasants, who flew off in a great, sudden rush of wings. On the edge of this imperceptible depression there were even two or three stunted pines, no taller than a man, in which some magpies had built their nests. Nathanaël stuck his fingers into these empty pouches which had so recently held life.

Meanwhile, the whole sky had turned pink, not only in the east as he had expected, but in all directions, the low clouds reflecting the dawn. It was hard to orient oneself: the Orient seemed to be everywhere. Standing in the bottom of this gently sloping hollow, he saw the dunes on every side rolling like whitecaps toward the sea. But the resounding crash of the surf could not be heard at this distance. It was comfortable here. Cautiously, he lay down in the short dune grass near a grove of arbutuses which sheltered him from the bit of wind. He could sleep a little before going back, if his heart told him to. He was thinking, though, that if by chance he were to die there, he would be spared all the usual human formalities: no one would look for him where he was; old Willem would certainly never suppose that he would have tried to wander so far. What one would find when spring came and the poachers who stole eggs from the nests arrived wouldn't even be worth burying.

All of a sudden, he heard a bleating sound. He wasn't surprised: some sheep who had turned wild lived in the center of the island, and they, like him, had found a safe shelter.

The pink sky had faded now. Lying on his back, he

watched the great clouds forming and dissolving above him. Then, abruptly, he was once more seized with a coughing fit. But he felt it no longer mattered that he clear his congested lungs, and he tried not to cough. Inside his ribs, it hurt. He raised himself a little to get some relief. A warm, familiar liquid filled his mouth; he spat weakly, watching the thin trickle of foam disappear into the clumps of dune grass that covered the sand. He choked a bit, hardly more than usual. Resting his head on a tuft of grass, he bedded down, as if to sleep.

A
LOVELY
MORNING

to Johan Polak

"Well, did you see them?"

"I did more than see them. I talked with them. Can you keep a secret? I'm leaving."

"Where are you going?"

"To Denmark. It seems it's in the north somewhere and they treat actors well there."

"They hired you?"

"They needed somebody, you know, since their young leading lady got his head bashed in at the Brown Bear."

"Does Loubah know?"

"No, better she doesn't. But she'll find someone else to carry the beer mugs and coffee to her clients."

"And they're leaving tomorrow?"

"Yes. Early. Don't worry, Klem. We'll come by here on our way back from Denmark. By the way, I owe you thruppence from our last bet."

"Oh, never mind . . ."

They embraced.

For the dozen years now that he'd been on this great turning ball, the boy had wandered round and round a good deal himself, but only in the lanes and alleyways of Amsterdam. At night, all dressed up like a little valet, he would open the door for Loubah's clients, bowing down to the ground; from time to time, when the bells were ringing furiously, he was sent to carry the drink or tobacco they needed to those visitors who were worth making a fuss over in little ways. And, anyhow, that was the only sort of person Mevrouw Loubah let in.

The men lying against the cushions with one or the other of the two nieces, or else with a third, who was black, paid no attention to the tousle-headed little boy; they would absentmindedly tell him to look in the pocket of their jacket hanging on the back of a chair and take a coin for himself. Once or twice, Lazarus acquired a gold piece that way, which caused him some embarrassment, since he didn't know where to change it without getting himself accused of theft. In the end, the black girl would burst into a big guffaw and change it for him herself. The nieces were pleasant enough, but they rose late; the servants never seemed to finish with making their beds, getting them washed, and ironing their sleeves or coifs or polishing their shoes. The hairdresser, who came every day to curl their hair, let the boy warm the irons and blow on them to cool them when necessary, but the smell of scorched hair revolted him.

The best was when they asked him to help out at the inn. Loubah, who wasn't a bad woman and who tried to stay on good terms with her neighbors, never prevented him from going and didn't even take a part of his tips. As far as school went, they managed. In any case, he was getting a bit old for school.

The inn was a whole world in itself. It had everything: fat farmers who came for one of the fairs, sailors from all over, Frenchmen who were always anxious and penniless and called themselves men of letters (but Lazarus didn't know what that strange phrase meant, and the innkeeper quietly treated them as spies), servants of ambassadors for whom Their Excellencies didn't at the moment have a place where they could stay, and women with military officers. His mother must have been like those women. The packetboat from England almost always brought new clients. And that was when they really appreciated him, him, the boy Lazarus from Loubah's, not only because he could carry dishes or hold horses in the courtyard but because he could make himself understood in English with those people. A lot of English was spoken at Loubah's, and he had learned it early. Even the black girl, who came from Jamaica, spoke a kind of English gibberish. But there had also been that great occasion for Lazarus when Loubah had taken him to London for a few weeks, wearing his best lace collar and carrying some hard little sparkling balls in his pocket. Mostly, however, he remembered being seasick.

These days, there was a whole pack of Englishmen. You couldn't tell at first glance whether they were rich or poor; they brought a huge pile of badly done-up parcels. And their trunks were old, held together as well as possible with ropes. Some of them were fairly well got up, but their linen was a bit worn or mended, and others, rather sloppily dressed, wore dirty, threadbare clothing, yet sometimes under their jackets they had a fine scarf with sequins on it, a woman's scarf, or wore a huge diamond on their finger which Mevrouw Loubah would at once declare was a fake.

Lazarus recognized the actors immediately. He knew who they were. He had seen a couple of plays in London, and even here in Amsterdam theatricals were sometimes staged on trestle platforms set up at crossroads or in the coachyard of an inn. But those actors, who could only do acrobatics or play the clown, were no great shakes. In contrast, these (there were eighteen or twenty of them) had manners almost as good as Mevrouw Loubah's or those of Herbert Mortimer, whom Lazarus, won over by his great kindness, considered a close friend.

Herbert Mortimer had gone back to London around Christmastime, but Lazarus hadn't forgot him. He had a handsome face, even though he was nothing more than a broken old man, white-haired and very gentle. He had long, well-cared-for hands, which seemed to caress the knob of his cane without stop. But he also liked to pat the child's head and open up the handsomely carved knob in order to give him some sweetmeats, which both of them were fond of. He and Mevrouw Loubah, they were what you might call old friends. When he had arrived at her place two or three years before, he had with him some handsome clothes and a huge trunk full of pamphlets and books. He also had a little monkey big as your finger, but the monkey had died. Loubah had put Herbert in the room at the very top of the house, where she lodged people who didn't like to be disturbed. He rarely came downstairs; the child, who carried his meals up to him, thought that was probably because of the stairs, or else because he was afraid. Nobody used so many wax candles (he hated the tallow ones), but Loubah, for once, didn't get upset by that. Given how considerate they were of each other, Lazarus thought they must often have woken up, the way lovers do, with their heads on the same pillow, yet that must have been some time ago, because Loubah, despite her rouge, her powder, and her henna, was pretty long in the tooth, and he, Herbert, didn't hide the fact that he was old. Certainly he was sixty if he was a day. But in one respect at least he was completely different from other old people: he was generous. He shared with the boy the cups of hot chocolate and the biscuits that were sent up to him.

Late at night, going up to his attic room, Lazarus would see a ray of light under Herbert's door and hear him talking to himself. Or rather, you would have said he was talking to other people who were answering him, yet Lazarus was sure there was no one else in his room. Unless he was talking to ghosts, which would have been pretty scary; but one day Lazarus looked through the keyhole and he didn't see any ghosts. The strangest thing was that the old gentleman's voice was always changing: sometimes it was the strong voice of a man you would have said was very young, one of those voices that suggest full lips and fine teeth. At other times, it was a young girl's voice, very sweet, which laughed and babbled like a spring. There were also several voices of rustics which sounded as if they were arguing among themselves. But the most beautiful thing was when he spoke in a majestic voice so weighty that it was surely the voice of some bishop or king.

One night, the boy scratched at the door. The old man opened it with a kindly air, a book in his hand. "It's you, is it? For a long time now I've heard you panting behind the door like a puppy."

Lazarus, playing his canine part, barked softly, sat down on the floor, and rested a paw on Mister Herbert's knee. The man stroked his head and went back to reading aloud softly, but the boy thought he was reading better than ever now that he knew someone was watching and listening to him. From that evening on, they were constantly in each other's company. Soon he also became his pupil. One night, the old man said to him, handing him some torn pages: "You know how to read. Give me the cues: it'll be more fun that way."

It was in fact more fun, because they both laughed a lot whenever Lazarus made a mistake, something that happened often. He didn't know how to read printed words all that well.

They almost always ate together now, and their meals were often spent pretending that the knife was a dagger thrust between someone's ribs, and the fork a flower proffered to some lady or, depending on the circumstances, a scepter. Two or three times, when Loubah invited him, Mister Herbert had agreed to come down to dine with his hostess, but her nieces and their invited guests bored him; the boy realized that Herbert made most of these fellows ill at ease with his beautiful table manners and his exceedingly polite conversation, since, it goes without saying, Loubah's guests were often pretty crude, even the rich ones, or else stiff and on their guard. Mevrouw Loubah herself, so well turned out and trim in her lace, was used to their loud laughter, their belches, and their gobbets of spit aimed at the stove. And then too, Mister Herbert, who spoke the English of kings and queens with such eloquence, didn't manage so well with the language of their country. They made fun of him, which annoyed him. The boy, too, didn't hesitate to laugh at his gaffes, but only when they were alone together.

One day, shortly before Christmas, when Mister Herbert was in Loubah's cozy little parlor, the boy heard him saying: "Such talent, such an ear for the rhythms . . . I see myself as I was at twelve, and even some quality I didn't have at that age—an elf, a sprite, Ariel . . ."

"Ariel?" repeated Mevrouw Loubah.

"Never mind," he said impatiently. "It's a shame to let this rich ground lie fallow . . . Under my tutelage . . ."

"Your profession, my dear, is one of those which begins and ends in starvation."

"But in between there are some fine moments," said Herbert, dreaming. "To stir an audience, to move people who wouldn't be moved if they saw a man killed in the street . . . And then, the court . . . And that special way of saluting Their Majesties without obsequiousness when you yourself are dressed as a king or prince . . . A profession in which you rub elbows with the great ones of this world. A bit like yours, if I may say so."

"At least I've never been asked to carry dangerous dispatches that can land their bearer in prison. You were lucky to get away . . ."

"Thanks to you, my adorable one. And it's only your charms which have spared you the same trip . . ."

"Oh," she said, "I've never been compromised by any of that political nonsense. That's nothing but air, my dear. I'm only for what's solid."

"For what's solid and exquisite," he responded gallantly. "But that boy . . ."

"No," she said. "If I ever send him back there, it'll be with a protector loaded with more gold than you. Always what's solid, you understand? You can just kiss your dream goodbye."

Then, getting up, she did something that astonished the child: she kissed her old friend on the lips. He gave her a prolonged kiss in return. Was it possible people still embraced at their age? The boy thought he heard Mevrouw Loubah say laughingly to Mister Herbert that a twelve-year-old brat was no rival.

But a few weeks later Herbert proudly displayed the safe-conduct, stamped with a lot of seals, that he'd been waiting for for a long time. The political skies had cleared for him.

"I advise you to stay here," said Loubah with prudence. "The theater over there is in parlous state because of the Roundheads. You run the risk of stepping into a real drama."

But it was to no avail. Several days later, the old man took the packetboat back to London, where Illiard Swanson had offered him a good role. The farewell between him and Mevrouw Loubah was affectionate but brief, like that of people who have often parted and met again. The child he embraced more tenderly, at least so it seemed to the boy, who thought he saw the eyes of his old friend become moist. "What a Juliet!" he murmured with an almost tremulous voice. "What a Juliet!" Fearing he would be badgered by the customs agents, who would rummage through his bags, he left a good part of his books and quartos with Loubah.

The child took advantage of them, but, since Mevrouw Loubah would not have been so generous to him with her wax candles, he used the ends of tallow ones he was able to snitch. At night, in the attic, he did his best to imitate the tones of voice and gestures of his old friend.

The actors staying at the inn could not pretend to have the splendid bearing of Herbert, who had, if you could believe him, often acted before King James. But they had some money in their pockets. It was known that they were about to leave on tour for Hanover (the Electress was English), Denmark, and, finally, Norway, but they were first getting ready to put on a comedy at a country festival a certain gentleman bon-vivant named M. de Bréderode, well thought of by the owners of the inn, was going to give in his park a few miles from there. The esteem in which he was held rubbed off onto the players. All the same, actors aren't much better than a herd of cattle, and they had only been given a large room in one of the outbuildings, which must once have been a stable but was now furnished with a round table and some stools. Some counterpanes heaped against the wall served for beds.

Lazarus, who liked to try and guess ages, thought the oldest of the troupe was probably fifty and the youngest about seventeen. The seventeen-year-old was nice. He soon learned that he was called Humphrey.

The boy went back and forth from the kitchen to the room with tin tankards. It became a sort of game. Lifting his thin arm high in the air, he took pride in his skill at making the beer flow in a long frothy stream.

"Bravo! Old man Jupiter's cupbearer!"

"And therefore look you call me Ganymede," exclaimed the boy, citing a verse from one Shakespeare.

The director could hardly believe his ears. "Where did you get that?"

"I know the part of Rosalind by heart," said the boy proudly.

"If that's so, it's better than a good omen," said the director, addressing his remarks to the whole company; "it's a godsend we can't let slip by."

"We're not sure Edmund won't be ready," said the stage manager, who liked to contradict and who, in any case, was fond of Edmund.

"Come on! He's out for three weeks, if he ever does recover, and we're performing tomorrow. Anyway, a Rosalind with a bashed-in face . . ."

"You, you lousy little Jew, how is it you know English?" asked the stage manager ferociously. Onstage, he was used for tyrants and King Herod. "And where did you learn Rosalind's part?"

"An old man named Herbert Mortimer used to live in our house."

The director sucked in his cheeks to produce a whistle. "You don't say! By the way, he just went back to London, Herbert did, with a valid safe-conduct. We needed him to play Caesar."

"Oh no, not Caesar! In these troubled times? That's a dangerous play . . . No . . . For the Moor of Venice, now . . . Fixed up, of course, because, after all, it's a damned old play. Still, it has to be said, Herbert isn't bad with walnut stain on his face and a turban on his head . . ."

"All the same! Everyone's well aware that he's no longer young enough to couple with Desdemona."

"Oh, forget it! In the theater, age, you know . . . and even in life . . ."

The fat, fair-haired director never took his eyes off the boy everyone else seemed to have forgot about. "Give him the cues, Orlando," he said to Humphrey. "We'll see whether or not he can play Rosalind. He's a sweet boy, in any case . . ."

"It's not fair," said a surly, rather pudgy lad who was nibbling at some smoked herring on a hunk of bread. "It's me, Aliena, who ought to take over Rosalind . . ."

"Content yourself with Aliena, my girl," said the director, whom they also called "the good duke." "Already you don't look so good in skirts, and to play the part of a girl who dresses up as a boy is like making three leaps one after another. You've really got to know how to manage that."

"Anyway," said Humphrey, "your waist size would make it hard for me to lead you in the dance."

He sat back on his heels, wiping his eyes to hide his bashful lover's tears, alternately laughing and imploring. He was a good actor: as Orlando he was simply a bit more, and a bit more gaily, himself. The boy, his eyes shining with joy, answered him without a mistake. In his role of a girl who pretends to be a boy, both in order to console her comrade for the absence of his girl and to poke gentle fun at him, he managed to convey something like three persons within himself, three persons who were, so to speak, played against one another. For, to complicate matters, the girl dressed as a boy was in love with the boy she was bantering with, and he didn't recognize her in her man's breeches and doublet. They had to admit that Herbert had been a good teacher.

"You're getting mixed up," said Humphrey. "Don't skip over the best part. *As boys and women are for the most part cattle of this color.* Let's start back a bit."

"Whatever you say," said the boy. "But I'm mixed up because she's mixed up . . . She's rather embarrassed, you see, because she's in love with you, Humphrey."

He had decided right away that Humphrey-Orlando was worthy of Rosalind's love.

"What about me, then?" asked a very young lad with a red nose, who kept pulling a sort of peasant shawl up over his shoulders. "I'd do Rosalind well enough if you'd only give me her clothes."

"My dear Audrey, you're exactly the right girl for Touchstone," said the director—a remark which immediately angered an unshaven man with a whitened face, who didn't like to be reminded that he played the clown.

"But I'm the only one who can make them laugh," he said savagely. And as if to prove his skill, he twisted his face into a grimace with the gaping mouth of a gargoyle.

"Good," said the director, turning his back on this Touchstone. "Very good, in fact . . . A stroke of luck," he continued with jubilation, "and to think that I expected to have to change the play . . . But we still have to see if he looks good dressed as a girl. After all, she's my own daughter."

Humphrey went to rummage in a trunk. He returned with his arms full of cheap finery.

"Put that on. Don't bother to take off your clothes. You're thin enough that we can see what it will look like."

And, turning to the director-duke, he added: "I brought her wedding dress, since it's the prettiest. We'll be able to tell better."

The boy had trouble finding the hooks of the full skirt of crimson moiré with its strips of cloth-of-silver.

"Be careful: that one's a bit torn. It has a low neckline, but that'll be all right once you're not wearing that thick shirt which bulges out the top . . ."

"It's rather ample in front," said Aliena, sneering.

"That's all right. We'll stuff it with rags. Turn around."

The boy turned obediently, revealing beneath the skirt an old, worn-out shoe which was too big for him.

"My God!" said the director-duke. "I almost forgot. Do you live with your parents?"

"I've got a grandmother of sorts."

"What does she do?"

"She receives gentlemen who dance with her three nieces."

"I don't think this is going to pose any difficulties," whispered the director to the stage manager. "And your mother?"

"My mother was hanged in public," said the boy unabashedly, for he was proud of that episode. It seemed to him that his mother (whom, in any case, he didn't remember, since he was very young at the time) had died on the stage of a great theater.

"And your father?"

"Don't know," said the boy. "I don't think I had a father."

"Everyone has a father," said Humphrey sententiously, rubbing his backside as if he remembered the strokes of a cane.

"Listen," said the director, holding the boy by the arms. "God's sent you to us. You're a Jew, I think, but even so you believe in God, don't you? Well then, the day before yesterday, the day we arrived from London, Edmund (sometimes called Edmunda) went out to wander about the town and got into a fight with someone. The Dutch, they're no joke, and then, too, he'd drunk more of their jenever than he should have. I don't know who was right and who was wrong in all that, but he was found on the pavement with his head bashed in. And tomorrow we've got to have a Rosalind to perform at M. de Bréderode's."

"And afterwards," continued Humphrey, "it's even better. We're going to Hanover, because the Electress is from our country and wants to see the plays from London they put on in her youth. Then to Denmark. Our contract calls for real rooms in the attic, and two geese or swans a day, with all the trimmings. And afterwards, if we feel like it, we'll go to Norway, and we'll come back through here on our way back to England, where they'll get bored without us. How about it?"

"*I am your Rosalind,*" said the boy, still acting.

"I think it'll be best if he doesn't tell his old lady about this," mused the director-duke. "Does she love you, your grandmother?"

"I carry the dishes and open the door for her."

"Oh well, she'll find someone else who can open the door and carry the dishes. Sneak out quietly tomorrow and meet us at dawn."

"And you'll see what a lark it'll be," added Humphrey. "The ladies will kiss you and call you their page. They'll give you sweetmeats. And sometimes the gentlemen will give you a gold piece from their pocket. I was a girl once myself, and I know what happens. Since I turned eighteen, though, I've been a boy again."

"That hasn't deprived you of women's kisses or of gold pieces," said Aliena bleakly.

"That's all well and good, my children, but we can't let the boy get himself ensnared and stay in Denmark as Her Highness's page," said the director-duke. "If you're a good boy, we'll take you back to London with us."

"I've already been to London."

"Better and better. You'll feel right at home. Keep an eye on him, Humphrey. He may be a bit featherbrained, our little prodigy."

Humphrey took the boy back out into the courtyard. Lazarus paused to put his arms around a horse's neck.

"Don't say goodbye to anybody but the horses. Anyway, it's not goodbye; we'll be coming back through here. I wish I could keep you here to sleep in the big room, but that would put the wind up your old lady. Slip out quietly at dawn and wear your best clothes. Do you have any? We've got a handsome Ganymede costume for you in the scenes where you wear hose, but it's too good to wear on the street. And don't take any money, or at least not much. She could come after you."

"I've already thought of that," said the boy with a toss of his head.

He ran back home. The house was close by, but it was nearly the time when they would be expecting him to put on his best suit and open the door. He only stopped for a minute to tell Klem all about it; Humphrey had warned him not to do that, but Klem could be trusted; he'd let them beat him to death before he said anything. Loubah's drawing room was full of people. He thought he'd never get done that night. When finally there were only two or three clients left, who had paid to spend the night, Mevrouw Loubah poked at the fire in the kitchen, separating the logs and removing them from the heap of still-hot ashes. Lazarus thought she looked like a witch or a fairy (in Herbert's books, there were also sibyls), and that, in her own way, she was really quite beautiful. In the theater, she could easily have played the part of aged queens.

As he went step by step up the long staircase, it occurred to him that she had never struck him, much less beat him. She had never given him a talking to, except on the subject of the mistakes you can make with your body, such as blowing your nose too hard or not combing your hair. As far as he could see, she was good to the nieces, and good to her clients, whom she didn't criticize even when they threw up after they'd drunk too much. She was very good to Herbert, and he'd never seen him give her any money. And he remembered how once, in his presence, she had put a gentleman's purse back into his pocket when he'd dropped it as he was tipping back in his chair. Mevrouw, who wasn't given to speaking moralistically, had said to the astonished boy: "You've always got to be honest in little things. You'll understand that one day."

No, she wasn't a bad grandmother. Still, he didn't love her enough to tell her he was going.

Once in his attic, he carefully removed his supply of candle ends from between two beams and by their light reread the complete part of Rosalind to be sure he wouldn't stop short in the middle of some speech. "Anyway," he thought, "if I do forget, I'll make something up. Humphrey will help me." He made a parcel of Herbert's quartos (the books were too heavy to take with him) and put it on his pillow. Resting his head on this hard package, he slept with half-closed eyes . . . or rather, instead of sleeping, he dreamed.

It was a long dream. It was about him, Lazarus the child, who knew everything there was to know in the streets of Amsterdam—the thieves, who, you had to hand it to them, had never stolen anything from him; the drunks, who are often quite kind when they've drunk a lot; the poor and the rich (you can tell them from their clothing); the beggars, who are afraid someone's going to compete with them; the gentlemen young and old, those who pay you a few pence to deliver a letter to some woman and give you a tip in addition when you bring them back an answer, before they've even read what it says inside (and sometimes what's inside makes them burst into tears); those who hug you in their arms (God knows why) in some dark corner, as if they would squeeze you to death, and sometimes they reward you with a silver coin; those who give you money for holding their horse, and sometimes the horse is bad-tempered and kicks, but most horses liked him and he liked feeling their saliva on his hand when he offered them an apple core . . . And those who distrust you (the merchants) and chase you away with a stick if you stand too long looking in their windows, especially the bakers.

And it was about Lazarus the boy, who played with Klem and whom Mevrouw Loubah was good to, except that she never kissed him, but then he'd never seen her kiss anyone but Herbert, who was very old. Yet it seemed to him that these small Lazaruses were not so much dead or forgotten as somehow outgrown, like the small boys with whom he had played in the street.

And it was about Herbert, who had taught him to act and talk like someone else. Herbert's room had been full of an endless number of people, and of battles, and of processions, and of wedding feasts, and of cries of joy or pain that would shake the house down, but you cried out in a soft voice so that no one would hear, and this whole crowd including the kings and queens had comfortably fitted into the space between the trunk and the small stove. And Herbert had gone away the way people go away in dreams, or the way actors sometimes disappear into the wings and you don't know why, and in the same way, tomorrow, little Lazarus would go away with the players.

It didn't matter that Herbert was pale and feeble: he was ageless. When he wanted to, he could be as small and sweet as the children of Edward who had been killed in the Tower, and sometimes as gay and full of laughter as Beatrice, who danced as the stars dance, and at those moments he was fifteen, and at other times, when he wept over his lost kingdom or his dead daughter, he was so old he seemed a thousand. And he no longer had a body. When he would make little Lazarus laugh so hard by becoming Falstaff, then he was big and fat, with legs as curved as the hoops of a barrel, while the rest of the time he was as thin as the melancholy Jacques (tomorrow, at M. de

Bréderode's, there would be no melancholy Jacques like
him), and when he was Cleopatra he was ravishingly
beautiful.

And Lazarus, too, would be all these girls, and all these
women, and all these young men, and all the old ones, too.
Already he was Rosalind. Tomorrow he would depart from
Mevrouw Loubah's house with its Venetian mirrors in
which the nieces and their gentlemen liked to look at
themselves naked. He would be dressed as usual, as a boy,
but he would really be Rosalind, when she had fled in disguise from the handsome palace from which her father
the good duke had been chased out. She would call herself
Ganymede and would go deep into a forest so large that if
you wanted to put that many trees on the stage all the
copses and woods around Amsterdam put together wouldn't
be enough.

She would leave in the company of Aliena, her good
cousin (he would have to remember to be nice to Aliena),
and a white-faced clown Lazarus was a bit afraid of, but it
was better not to let anyone see he was afraid. And on
the day of his wedding to Orlando, he would dance in his
beautiful gown with strips of silver (he didn't know how to
dance, but it would be enough to hop up and down in
time), and he'd have to be careful not to rip the strips any
further, as they were already torn.

And he would be other beautiful girls too, but first he'd
have to learn by heart all the speeches they delivered and
not merely a few words that came to him because Mister
Herbert had, as it were, sung them out. He would be Juliet,
and now he understood why Mister Herbert had called
him by that name when he left. He would be Jessica the
Jewess, dressed like the pretty girls of the Jodenstraat; he
would be Cleopatra and give his tiny hand to be kissed by
a general named Antony; he looked in vain for an actor in

the big room who could be magnificent enough to be Antony. And then he would die, killed by a snake, but he hoped the snake bite wouldn't hurt too much.

When a good deal of time had gone by, when he would be eighteen or possibly nineteen or (who knows?) even twenty, he would become a boy again, like Humphrey: he would struggle shoulder to shoulder with the brute who would attack him in the lists, but first he'd have to develop his biceps and strengthen his fists. And he would be Romeo weeping over the Juliet he would remember having been; it would be easy for him to climb up to the balcony, he who so nimbly climbed the trees along the quayside.

He would be the Duchess of Malfi, weeping in a madhouse over her little children, and then, one day, when he no longer looked very good in women's clothing, he would be one of the evil men who strangled her. And he would be Hotspur, the knight with the fiery spurs, so young and brave, and also his wife, Kate, who, when she bids him farewell, tries to laugh so as not to weep, and Hal, so brave and full of gaiety with his joyful comrades.

Much later still, when he had reached a really advanced age, say forty, he would be a king with a crown on his head, or else Caesar. Herbert had shown him how to fall and arrange the folds of his toga in such a way that he didn't expose his naked legs indecently. And he would also be those ladies weighed down with all the evil they had committed in their lives: a fat queen of Denmark, swollen with crimes, or Lady Macbeth with her knife, or even those bearded witches who boil up filthy things in their cauldron.

Or else he'd play the clown, like that grimacing, white-faced fellow last night: making people laugh would be another way of amusing them and giving them pleasure, the way you amuse them and give them pleasure when you are a girl and kiss someone before their eyes (and

sometimes they wait in the wings, too, to be kissed themselves) or (strange to say) when you die young and beautiful before their eyes. And then, when he'd got to fifty
(that was a long time, fifty years), they'd give him the
really old parts: an Orlando who wouldn't be Humphrey—
for Humphrey would perhaps be dead by then since he
was already eighteen now—would tenderly carry him in
his arms as the old servant Adam, hoary with age and full
of wrinkles, toothless, feeble, but faithful. It would be nice
to have been faithful for fifty years.

And quite possibly, after having been Jessica, the lovely,
laughing Jewess who runs off taking the ducats with her,
he'd be her father Shylock with his miserly fingers, and
they'd treat him like a lousy old Jew, the way the stage
manager had treated him as a lousy young Jew yesterday,
because that's the way things are. Still, it must be hard for
an old man to lose both his daughter and his ducats, and
maybe, instead of making people laugh when he was
Shylock, he'd make them cry.

Or else, in contrast, everything would take place before
a blue sea under a pinkish sky, and he would be Prospero
the Magician, who, like Herbert, has no age because he is
practically God, and he would remember how he had
been, years earlier, his own daughter, the innocent
Miranda, who falls in love with a man because he's handsome. And after calming the earth and the waves, he
would recite those wonderful words about things that pass
as in a dream, in the depths of a dream with which our
little life is rounded (he didn't know the passage by heart
too well), and then when he had broken his magic staff,
everything would be over.

And when there was no longer a place for him on the
boards, he would become the candle snuffer, the man who
lights them and then, at the end, puts them out one by one.

But since he'd know all the parts, they would take him on as a prompter: his voice would be, as it were, in all the voices. He was overcome with a feverish joy at the thought of being in one instant so many people living out so many adventures. Little Lazarus had no limits; and it was in vain that he gave a friendly smile to his own reflection, which came back to him from a bit of mirror stuck between two beams, for he had no specific shape. He possessed a thousand shapes.

In any case, that particular morning he was invisible in the gray light of daybreak as he came barefoot, his old shoes in his hands, down the back stairs of Loubah's house and slipped out by the kitchen door, whose latch he had oiled with a bit of fat the day before. The sky was half gray, half rose. It was going to be a lovely morning.

In the street, he put on his shoes; he was already overladen with his best clothes folded over his arm, his Sunday shoes hanging from his belt, and the large parcel of Herbert's quartos. In the kitchen, five pennies were lying on the table for the milkman. He had taken them. It wasn't really a theft; it was a windfall.

The street was still practically empty except for some country folk going to market with their baskets full: they must have got up by candlelight. A vendor of fritters was already in place to appease the hunger of those who passed by. Lazarus parted with a penny and put the delicious big, warm ball into his mouth. Some scrawny dogs were scavenging in the piles of garbage visited by rats during the night; he would have liked to pat all the dogs one by one. He would also have liked to lend a supporting hand to the drunk reeling home, who was in danger of falling into the gutter; but his hands were full of his clothing and parcels. And he was in a hurry to get to the inn.

Humphrey was waiting for him at the door, an old horse blanket draped over his shoulders. "Put your costume on right away. Your dress is in the little room next to the carriage house. And be careful not to catch cold: the early morning air can make you hoarse."

As they crossed the courtyard, he pointed to a coach they were beginning to harness up. "M. de Bréderode sent it to take us to the castle. He wants us to arrive dressed up in our costumes to look more festive."

Then, lifting aside the flaps of the old blanket he was using as a cape, he exclaimed: "Look how handsome I am!"

Indeed he was, in his hose of yellow leather, his buckled boots, and his red jerkin sprinkled with gold. He had put rouge on his cheeks.

"Take off all your clothes. I've got some women's underclothes and stockings all of silk for you."

"But where's the beautiful skirt with the strips of silver?" asked the boy, somewhat disappointed when Humphrey handed him a dress of blue velvet.

"Idiot! That's for the end, for your wedding scene. And for the scenes in the middle, when you're dressed up as a boy, you've got a splendid black and rose-colored suit. Your jacket from home will be good enough for the trip."

Shivering slightly in the damp coachhouse, he carefully smoothed out his silk stockings. Humphrey pushed a pair of embroidered slippers toward him. "Make sure you walk like a girl, with little steps. And if the shoes hurt you, too bad. The waistline is too big, but I've got some pins. I've padded the bodice so that it looks right."

He put a paste necklace around the child's neck. Then,

opening the door of the little room a bit to let more light in, he said: "You're beautiful! Your hair will be fine when it's been combed. I forgot to bring the rouge pot, but we'll fix you up once we get there. Anyway, you've got naturally rosy cheeks. Come on. They're finishing getting ready in the room."

He helped the boy put his clothes in a bag. "You can throw away those worn-out shoes. No, keep them. You can use them for clogs on rainy days."

In the large room, people were getting dressed, swearing over a missing ribbon or a belt buckle stolen by some comrade. Audrey had already drunk a bit too much and was wearing her peasant's cap askew. Touchstone had added to his powdered face some large red circles. Covered with the gold chains he also used in his roles as majordomo, the duke moved from group to group with a ducal dignity. Everyone applauded at Rosalind's entry, but Aliena remained grumpy.

"Do me the favor of not tripping him," whispered Humphrey. "I've got my eye on you."

Without protesting too much, Aliena took her cousin by the hand. They piled the trunks on the roof of the coach, and the bags were thrown inside to serve as cushions. M. de Bréderode must have sent them the most dilapidated of his carriages, for the interior contained only one remaining fringed seat, on which the duke placed himself next to a tall, thin, pale youth, already some thirty years old, whom Lazarus concluded was the melancholy Jacques because he did his best to look sad. But they didn't mind the lack of other seats: it was just as easy to sit Turkish fashion, and some damp straw, which smelled delicious, had been spread over the floor of the coach.

. . .

An incident took place, however, which caused the duke to descend from the coach. There was a discussion in the courtyard. When the coachman had arrived late the night before, he had proceeded to knock back tankard after tankard of ale; a dousing of cold water from the pump hadn't managed to sober him up. Lying on the pavement of the courtyard, all puffy with drink, he looked like a dead slug. But he was snoring, which at least proved that he was still alive. A thin, misty rain began to fall.

"We'll do without him," decided the good duke. "You there, giraffe!"

A tall, gawky fellow appeared and got up on the driver's seat with an air of resignation. Over his old clothing he had thrown a white bedsheet, which covered him from head to foot, and in his hand he held a scythe, which he put down to pick up the reins.

"He's the one who drives us when we hire a cariole," explained Humphrey. "He almost never lands us in a ditch. And with the sheet he's wearing, his clothing won't get spoiled even if there's rain or wind."

"He scares me a bit," muttered the boy.

"There's no reason to be scared. Onstage, they paint his face white to make him more frightening. He plays Death, who carries off a rich man in an old farce we give from time to time to open with. Touchstone acts the devil in it with a long tail. The other one, the tall, white-faced man, also plays the ghost of a murdered King of Denmark. But that's not a play you can put on in Copenhagen."

By now, the rain had become heavy. Everyone crowded into the interior of the coach. Aliena, sitting next to her cousin, discomforted her by chewing a clove of garlic. Rosalind rested her head on the knees of Orlando, who had thrown a corner of his old blanket over her. The boy was hungry and told himself he should probably have had two fritters. At the same time, it was good to know he still had fourpence left that he could share with Humphrey. Two pair of hunters from the duke's entourage, dressed in green and camouflaged with leaves, carried on with their game of tarots in the corner. Touchstone, his head on his chest, softly sang a mournful lament. Through the dirty windows you could see the fields and meadows with cows in them, and that delighted Lazarus, since the boy had rarely gone outside the town before. The burgeoning trees of springtime spread their fresh greenery. It continued to rain in sheets, but the clouds racing after one another seemed to be playing in the sky, and here and there were large patches of blue. They would have good weather for their performance in the park.

The journey, however, seemed long. The jolting of the coach, which he got used to, made the boy sleepy. Everything blurred together in his drowsiness: the beating of the rain on the roof (a drop of water trickled down over the blanket), Lazarus's little ouches when Humphrey, for all his care, pulled his hair as he was untangling it, the mournful lament of the clown, Audrey's smelly breath, the figures of the tarot pack whose meaning isn't quite clear, and Copenhagen, which seemed very near, just around the next bend in the road, and, through the streaming windows of the coach, the beautiful patches of clear sky, and the sweetmeats M. de Bréderode's majordomo would surely have saved for the actors, and the great skirt with its strips of silver.

ANNA,
SOROR ...

She was born in Naples, in 1575, behind the thick walls of the fortress of Castel Sant'Elmo, of which her father was the governor. Don Alvaro, by then an inhabitant of the peninsula for many years, had won the favor of the Viceroy but also the enmity of both the populace and the members of the Campanian nobility, who found the abuses of the Spanish functionaries hard to endure. Yet no one, at least, questioned his integrity or the superiority of his blood. Thanks to a relative of his, Cardinal Maurizio Caraffa, he had married the granddaughter of Agnese da Montefeltro—Valentina, the last flower of an exceptionally gifted line, in whom it had exhausted its vigor. Valentina was beautiful, with a pale complexion and a narrow waist: her perfection disheartened the sonneteers of the Two Sicilies. Worried about the risk to his honor such a marvel might create, and naturally mistrustful of women, Don Alvaro imposed a virtually claustral existence on his wife, so that Valentina's year was divided between the melancholy estates her husband possessed in Calabria, the convent on Ischia where she passed Lent, and the small, vaulted chambers of the fortress, in whose dungeons suspected heretics and opponents of the regime rotted away.

The young woman accepted her fate with equanimity. Her childhood had been spent at Urbino, in the most refined of polite societies, amidst ancient manuscripts, learned conversations, and viole d'amore. The last verses of the dying Pietro Bembo had been composed to celebrate her impending birth. Her mother herself, as soon as she was able to rise from her childbed, took her to Rome, to the Cloister of Santa Anna. A pallid lady, whose mouth was drawn with sadness, took the child in her arms and blessed her. It was Vittoria Colonna, the mystical friend of Michelangelo, widow of Ferrante d'Avalos, who had won the battle of Pavia. From having received the blessing of this austere Muse, Valentina acquired early a singular gravity and the calmness of those who do not even aspire to happiness.

Preoccupied by ambition and crises of religious hypochondria, her husband, who neglected her, had forsaken her completely after the birth of a son, their second child. He inflicted no rivals on her, however, never having had any amorous adventures in the court of Naples beyond what was necessary to establish his reputation as a gentleman. Beneath his outward demeanor, Don Alvaro was thought to prefer, in those moments of low spirits when a man gives in to his desires, the Moorish prostitutes whose favors were negotiated for with brothel-keepers squatting under a smoky lamp or beside a brazier in the port area. Donna Valentina did not take offense at that. Herself an irreproachable spouse, she never took lovers, heard Petrarchizing gallants with indifference, refused to take part in the cabals the former mistresses of the Viceroy formed amongst themselves, and singled out from among her entourage neither confidantes nor favorites. To observe the proprieties, at court festivities she wore the magnificent garments appropriate to her age and rank, yet she never paused to look at herself in the mirrors and correct a pleat or adjust a necklace. Every evening, Don Alvaro found on his desk the household accounts verified in the clear handwriting of Valentina. It was the epoch when the Holy Office, recently established in Italy, spied on the slightest falterings of conscience; Valentina carefully avoided any conversations concerned with matters of faith, and she was properly dutiful in religious observances. No one was aware that she secretly caused linens and thirst-quenching drinks to be supplied to the prisoners in the fortress dungeons. In later years, her daughter Anna could not recall ever having heard her pray, but she had often seen her in her cell in the convent on Ischia sitting with a *Phaedo* or a *Symposium* on her knees, her beautiful hands resting on the ledge of the open window, musing silently for extended periods before the magnificent bay.

Her children worshipped her as if she were a Madonna. Don Alvaro, who planned to send his son to Spain presently, rarely required the presence of the young man in the antechambers of the Viceroy. Miguel spent long hours sitting beside Anna in a small room gilded like the inside of a coffer, upon the walls of which was embroidered the device of Valentina: *Ut crystallum.* From childhood, they had been taught by her to read Cicero and Seneca: as they listened to her soft voice explaining some argument or maxim to them, the hair of one child would become entangled with that of the other upon the page. At that age, Miguel looked very much like his sister; had it not been that her hands were delicate and his hardened from using the bridle and the épée, one could have been mistaken for the other. The two children, who were fond of each other, were often silent, not needing words to enjoy each other's presence; Donna Valentina, warned by the sharp instinct of those who feel they are loved but not understood, also spoke little. In a small chest, she kept a collection of Greek intaglios, many of which were decorated with nude figures. From time to time, she would mount the two steps leading to the deep embrasures of the windows in order to hold up to the last rays of sunlight the transparency of sards; enveloped in the slanting gold of the sunset, Valentina seemed herself as diaphanous as those gems.

Anna would lower her eyes, with that shyness that, in pious girls, grows even greater as they approach marriageable age. Donna Valentina would say, with a limpid smile: "Everything that is beautiful is illumined by God."

She spoke to them in Tuscan; they responded in Spanish.

In August, 1595, Don Alvaro announced that before Christmas his son was to go to Madrid, where his relative, the Duke of Medina, had done him the honor of selecting him as a page. Anna wept in secret but, out of pride, kept her composure in front of her brother and her mother. Contrary to what Don Alvaro had expected, Valentina raised no objection to Miguel's departure.

From his Italian family, the Marqués de la Cerna possessed large domains interspersed with swampland, which brought in little revenue. Upon the advice of his stewards, he attempted to naturalize the best vine stocks from Alicante on his estate at Agropoli. He achieved only mediocre success; yet Don Alvaro did not become discouraged, and every year he himself presided over the grape harvest. Valentina and the children accompanied him. That particular year, however, Don Alvaro, prevented from going himself, asked his wife to oversee the estate alone.

The trip there took three days. Donna Valentina's carriage, followed by others filled with servants, rolled across the bumpy roads toward the valley of the Sarno. Donna

Anna sat across from her mother; Don Miguel, despite his love of traveling on horseback, rode seated beside his sister.

The house, built in the time of the Sicilian Angevins, had the appearance of a fortified castle. At the beginning of the century, a whitewashed structure had been attached to it, a sort of farmhouse with a portico sticking out into the interior courtyard, a flat roof on which fruit from the orchard was dried, and a row of stone winepresses. The steward lived there with his perpetually pregnant wife and a gaggle of children. The passage of time, neglected repairs, and the inclement weather had made the great hall uninhabitable, and it was infiltrated by the surplus produce of the farm. Piles of grapes already sticky with their own juice and alive with flies smeared the Moorish tiles on the floor; bunches of onions hung from the rafters; flour oozing from sacks was mixed with the omnipresent dust; the pungent odor of strong cheese caught in one's throat.

Donna Valentina and her children installed themselves on the *piano nobile*. The bedrooms of brother and sister were across from each other; through the narrow casements, he was able to discern Anna's shadow coming and going by the light of a small lamp. She undid her hair, pin by pin, then proffered her foot to a maid so that she could remove her shoe. Out of a sense of decency, Don Miguel drew the curtains.

The days dragged on one like another, each of them long as an entire summer. The sky, almost always filled with a mist which seemed glued onto the plain, flowed down from the low mountain to the sea. In the *farmacia*, which was falling into ruin, Valentina and her daughter labored to produce medicines for those afflicted with malaria. Bad weather slowed the finish of the grape harvest; some of the workers, overcome with fever, could not leave their pallets; others, languishing from the sickness, stumbled through the vineyard like drunkards. Although Donna Valentina and her children never spoke of it, the imminent departure of Miguel saddened the three of them.

At evening, in the abrupt darkness of the *tramonto,* they ate together in a small downstairs room. Valentina would go to bed early, exhausted; left alone, Anna and Miguel would stare at each other in silence; after a while, Valentina's clear voice would be heard, calling her daughter. They would then mount the stairs together. Stretched out on his bed, Don Miguel would count the weeks until his departure, and although it pained him to leave Anna and their mother, he perceived with relief that the approach of this journey was already putting a distance between the two women and himself.

Troubles had broken out in Calabria, and Donna Valentina requested her son not to go too far from the village and the castle. Among the lower classes, discontent against the Spanish officers and civil servants was smoldering, and certain monks, especially, were agitating in their impoverished hillside monasteries. The more educated of these friars, those who had studied for a few years in Nola or Naples, looked back to the time when this land had been Greek, full of marble statues, gods, and beautiful naked women. The more daring ones denied or cursed God and, it was said, plotted with the Turkish pirates who dropped anchor in the coves. Strange sacrileges were spoken of— crucifixes trampled underfoot and Communion wafers carried under virile members to increase their vigor; one band of monks had kidnapped a group of young people from a village and held them prisoner in the monastery, where they indoctrinated them with the idea that Jesus had carnally known Mary Magdalene and Saint John. Valentina would quickly put a halt to such gossipmongering in the steward's house or the kitchen. Miguel would often think about it despite himself, then would chase it from his

mind, the way one delouses oneself; yet he was troubled
nonetheless by the thought of those men whose desire carried them so far that they dared do anything. Anna had a
horror of Evil, yet sometimes in the little oratory, before
the painting of the Magdalene swooning at the feet of
Christ, she would dream of how sweet it would be to
enfold in one's arms what one loved and would imagine
that the saint was no doubt burning to be lifted up by
Jesus.

Some days, disobeying the interdictions of Donna Valentina, Miguel got up at dawn, saddled his horse himself,
and rode, with no predetermined destination, far off into
the low-lying countryside. The earth stretched before him
black and naked; motionless oxen, lying in dark masses,
seemed from a distance like clumps of rock fallen off the
mountains; volcanic hummocks rose out of the heath; a
strong wind blew ceaselessly. When he observed thick mud
being thrown up by his horse's hooves, Don Miguel would
rein up abruptly at the edge of a marsh.

Once, just before sunset, he came upon a group of columns rising at the edge of the sea. Fluted drums lay on
the ground like great tree trunks; others, still upright and
horizontally reduplicated by their shadows, rose against
the reddening sky; the pale, mist-covered sea could be
dimly descried behind them. Miguel tied his horse to the
drum of a column and started walking amongst these
ruins whose name he did not know. Still somewhat dazed
by his long gallop over the barren plain, he experienced
that feeling of lightness and slackness one sometimes has
in dreams. But his head ached. He knew vaguely that he
was in one of those cities where the philosophers and poets
Donna Valentina spoke of had lived; those people had
existed without the agony of a hell yawning beneath their
feet which sometimes overcame Don Alvaro, who at such
moments was as tortured as the prisoners of Sant'Elmo.

And yet, those people had had their laws. Even in their day, unions had been severely punished which must have seemed legitimate to the offspring of Adam and Eve at the beginning of time. There had been a certain Caunus who had fled the advances of the sweet Byblis from land to land . . . Why did he think of Caunus, he whose love no one had yet sought? He lost himself in the maze of broken stones. On the steps of what must have been a temple, he noticed a girl sitting. He went toward her.

She was probably still a child, but the wind and sun had modeled her face. Don Miguel observed her eyes, which troubled him. Her face and skin were gray as dust, and her skirt exposed her bare feet on the stones and her legs as far up as the knees.

"Sister," he said, troubled in spite of himself by this chance meeting in that lonely spot, "what is the name of this place?"

"I have no brother," the girl said. "There are many names it is better not to know. This place is evil."

"Yet you seem at ease here."

"I am among my people here."

Her lips puckered into a quick whistle, and, as if making a sign, she pointed with her toe to a crack in the stones. A narrow, triangular head emerged from the fissure. Don Miguel crushed the viper with his boot.

"God forgive me!" he exclaimed. "Are you a witch?"

"My father was a snake charmer," the girl replied. "At your service. And he made a lot of money. Because vipers, sir, they're everywhere, not counting those in the heart."

Only then did Miguel think he noticed that the silence was replete with quiverings, rustlings, slitherings; all sorts of poisonous creatures were creeping through the grass. Ants scurried about, and a spider was weaving its web between two of the drums. Innumerable eyes, yellow like the girl's, formed stars on the ground.

Don Miguel wanted to step back but didn't dare.

"Go away, my lord," said the girl. "And remember that elsewhere there are serpents too."

It was late when Don Miguel got back to the castle of Agropoli. He tried to find out from the farmer what the city of ruins was called, but the man was not even aware of its existence. At the same time, Miguel learned that, that evening, as she was sorting fruit, Donna Anna had seen a viper in the straw. She had cried out; her maid, running to her assistance, had killed the creature with a stone.

That night, Miguel had a nightmare. He was lying in bed, with his eyes wide open. A huge scorpion came out of the wall, then another, then another; they crawled across his mattress, and the complicated patterns on the borders of his bedspread turned into vipers' nests. The brown feet of the girl rested on them peacefully, as if on a bed of dry grass. The feet began to dance; Miguel felt them tread on his heart; he saw them become whiter at each step; now they reached his pillow. As Miguel reached out to embrace them, he recognized them as Anna's feet, naked in their black satin mules.

Shortly before matins, he opened the window and leaned out to breathe. A slight cool wind blowing off the gulf chilled his sweat. Anna's shutters were open; Don Miguel resolutely watched, in the opposite direction, a herd of goats being led along the walls to pasture; he counted them with a maniacal obstinacy; he lost count; in the end, he turned his head. Donna Anna was at her prie-dieu. As she arose, he thought he saw, between her nightclothes and the satin of her mule, the golden hue of her naked foot. She greeted him with a smile.

He went out into the gallery to wash. The coldness of the water, awakening him completely, calmed him.

163

Often, when he was alone, he rode in the direction of the ruins. But whenever he came in sight of the columns, he would turn the bridle; sometimes, however, enticed despite himself, or ashamed of himself, he would go on in. Tiny lizards would follow him in the grass. But Don Miguel never saw any vipers, and the girl was no longer there.

He asked about her. All the peasants knew her. Her father, a native of Lucera, was of the Saracen race. His daughter had inherited magic powers from him; she went around from village to village, where she was well received at the farms, since she would rid them of their vermin. Fear of an evil spell and possibly, without his being aware of it, the instinct of a race which was itself crossed with Moorish blood kept him from harming this Saracen girl.

Every Saturday, he made his confession to a nearby hermit, a pious and revered man. But one does not confess one's dreams. Since his conscience was uneasy, he was surprised to find that he was unable to accuse himself of any sin. He attributed his nervousness to his approaching departure for Spain. And yet he was hardly making any preparations for it.

One hot day, returning from a long ride, he dismounted and knelt to drink straight from a spring. A thin stream flowed out of a waterhole a few steps from the road; high grass grew at its tallest near this source of water. Don Miguel lay flat on the ground to drink, like an animal.

There was a rustling in the undergrowth; he jumped up at the sight of the Saracen girl. "Ah, false serpent!"

"Beware, my lord," said the possessor of magic powers. "The water flows down, turns, writhes, glistens, and its poison chills your heart."

"I'm thirsty," said Don Miguel.

He was still close enough to the pool formed by the

spring to perceive, in the faintly trembling water, the reflection of the narrow face with its yellow eyes. The girl's voice had become a hissing sound. "My lord," he thought he heard, "your sister is waiting for you nearby with a goblet of pure water. You will drink together."

Don Miguel staggered as he remounted his horse. The girl had disappeared, and what he had taken for a presence and words had been nothing more than a hallucination. Perhaps he was feverish. Yet perhaps fever had allowed him to see and hear what is otherwise not seen or heard.

Supper was cheerless. Don Miguel, his eyes focused on the tablecloth, thought he felt Valentina looking at him. As usual, she ate only fruit, vegetables, and herbs, but that evening she seemed hardly able to raise even this nourishment to her lips. Anna neither spoke nor ate.

Don Miguel, terrified at the prospect of being alone in his room, suggested they go and take the air on the esplanade.

The wind had fallen with the light. The heat had made cracks in the soil of the garden; one after another, the shimmering, narrow puddles of the marsh grew dark; there were no lights from any of the villages; the limpid darkness of the sky curved against the thick darkness of the mountains and the plain. The heavens, the heavens of diamond and crystal, revolved slowly about the pole. The three of them, their heads bent back, watched. Don Miguel asked himself what evil planet was rising for him in his house of Capricorn. Anna, no doubt, was thinking of God. Valentina was probably dreaming of the musical spheres of Pythagoras.

She said: "Tonight the earth remembers . . ."

Her voice was clear as a silver bell. Don Miguel debated whether it would not be better to share his torment with his mother. Yet, as he searched for the words, he realized that he had nothing to confess to her.

In any case, Anna was there.

"Let us go in," said Donna Valentina softly.

They returned to the house. Anna and Miguel went first; Anna came up close beside her brother, but he drew away; he seemed fearful of communicating his unhappiness to her.

Donna Valentina was obliged often to halt and lean on her daughter's arm. Under her cape, she was trembling.

Slowly, she ascended the stairs. When she arrived at the second-floor landing, she remembered that she had left behind on a bench her handkerchief of Venetian lace. Don Miguel went down to look for it; when he returned, Donna Valentina and her daughter were already in their chambers; he had the handkerchief delivered by a maid and retired without having kissed, as he usually did, his mother's hand and that of his sister.

Don Miguel sat with his head in his hands at his table, without even bothering to take off his doublet, and passed the night trying to think. His thoughts circled about a fixed point like moths about a lamp; he was unable to arrest them; the most important one eluded him. Late in the night, he dozed, just sufficiently awake to realize that he was sleeping. Perhaps that girl had bewitched him. He didn't like her. Anna had much whiter skin, for example.

At dawn, there was a knock on his door. He perceived that it was already day.

It was Anna, also still fully dressed; he assumed she had got up early. Her frightened expression seemed to Don Miguel so like his own that it was as if he were seeing his reflection in a mirror.

His sister said to him: "Mother has caught the fever. She is very ill."

Letting her precede him, he went into Donna Valentina's room.

The shutters were closed. Miguel could hardly make out his mother in the great bed; she shivered feebly, more comatose than asleep. Her body, warm to the touch, shuddered, as if the breeze from the marshes were still blowing on her. The woman who was taking care of Donna Valentina led them into an embrasure.

"Madame has been ill for some time," she told them. "Yesterday she was so overcome with weakness we thought she was dying. She's better now, but she is too calm: that is a bad sign."

Since it was Sunday, Miguel and his sister went to hear Mass in the chapel of the castle. The curate of Agropoli, a vulgar man who was often a bit drunk, celebrated Mass for them. Don Miguel, reproaching himself for having proposed the walk on the esplanade the previous night in the dangerous cool of evening, began to look for the leaden pallor of fever in his sister's face. Some of the servants were also attending Mass. Anna prayed fervently.

They took Communion. Anna's lips opened to receive the Host; it seemed to Miguel that such a movement gave them the shape of a kiss; then he rejected the idea as a sacrilege.

As they returned, Anna said to him: "We must get a doctor."

A few minutes later, he was galloping in the direction of Salerno.

The open air and the speed of his horse effaced the traces of his sleepless night. He galloped into the wind. It was as intoxicating as a struggle against some adversary who still resists even while retreating. The gusts of wind swept his fears behind him like the folds of a long cloak. The ecstasies and the tremors of the day before had ceased, borne away on a surge of youth and strength. Donna Valentina's attack of fever, too, might be nothing more than a passing crisis. In the evening, he might once more find his mother's handsome, serene visage.

As he came into Salerno, he slowed his horse to a walk. His worries returned. Perhaps the fever was like a curse from which one could free oneself only by passing it on to others, and he had unwittingly communicated it to his mother.

He had trouble finding the doctor's residence. At last, in a blind alley near the port, a shabby-looking house was pointed out to him; a half-fastened shutter was banging in the breeze. In response to his knock, a woman with her bodice unlaced appeared, gesticulating; she asked the horseman what had brought him; he was obliged to explain in detail, shouting to make himself heard. Some other women began loudly to bewail the sick woman they didn't know. In the end, Don Miguel comprehended that Messer Francesco Cicinno was attending Mass.

They placed a stool outside for the young nobleman. When the Mass was over, Messer Francesco Cicinno came down the street in his doctoral robes, walking with tiny steps, gingerly choosing the best paving stones. He was a small, elderly man, so tidy that he seemed as new and meaningless as some unused object. When he heard Don Miguel's name, he fell all over himself with politeness. After considerable hesitation, he agreed to mount behind the rider. Nevertheless, he insisted that he be permitted to eat something first. The maidservant brought a piece of bread dipped in olive oil to the doorstep; he took a long time wiping off his hands.

Noon found them in the middle of the marsh. It was warm for the end of September. The sun, falling almost vertically, dazed Don Miguel; Messer Francesco Cicinno was discommoded by it too.

Farther along, near a thin grove of pines beside the

road, Don Miguel's horse started at the sight of a viper.
Don Miguel thought he heard a laugh, yet there was nothing around him but empty countryside.

"You have a skittish horse, my lord," said the doctor,
who was oppressed by the silence. Then he added, shouting a bit so that he could be heard by the rider: "Viper
broth is not a remedy to be disdained."

The women were anxiously awaiting the doctor. But
Messer Francesco Cicinno was so self-effacing that his
presence was scarcely noticed. He supplied numerous explanations about the dry and the humid and proposed to
bleed Donna Valentina.

Very little blood flowed from the puncture. Donna
Valentina fainted a second time, worse than the first, and
they had great difficulty reviving her. When Anna begged
Messer Francesco Cicinno to try something else, the little
doctor made a sign of defeat. "It is the end," he whispered.

With the sharp hearing of the dying, Donna Valentina
turned her lovely face toward Anna, smiling once more.
Her women thought they heard her murmur: "Nothing
ends."

Life visibly drained out of her. Under the baldachin of
the great bed, her thin body lay stretched out, molded by
the sheets like some recumbent tomb sculpture on its catafalque of stone. The little doctor, sitting apart in a corner,
looked as if he were afraid he might disturb Death. It was
necessary to silence the servants, who were suggesting
miraculous remedies; one woman spoke of asperging the
patient's forehead with the blood of a rabbit dismembered
live. Again and again, Don Miguel begged his sister to
leave the room.

Anna placed great hope in the Extreme Unction; but
Donna Valentina received it with no emotion whatsoever.
She asked that the curate, who had burst into clamorous
homilies, be taken back to his house.

When he had gone, Anna knelt at the foot of the bed, weeping. "You are leaving us, my lady mother."

"I have seen the winter forty-seven times, forty-seven times the summer," murmured Valentina faintly. "That is enough."

"But we are still so young," said Anna. "You will not see Miguel achieve fame, and me, you will not see me . . ." She was about to say that her mother would not see her married, but suddenly the idea horrified her. She stopped herself.

"You are both so distant from me already," said Valentina in a low voice.

They thought she had become delirious. Yet she still recognized them, for she gave Don Miguel, who was also kneeling, her hand to kiss. She said: "Whatever happens, never come to hate each other."

"We love each other," said Anna.

Donna Valentina closed her eyes. Then, very softly: "I know."

She seemed to have passed beyond pain, fear, and uncertainty. She spoke once more, but they didn't know whether she was talking about the future of her children or about herself: "Do not worry. All is well."

Then she fell silent. Her death without suffering was also almost without words. Valentina's life had been one long drifting into silence; she surrendered without a struggle. When her children realized that she was dead, there was no surprise mingled with their sadness. Donna Valentina had been the sort of person one was surprised to see existing.

They decided to take her back to Naples. Don Miguel had to make the arrangements for her coffin.

The vigil was held in the great ruined hall, emptied of its farm produce, furnished only with several large coffers

with broken panels. The weather and the insects had done
their work on the cordovan hangings. Donna Valentina
was laid out between four tapers in her long white velvet
robe; her smile, half haughty, half tender, still curved the
corners of her mouth, and her face with its high, deeply
sculpted cheekbones recalled that of the statues that were
sometimes dug up out of the earth of Magna Graeca between Crotona and Metapontum.

Don Miguel thought about the presages that had assailed him for weeks now. He recalled that Donna Valentina's mother, herself descended on her mother's side from
the Lusignans of Cyprus, had considered the sudden appearance of a snake an augury of death. He was in some
vague way reassured by that. This grief that confirmed
his presentiments gave him a kind of calm.

The wind blowing in through the large open windows
caused the flames of the lamps to flicker. To the east, the
mountains of the Basilicata were still dark with night;
brush fires indicated the course of dried-up streams.
Women were moaning threnodies in the accent of Naples
or the dialect of Calabria.

A feeling of infinite solitude enveloped the children of
Valentina. Anna made her brother swear never to leave
her. When he went back to his room to prepare for their
departure, he took heart in thinking that, happily, at
Christmastime he would be setting sail for Spain.

Their trip back, infinitely slower than the trip down,
lasted almost a week. Anna and Miguel were seated side
by side, with their mother's coffin opposite them on the
floor of the heavy carriage which had brought them from
Naples. The servants followed in carriages draped with
crepe. They went at a slow pace; penitents accompanied
the carriage on foot, reciting litanies and carrying candles.
They were replaced by others at each stop. At nightfall,

when there was no convent available, Anna and her maids found accommodations in some wretched inn. When the village had no church, the coffin of Valentina was placed in the square; a funeral vigil was organized around it; Don Miguel, who slept as little as possible, spent the greater part of the night in prayer.

The heat, which continued to be intense, was accompanied with unremitting dust. Anna seemed to grow gray. Her black headbands became covered with a thick white layer of dust; her eyebrows and eyelashes became invisible; both of their faces took on the tones of dried clay. Their throats burned, but Miguel, fearing fever, forbade Anna to drink cistern water. Outside, the wax candles bent in the hands of the penitents. By day, the harassment of flies replaced the nervous irritation caused at night by vermin and mosquitoes. To rest her eyes from the shimmering road and the trembling tapers, Anna had the curtains of the coach pulled shut; Don Miguel protested strongly, insisting they would suffocate.

They were ceaselessly beset by beggars whimpering prayers. Squealing urchins hung on to the axles, risking being maimed or crushed by a fall at each turn of the wheels. From time to time, Don Miguel would toss a coin into the road in the vain hope of getting rid of this rabble. At noontime, the campagna was almost always empty; they drove forward as if through a mirage. Then, at evening, peasants in rags would, for lack of flowers, bring armfuls of aromatic herbs. They were strewn as well as could be over the coffin.

Donna Anna no longer wept, conscious of how much her tears upset her brother.

He huddled in a corner, as far away from her as possible, in order to give her more space. Anna held a small lace handkerchief against her mouth. The slow rocking of the coach and the litany of the candle bearers plunged them into a sort of hallucinatory somnolence. At the worst places in the road, the bumps flung them against each other. At times they trembled with fear at the thought of seeing the coffin, which had been put together in haste by the cartwright of Agropoli, fall and break open. Soon, in spite of the double planks, a faint odor began to mix with the perfumes of the dry herbs. The flies multiplied. Each morning they doused themselves with scented water.

At noon on the fourth day, Donna Anna fainted.

Don Miguel called one of his sister's women. She was slow in coming. Anna appeared to be dead, and he unlaced her bodice; anxiously, he searched for the location of her heart; her heartbeat recommenced beneath his fingertips.

At last, Anna's chambermaid brought some aromatic vinegar. She knelt before her mistress to sponge her face. As she turned to pick up the bottle, she started at the sight of Don Miguel. "My lord is ill?"

He was standing, leaning against the door of the carriage, his hands still trembling, even paler than his sister. He was unable to speak. He said no with a shake of his head.

Since there was room for three people on the seat of the carriage, Miguel, fearing that Anna might faint again, ordered the chambermaid to sit beside her.

The trip lasted two more days. The heat and dust persisted; from time to time the chambermaid would sponge Anna's face with a damp cloth. Don Miguel continually rubbed one hand against the other, as if to wipe away something.

They got back to Naples at dusk. The populace knelt along the route of Valentina's coffin: she had been much loved. Hostile whispers against the governor of Sant'Elmo accompanied the exclamations of pity: the enemies of the regime accused Don Alvaro of having sent his wife to die of the fevers in that unhealthy region.

The funeral was celebrated two days later in the Spanish church of San Domenico. Brother and sister were present side by side. When they returned, Don Miguel asked for an audience with his father.

The Marqués de la Cerna received him in his study, seated at his desk covered with informers' reports and lists of political prisoners or suspects spied on by order of the Viceroy. Don Alvaro's chief function was to repress outbreaks or sometimes, if necessary, to foment one in order better to catch the agitators in his net. His black garments were worn not only for his wife; since the death, years before, of a son by his first wife, this man, faithful in his own way, had worn mourning.

He did not ask for the slightest detail about Donna Valentina's death. Miguel, claiming that Naples had become too melancholy for him without his mother, asked if it would not be possible to hasten his departure for Spain.

Don Alvaro, who went on reading the letters newly arrived from Madrid, answered without lifting his head: "This does not seem to me the right moment, sir."

When Don Miguel continued to stand there, silently biting his lips, he added as a dismissal: "Speak to me about it another time."

Nevertheless, when Miguel got back to his room, he began some of the preparations for his voyage. For her part, Anna started to put in order the things that had belonged to her mother. It seemed to her that Miguel's filial love was taking precedence over his fraternal love; they scarcely saw each other: their intimacy seemed to have died with Donna Valentina. Only then did she comprehend the change this disappearance had effected in her life.

One morning, as he came back from Mass, he met Anna on the staircase. She was terribly sad. She said to him: "It's been more than a week since I've seen you, brother."

She held her hands out to him. Anna, for all her pride, abased herself so far as to say to him: "Ah, brother, I feel so alone!"

He pitied her. He was ashamed of himself. He reproached himself for not loving her enough.

They took up once again their former life.

He came every afternoon, at the hour when the sunlight filled her room, and would sit in front of her. Anna was supposedly sewing, but most of the time her needlework lay on her knees in her listless hands. They each kept silence; through the half-open door could be heard the reassuring hum of the servants spinning.

They did not know how to fill up the time. They undertook new reading, but Seneca and Plato lost something in no longer being modulated by the soft voice of Valentina and commentated upon by her smile. Miguel would leaf through the volumes impatiently, reading a few lines, and then pass on to others, which he would put aside just as quickly. One day, he found on a table a Latin Old Testament which one of their Neapolitan relatives, converted to Evangelism, had entrusted to Valentina before leaving for Basel or England. Opening the book at various points the way people do who attempt to come upon a line by chance which will serve to enlighten them about the future, Don Miguel read several verses here and there. Abruptly, he stopped, casually put down the book, and carried it off with him as he left.

He could hardly wait to get back to his room to reopen

the book to the page he had marked; and when he had
finished reading it, he began again. It was the passage in
the Book of Kings where the story is told of the violence
done by Amnon to his sister Thamar. A possibility he had
never dared face presented itself. It filled him with horror.
He threw the Bible into the back of a drawer. Donna
Anna, who was in the process of putting her mother's
books in order, asked for it more than once. He always
forgot to give it back to her. She ceased to think about it.

Sometimes she entered his room when he was not there.
Afraid that she might open the book to that page, he carefully locked it up whenever he went out.

He read her the mystics: Luis de León, Juan de la
Cruz, the pious Mother Teresa. But those sighs mingled
with sobs exhausted them; the ardent, vague vocabulary
of the love of God moved Anna more than that of the
poets of worldly love, even though the words were, in the
end, virtually the same. Those effusions which had emanated not long before from holy persons she could never
have seen, cloistered as they were behind the walls of their
convents in Spain, became a heady wine which inebriated
her. Her head bent back and her open lips reminded Don
Miguel of the languorous abandon of saints in ecstasy,
whom the painters depict as almost voluptuously possessed by God. Anna felt her brother's gaze upon her;
embarrassed without knowing why, she sat up straight in
her chair; the entrance of a maid caused them to blush,
as if they were accomplices.

He became hard. He reproached her incessantly for her
inactivity, her bearing, her dress. She received these re-
proaches without complaint. Since he was horrified by
the low-cut dresses of fashionable ladies, Anna swathed
herself in wimples to please him. He bitterly criticized her
verbal effusions, so that she came to imitate Miguel's own
severe taciturnity. At that point, he began to fear she sus-

pected something; he watched her clandestinely; she felt
spied upon; and the most insignificant incidents provoked
quarrels. He ceased treating her with the affection due a
sister; she became aware of it and wept about it at night,
wondering how she had offended him.

They often went together to the church of the Dominicans. To do so, they had to cross the whole of Naples. The
coach, filled with memories of the funereal return, was
hateful to Miguel; he insisted that she bring along her
maid-in-waiting, Agnesina. She suspected he was attracted
to her. She could not tolerate such a relationship; the
effrontery of that girl had always offended her; and so,
on some pretext, she dismissed her maid.

The first week of December arrived. Don Miguel had
his trunks brought up and even engaged an equerry for
the journey. He counted the days, endeavoring to be
pleased that they passed so quickly but actually more
grief-stricken than relieved. When he was alone in his
room, he would try to fix in his memory the slightest details of Anna's physiognomy, in the way he unquestionably would once he was far from her, in Madrid. But the
harder he tried, the less he could see her, and the impossi-
bility of recalling the precise curve of her lip, the special
shape of her cheek, or the beauty spot on the back of her
pale hand tortured him in advance. Then, overcome with
a sudden determination, he would go to Anna's room and
stare at her in avid silence.

One day she said to him: "Brother, if this journey torments you, our father will not force you to make it."

He said nothing. She believed he was content to go, and
although this feeling indicated little love on his part, she
was not unhappy because of it: she knew at least that no
other woman was keeping Don Miguel in Naples.

At about ten o'clock on the evening of the next day, he
was called to his father.

Miguel was sure it was only a matter of some advice concerning his journey. The Marqués de la Cerna motioned him to be seated and, picking up from his desk an opened letter, handed it to him.

It was from Madrid. In it, one of the governor's secret agents recounted, in prudently veiled terms, the abrupt fall from grace of the Duke of Medina. He was the relative for whom Miguel was to serve as a page in Castile. Miguel slowly turned the pages and then handed the letter back in silence.

His father said to him: "Well, there you are: back from Spain."

Don Miguel seemed so stricken that the Marqués added: "I had no idea you were so eager to give rein to your ambitions."

And, with polite condescension, he promised vaguely that he would see at once about finding some other situation worthy of his rank which would compensate Miguel. Then he added: "But your love for your sister ought to make you prefer not to leave Naples."

Don Miguel looked up at his father. The gentleman's face was as impenetrable as always. A servant wearing a turban in the style of a Turkish page brought the governor his evening wine. Don Miguel left.

Once outside, he was overcome with a flood of joy. He said over and over to himself: "It was not God's will."

And then, as if the involuntary change in his fate, by discharging him of all responsibility, had justified him in advance, he experienced with a kind of intoxication a sudden ease in letting himself career downhill. He ran to Anna's rooms; she ought to be there alone at that hour. He himself would inform her that he was staying. She would be very happy.

The corridor and antechamber of Anna's apartment were plunged in darkness. A faint ray of light issued from under the door. As he drew near, he heard Anna's voice praying.

Immediately, he could imagine her, whiter than her linen, completely absorbed in God. In the whole immense sleeping fortress, that low monotone was the only sound he heard. The Latin words fell one by one into the silence like drops of cool, soothing water. Unconsciously, Don Miguel clasped his hands and joined in the prayer.

Anna ceased; the ray of light went out. She must have gone to bed. Very slowly, Don Miguel moved away from her door. Finally, the thought came to him that some servant might encounter him in the antechamber or on the landing. He returned to his room.

A frenzy of dissipations swept him away. His godfather, Don Ambrosio Caraffa, had recently sent him two Barbary jennets for his nineteenth birthday. He started hunting again. Since his room was situated on the same floor as Donna Anna's, and in the same part of the fortress, he exchanged it for another at the opposite end of the castle, not far from the governor's personal stables.

His father believed he was mourning his Spanish ambitions. Anna, offended by this separation, feared that he suspected her of having opposed his departure. She did not dare attempt to explain herself to his face; and although her pride prevented her from complaining, her unhappiness was only too visible. On the rare occasions when he encountered her in the great hall or in the corridors of Castel Sant'Elmo, Don Miguel would harshly ask her the reason for her sadness.

He forced himself to attend the Viceroy's court. There were very few friends there, for the Spanish intransigence of the governor had begun to turn the nobility of the peninsula against him. Miguel would wander alone amongst this crowd, and the plump Neapolitan beauties, tricked out with makeup and jewelry, their breasts exposed in the glow of the lamps, irritated him with their lasciviousness cloaked in Petrarchism. Sometimes Anna was obliged to appear at these festivities. He would see her from afar, all in black, her hips monstrously enlarged by the width of her farthingale. They would be separated by the crowd; a great weight of boredom would descend from the corniced ceilings, and the rest of the people there would seem nothing more than opaque ghosts to him. In the morning, Don Miguel would find himself on the doorstep of some low tavern in the port, sick, shaking with cold, stupefied with fatigue, as cheerless as the sky at the approach of dawn.

More than once, he encountered Don Alvaro in the hallway of a brothel. Each pretended not to recognize the other, and in any case, Don Alvaro wore a mask, as was the custom in that sort of place. On the days following, however, whenever Miguel would encounter his father at the postern gate of Sant'Elmo, he thought he discerned a sarcastic smile on that hermetically closed face.

He tried courtesans. But even the youngest seemed to him old as the sins of Herod, and he would sit with his elbows on the table, lost always in the same thoughts, paying for the drinks of chance acquaintances while the women of the tavern leaned on his shoulder.

One night, in a tavern in via Toledo, sitting with his elbows on his knees and his head in his hands, he watched a girl dance. She was somewhat surly and not beautiful; at the corners of her mouth she had the bitter smile of those who serve the pleasure of others. She was probably not more than twenty, but it was impossible to see her wretched body without thinking of the countless embraces that had already worn it out. Some client, waiting for her upstairs, must have been growing impatient, for the bawd leaned over the banister and cried out: "Anna, are you coming?"

Drunk with disgust, he got up and left.

At once, he felt he was being followed. He ducked into a side street. It was not the first time he had had the sensation of having a spy on his trail, and he began to walk more rapidly. The climb up to Castel Sant'Elmo was long and rugged. As he went in, he observed, as he always did when he came back at dawn, that Anna's shutters were ajar. When he arrived at the esplanade, he turned and saw his own equerry, Meneguino d'Aia, mounting the slope of the Vomero behind him.

Before entering Don Miguel's service, this man had been for a long time with Don Ambrosio Caraffa, who had trusted him completely. He was fairly wellborn and was said to have known better days. From the beginning, his air of frankness had pleased his new master; and yet, for several weeks now, Don Miguel had felt himself spied upon by this too-faultless servant. In the corridors of the castle, he would come upon mysterious confabulations between Meneguino d'Aia and his sister's women. And then, two or three times, he had seen him go into Donna Anna's apartment conducted by a maid. His inner struggles had so exhausted his mind that they left him prey to suspicions he himself considered ignoble. His acquaintances in the court and in the tavern had taught him to fear the dangerous fantasies of women.

He was tempted to listen at doors. His pride protested at such low conduct.

Anna, in this season of Carnival, multiplied her prayers. She had been apprised by Meneguino d'Aia of Don Miguel's deeds and movements; those banal sins seemed more execrable to her once she knew they had been committed by her brother. What she imagined about them caused her despair and worry at the same time. From day to day, she put off speaking to him.

One morning, as he was getting ready to attend Mass, he saw her come into his room. She stopped short when she perceived that he was not alone. Meneguino d'Aia was in the window embrasure, repairing a harness. Pointing to him, Miguel said to Anna: "There's the man you're looking for."

Anna paled. Their mutual silence would have lasted for a long time if Don Ambrosio Caraffa's man had not come forward.

"My lord," he said, "I have been at fault in concealing something from you. Donna Anna has been worried about your conduct and asked me to look out for you. She is somewhat older than you. I can't believe you will hold it against your sister that she is too fond of you."

Miguel's face suddenly changed its expression and seemed to clear. At the same time, his anger seemed to grow. He shouted: "Wonderful!"

And, turning to his sister: "So, it was to spy on me that you won over this man! Every morning when I come back you are waiting for me like an abandoned mistress! What right do you have? Are you in charge of me? Am I your son or your lover?"

Anna hid her head in the back of an armchair and sobbed. The sight of her tears seemed to make Miguel more tender. He said to Meneguino d'Aia: "Accompany her back to her room."

When he was alone, he sat down in the chair she had just got out of. Exultant, he exclaimed: "She is jealous!"

Getting up, he went and stared into the mirror, until his eyes grew tired from focusing on his reflection and he perceived nothing but a haze. Meneguino d'Aia came back. Don Miguel paid him his wages and dismissed him without a word.

The window of his room looked out on the ramparts. Leaning out, one looked down on an old guard walk, no

longer used, but to which the governor had access. The
staircase of the bastion joined it farther along, and into
its abandoned chambers Don Alvaro was thought to bring
loose women from time to time. Sometimes at night one
could hear the muffled laughter of the bawds and the girls.
Their powdered faces would be lit up by a trembling lantern as they mounted the stairs; but these creatures, who
revolted Miguel, managed to obliterate his scruples by
demonstrating to him the universal power of the flesh.

Several days later, coming back to her room, Anna
found Donna Valentina's Old Testament, which she had
so often asked her brother to return to her. The book was
lying open, upside down on the table, as if whoever had
been reading it had been interrupted and had wanted to
mark his place. Donna Anna took it, put a marker between
the pages, and carefully put it on the shelf. The next day,
Don Miguel asked her if she had looked at those pages.
She replied no. He was afraid to insist.

He no longer denied himself her presence. His attitude
had changed. No longer did he forbid himself allusions he
assumed were quite clear. They were so only for him; but
now everything seemed to him only too obviously to refer
to his obsession. So many enigmas threw Anna into confusion, but she didn't attempt to make sense of them. An
inexplicable anguish overcame her in her brother's presence; he felt her tremble at the slightest touch of his hand.
And so, he drew back. At night in his room, exhausted to
the point of tears, hating his desires and his scruples in
turn, he asked himself in horror what would have tran-
spired by the same hour on the morrow. Days passed, but
nothing changed. He was persuaded she did not wish to
understand. He began to hate her.

He no longer repressed his nightly fantasies. He awaited
with impatience the half consciousness of the mind falling

asleep; with his face buried in his pillows, he gave himself over to his dreams. He would awake from them with
his hands burning, his mouth stale as if from a fever, and
more obsessed than the day before.

On Maundy Thursday, Anna sent a message to her
brother asking if he did not wish to accompany her on her
visit to the seven churches. He answered that he did not.
Anna's carriage was awaiting her. She departed alone.

He paced back and forth in his room. After a while,
he could stand it no longer. He got dressed and went out.

Anna had already visited three churches. The fourth
was to have been that of the Lombards; the carriage
stopped in Piazza Monteoliveto, in front of the low porch
where a yapping group of sick beggars was assembled.
Donna Anna crossed the nave and entered the Chapel of
the Holy Sepulcher.

An Aragonese King of Naples had caused himself to be
depicted there with his mistresses and his poets, in the
postures of a funeral vigil that would last forever. Seven
people in terra-cotta, life-size, knelt or crouched on the
flagstones, mourning the cadaver of the God-Man they had
followed and loved. Each of them was the faithful likeness
of a man or woman dead for hardly a century, yet their
desolate effigies seemed to have wailed in place since the
time of the Crucifixion. They were still decorated with
bits of color: the red of Christ's blood was flaking off like
the scabs of an old wound. The filth of time, the candles,
and the counterfeit daylight of the chapel gave the Jesus
the appallingly dead look that the Jesus of Golgotha must
have had a few hours before Easter, when the rot had begun its work and the angels themselves had begun to
doubt. The continuously renewed crowd strolled through
the narrow space. People in rags jostled gentlemen; eccle-

siastics, as busy as if at a funeral, pushed their way through sailors from the fleet with their faces tanned by the sea and slashed by Turkish sabers. Rising high above the bowed faces, other statues of Virgins and saints stood in niches, shrouded according to ancient custom in violet-colored veils in honor of this mourning which surpasses all others.

People stepped back to give Anna space; her name was whispered from lip to lip; her beauty and the magnificence of her garments interrupted the clicking of rosaries for an instant. A small cushion of black velvet was slid in front of her; Donna Anna knelt. Leaning over the corpse of clay lying on the flagstones, she devoutly kissed the wounds in the side and the hands. Her veil, which covered her face, got in her way. As she rose up a bit to fold it back, she thought she felt someone looking at her, and turning her head to the right, she saw Don Miguel.

The violence with which he fixed his gaze on her was terrifying. They were separated by the width of a bench. Like her, he was clad in black and she, alarmed and whiter than the wax of the candles, stared at that dark statue at the foot of the violet-clad ones.

Then, reminding herself that she was there to pray, she knelt once more to kiss the feet of Christ. Someone leaned over her. She knew it was her brother. He said: "No."

Then, still in a low voice: "I shall wait for you at the entrance."

Anna did not even dream of disobeying him. She rose, and crossing the church abuzz with litanies, she came to the edge of the porch.

Miguel was waiting for her. On these last days of Lent, both of them were struggling against the exhaustion caused by prolonged abstinence. He said: "I trust your devotions are finished."

She waited for him to continue. He went on: "Aren't there other churches, less populated? Haven't people stared at you long enough? Is it really necessary to show people how you kiss?"

"Brother," said Anna, "you are quite ill."

"You can see that?" he asked.

Then he asked her why she hadn't gone to the convent on Ischia for the retreat of Holy Week. She did not dare tell him she had not wanted to leave him.

The carriage was waiting for them. She got in. He followed. Abandoning the remaining churches, she ordered that they be taken back to Castel Sant'Elmo. She sat erect in her seat, anxious and rigid. Watching her, Don Miguel thought of his sister's fainting spell on the road from Salerno.

They arrived. The carriage stopped at the postern gate. They went up to Anna's room together. Miguel realized that she wanted to speak to him.

As she removed her veil, she said: "Are you aware that our father has proposed a Sicilian marriage for me?"

"Ah?" he said. "Who is it?"

She answered meekly: "You know perfectly well I shall not accept."

Then, explaining that she would prefer to withdraw from the world, perhaps forever, she spoke of entering the convent on Ischia or that of the nuns of the order of Santa Chiara in Naples, a handsome convent that Donna Valentina had visited often.

"Are you mad?" he cried.

He seemed beside himself, and said: "And you would live there, bathed in tears, wasting away with love for a wax figure? I saw you just now. And I should allow you a lover just because he has been crucified? Are you blind? Or are you lying? Do you really think I am able to surrender you to God?"

She stepped back, terrified. Again and again he repeated: "Never!"

He was leaning against the wall, already lifting the door-hanging to leave. A gasping sound filled his throat. He cried out: "Amnon, Amnon, brother of Thamar!"

He went out, slamming the door behind him.

Anna collapsed into her chair. The cry she had just heard still echoed within her. Vaguely remembered passages of Holy Scripture came back to her memory. Knowing in advance what she was going to read, she took down Donna Valentina's Old Testament and opened it to the place marked, to the passage where Amnon violates his sister Thamar. She went no further than the first few verses. The book slipped from her hands, and leaning back in her chair, stunned to realize how she had lied to herself for so long, she listened to the beating of her heart.

It seemed to her to expand until it filled almost her entire being. An irresistible languor overcame her. Shaken with spasms, her knees pressed tight against each other, she lay there absorbed into this inner beating.

That night, as he lay sleepless in bed, Miguel thought he heard something. He was not sure of it: it was less a sound than the tremor of a presence. Having often experienced similar things in his thoughts, he told himself that it was his fever, and attempting to regain his calm, he reminded himself that his door was locked.

He did not want to sit up. He sat up. It seemed to him that his awareness of his actions was more vivid the more involuntary they were. Experiencing for the first time this invasion of the self, he felt his mind gradually empty itself of everything except his sense of waiting.

He put his feet on the floor and very quietly got up. Instinctively, he held his breath. He did not want to frighten her; he did not want her to know he was listening. He feared she would flee, and feared even more that she would stay. The floorboards on the other side of the door creaked slightly under the weight of naked feet. He went silently to the door, pausing often, and at last leaned against the panel. He felt her leaning on the other side; the trembling of their two bodies passed through the wood. It was utterly dark: in the blackness, each of them listened to the sighs of a desire similar to his own. She dared not ask him to open the door. To dare open the door, he needed her to ask. He was frozen with the feeling of something immediate and irreparable; at one and the same time he wished she had never come and that she was already in his room.

The beating of his arteries prevented him from hearing. He said: "Anna . . ."

She did not respond. Abruptly, he undid the locks. His trembling hands were unable to lift the latch. When he finally opened the door, there was no one on the other side.

The long vaulted corridor was as dark as the inside of his room. He heard the flat, light, quick sound of naked feet fleeing and disappearing into the distance.

For a long time, he waited. He heard nothing more. Leaving the door wide open, he went back to bed. As he listened to the slightest noises in the silence, he began to imagine at times the rustling of a fabric, at other times a weak, timid cry. Hours went by. Hating himself for his cowardice, he consoled himself with thoughts of how she must be suffering.

When it was completely day, he got up and closed the door. Alone in the empty room, he thought: "She could have been here!"

The bedclothing he had thrown back formed large masses of shadow. He became enraged with himself. He flung himself down on the mattress and, tossing about, moaned aloud.

Anna spent the next day in her room with the shutters closed. She did not even dress: the long black robe in which her hairdressers enveloped her each morning floated about her in loose folds. She had forbidden anyone to be admitted to her room. Seated with her head against the hard back of a chair, she suffered without weeping, without thinking, humiliated both by what she had done and by having done it in vain, too exhausted even to feel her suffering.

Toward evening, however, her women brought her news.

That noon, Don Miguel had appeared before his father. But the nobleman was in the midst of one of his mystical crises, when he believed he was damned. At Miguel's insistence, the servants finally let him into the oratory, where he found Don Alvaro, who impatiently shut his Book of Hours.

Don Miguel announced his immediate departure on one of the armed galleys which chased the pirates who operated between Malta and Tangiers. Anyone was accepted aboard those vessels, which were often badly outfitted and old and whose crew was comprised of adventurers, sometimes even of old pirates or converted Turks, under the command of some chance captain. The servants had somehow learned that Don Miguel had signed his indenture papers that very morning.

Don Alvaro said to him dryly: "You have strange ideas for a nobleman."

It was a hard blow for him, however. He paled, and said to his son: "Remember, sir, that I do not have another heir."

Don Miguel stared fixedly in front of him. There was a quality of despair in that look, and, without a muscle of his face moving, his cheeks were suddenly streaming with tears. Don Alvaro appeared to understand then that some terrible struggle was taking place—for a long time now perhaps—in his son's soul. Don Miguel was about to speak, probably to confess everything. His father stopped him with a gesture.

"No," he said. "I suppose God has put you to some test. I do not wish to know about it. No one is entitled to put himself between a man's conscience and God. Do whatever seems best to you. I already have too many sins of my own for me to take on your troubles."

He shook his son's hand; the two men solemnly embraced. Don Miguel left. No one knew where he had gone after that.

Anna's women, seeing that she would not answer them, left her.

Anna remained alone. By now, it was completely dark. The heat was unusual for the fourth of April and quite stifling. Anna felt her heart throbbing again; she perceived with terror that the fever she had had the day before was about to begin again at the same hour. She was suffocating. She got up.

She went to the balcony, opened the shutters to let the night air in, and leaned against the wall to breathe.

The balcony was very large and communicated with other rooms. Don Miguel was seated in the farthest corner, leaning on the balustrade. He did not turn around. A rustling sound warned him that she was there. He made no sign.

Donna Anna stared into the darkness. The heavens, on

this night of Good Friday, seemed aglow with wounds. Anna stiffened in suspense. She said: "Why haven't you killed me, brother?"

"I have thought of it," he replied. "I would love you dead."

Only then did he turn around. In the darkness, she discerned his anguished face, which seemed eroded by tears. The words she had prepared died on her lips. She fell upon him with an agonized compassion. They embraced.

Three days later, in the church of the Dominicans, Don Miguel attended Mass.

He had left Castel Sant'Elmo at the first light of day on that Monday people call "la Pasqua dell'Angelo," since a heavenly messenger had once spoken on that day to some women beside a tomb. High up there in the great gray fortress, someone had accompanied him to the door of a chamber. Their farewells had been made in prolonged silence. He had had to unknot, very gently, the warm arms fastened about his neck. His mouth still tasted the bitter savor of tears.

He prayed desperately. Each prayer was succeeded by another, more ardent one; each time, a new thrust carried him on to a third prayer. With a drunken giddiness, he felt that lightening of the body which seems to free the soul. He regretted nothing. He thanked God that He hadn't let him leave without this viaticum. She had begged him to stay; but he had left on the appointed day. Keeping his word to himself confirmed him in his traditions of honor, and the immensity of his sacrifice seemed to him to engage God. His hands, between which he hid his face in order to block out everything else, were redolent of the perfumes of the body he had caressed.

Having nothing more to expect from life, he thrust himself toward death as toward some necessary completion. And, certain of achieving his death as he had achieved his life, he wept over his good fortune.

The faithful got up to take Communion. He did not follow them. He had not been to confession in preparation for his Paschal Communion; a sort of jealousy prevented him from revealing his secret, even to a priest. He merely went up as close as possible to the officiant standing on the other side of the marble railing, so that the influence of the Host might descend upon him. A ray of sun fell down the length of a nearby pillar. He leaned his cheek against the stone, as smooth and soft as a human touch. He closed his eyes. He returned to his prayers.

He did not pray for himself. Some obscure instinct, inherited perhaps from an unknown or disavowed ancestor who had fought under the banner of the Crescent, assured him that any man killed in combat against the Infidel is perforce saved. Death, in whose quest he was leaving, would dispense him from the need to be pardoned. He prayed to God, passionately, that his sister might be spared. He did not doubt that God would consent. Yet he demanded it, as a right. It seemed to him that by enveloping her in his sacrifice he would raise her up with him to some blessed eternity. He had left her, but he felt he had not abandoned her. The wound of separation had ceased to bleed. On this morning when tearful women had found nothing but an empty tomb, Don Miguel let his gratitude to life, to death, and to God mount on high.

Someone put a hand on his shoulder. He opened his eyes; it was Fernão Bilbaz, captain of the ship on which he was to embark. Together, they left the church. Once outside, the Portuguese adventurer told him that a calm was delaying the departure of their galley and that he should return home but hold himself ready for the slightest breeze. Don Miguel went back up to Castel Sant'Elmo, but he did not fail to attach a long scarf to the shutters of Anna's window, which he would hear snap in the wind.

Two days later, at dawn, they heard the rustling of the silk. Their farewells and their tears were renewed, the same as those of the day before, a little the way a dream repeats itself. But possibly neither of them any longer believed in the perpetuity of farewells.

Several weeks passed. Near the end of May, Anna learned how Don Miguel had met his death.

The boat commanded by Fernão Bilbaz had encountered an Algerian pirate ship halfway between Africa and Sicily. After the cannon fire, there had been the boarding party. The Saracen boat had sunk, but the Spanish vessel, victorious though disabled, its rigging broken and its mast shattered, had drifted many days at the mercy of the waves and the wind. A squall had finally driven it onto the beach not far from the little Sicilian town of Cattolica. In the meantime, most of the men wounded in the fight had died.

Some peasants from a nearby village, doubtless attracted by the lure of gain, went down to the wreckage. Fernão Bilbaz caused a grave to be dug and, with the assistance of the vicar of Cattolica, buried his dead. But Don Alvaro had large estates in this part of Sicily, and when the natives heard the name of Don Miguel, they piously placed his corpse in the church of Cattolica for the night; subsequently, they shipped his coffin to Palermo, whence it was put on board ship for Naples.

When Don Alvaro was apprised of his son's end, he limited himself to saying: "It was a handsome death."

And yet, it dismayed him. His first son had been car-

ried off by the plague, along with his mother, when he
was still a baby, several years before the birth of Miguel.
That double grief had led Don Alvaro to enter into a second marriage, but now that in turn had proved itself more
than vain. He regretted, as much as the loss of Miguel,
his fruitless efforts to increase and consolidate his fortune,
which, still being built up, would soon be without an
owner. His blood and his name would not survive him.
Without completely diverting him from his duties as a
nobleman, this outcome, in reminding him of the vanity
of all things, helped push him further into asceticism and
debauchery.

The corpse of Don Miguel was taken off the ship at
dusk and temporarily placed in the little church of San
Giovanni a Mare not far from the port. It was a soft,
stifling, slightly hazy evening in June. Anna came in the
dead of night and commanded that the coffin be opened.

A few torches lighted the church. A wound visible in
his left side caused Anna to hope that her brother had not
suffered long. But who could know? Perhaps, on the contrary, he had lain for a long time in his death agony
amidst the other dying men on the half-shattered bridge
of the ship. Fernão Bilbaz himself no longer remembered.
Two or three monks chanted psalms. Anna thought how
that partially decomposed corpse would continue to be
eaten away within the coffin, and she envied the rot. They
were about to reclose the lid. Anna looked for something
of hers which could be put inside. It had not occurred to
her to bring flowers.

Around her neck, she was wearing a scapular from
Mount Carmel. At the moment of his departure, Miguel
had kissed it a number of times. She removed it and placed
it on her brother's breast.

The Marqués de la Cerna, against whom the hostility
of the people continued to grow, decided it was prudent not
to be present at the transferal of the corpse to San Domenico, where the obsequies were to take place. It was accomplished at night, without ceremony; Anna followed in a
carriage. She aroused pity in her women.

The funeral was held the following day, in the presence
of the whole court. Kneeling next to the choir, Don
Alvaro stared vacantly at the high catafalque. Beneath the
mass of funeral hangings and emblems, the form of the
bier had disappeared. All sorts of visions passed through
the nobleman's mind, visions as arid as the earth of the
sierra, as harsh as a hair shirt, as poignant as a *Dies irae.*
He looked at the escutcheons, those emblems of lineal
vanity which, in the end, serve only to remind every
family of the number of its dead. The world, with its
vanities and pleasures, seemed to him a silken cerement
wound about a skeleton. His son, as well as he himself, had
tasted those ashes. No doubt Don Miguel was damned;
Don Alvaro, filled with religious horror, thought that he
probably would be too; he was engulfed by the thought
of those eternal torments inflicted on creatures of the flesh
in punishment for a few brief shudders of joy which is not
even happiness. Now he felt himself attached to the son
he had loved only slightly by a more intimate, more mysterious parentage: that which is established between men,
beyond the lugubrious diversity of sins, by the same anguish, the same struggle, the same remorse, the same dust.

Anna knelt across from him, on the other side of the
nave. To Don Alvaro, her face shining with tears recalled
that of Miguel on Good Friday, when his son had come to
announce his departure, on the threshold of death and, no
doubt, of sin. Old intimations which had finally come together in his mind, Anna's wild despair, and even certain

reticences of the servants caused him to suspect that which he forbade himself to know. He looked at Anna with disdainful hatred. The woman filled him with horror. He said to himself: "She killed him."

Quite suddenly, Don Alvaro's unpopularity worsened.

Don Ambrosio Caraffa had a brother, Liberio. This young man, brought up on the poets and orators of antiquity, had dedicated himself to the service of his Italian fatherland.

Amid the agitation that followed the uprisings in Calabria, he had inflamed the peasants against the tax collectors, formed a conspiracy, and been obliged to flee. There was a price on his head. He was thought to be in hiding in one of his family's castles, when it was suddenly learned that he had just been made a prisoner in Castel Sant'Elmo.

The Viceroy was away. Don Ambrosio Caraffa went to the governor to beg him to stay the execution. Don Miguel's godfather said to the Marqués de la Cerna: "I am asking you only for a stay. I love Liberio as if he were my own son. He is the same age as Don Miguel."

Don Alvaro answered: "My son is dead."

Don Ambrosio Caraffa realized that all hope was lost. He loathed and pitied Don Alvaro at the same time; nor was he without admiration for such inflexible firmness. He would have admired him even more had he known that the governor was obeying orders that had been personally given by Count Olivares, aware that he would be repudiated.

Several hours later, it was learned that Liberio's head had fallen. From that point on, Don Alvaro rarely, and then only when protected by an armed escort or else masked in the dead of night, dared go down into the city, to which he was drawn by his devotions and his pleasures.

He was recognized; stones were hurled at him; he retreated into Sant'Elmo and did not leave again. The citadel, suspended over Naples like the fist of the Catholic King, was hated by the people.

Every evening, Anna went to the church of San Domenico. Her father's worst enemies took pity on her as she passed by. She would have the chapel opened for her and would stay there, motionless and tearless, forgetting even to pray. The faithful who frequented the church at that late hour would watch her through the grille, not even daring to say her name lest they cause that figure resembling a statue on a tomb to turn around.

It was thought that she would enter a religious order. She never had the slightest intention of doing so. Outwardly, her life had not changed, but a virtually monastic rule governed her days, and she wore a hair shirt to remind her of her sin. At night, she would lie on a narrow pallet of wood which she caused to be placed beside the great bed in which she would no longer sleep. Dreams awakened her; she was alone. She began then to despair, telling herself that all that had gone by like a dream, that she could not prove it had ever happened, that she would end by forgetting it. To bring it all back to life again, she buried herself in her memories. No hope for the future stirred within her. So desolate was her feeling of solitude that Anna passionately would have liked to be expecting even that which most women, in a similar situation, would have been fearful of.

The Viceroy of Naples, Count Olivares, returned. Don Alvaro was called before him. Without any preamble, the Count said to him: "You knew I would disavow you."

Don Alvaro bowed.

Count Olivares went on: "Don't think that in so doing

I am acting in my own interests. I have just received from the King my letters of recall, and no doubt a greater monarch will call me soon to Him."

He was not lying. He was sick, swollen with dropsy. He continued: "The Marqués de Spinola is looking for a lieutenant for the war in Flanders who is familiar with the Low Countries. You once fought in that province. At this very moment we are sending a convoy of men there by way of Savoy. You will conduct it."

It was exile. Don Alvaro, taking leave of Count Olivares, kissed his flabby hand and said pensively: "All things are as naught."

Upon his return, he gave Anna warning that she should make arrangements for their imminent departure.

The governor passed his last days in Naples communing with himself in the Certosa di San Martino, a fortress of prayer next door to his own fortress. Anna went on with her inventory. She came to Don Miguel's room. Anna believed she had not even approached that door since the day when Miguel had tried to pick a quarrel with her over his equerry. As she opened the door she almost fainted; the forgotten incident took place once more in her mind's eye; Miguel was doing his best to scream insults at her, his tanned cheeks flushed with blood and rage. The room, still littered with valuable harnesses, was heavy with the odor of leather. She told herself—and knew even as she told herself that she was lying—that up to that moment nothing irreparable had taken place and that everything might have turned out otherwise. And then, much farther off in her memory although much closer in time, that other event . . . that moment of waiting outside a closed door, which she would have been so glad to forget . . . that sense of shame at the body's disappointment, which destiny had caused a brief happiness to wipe away.

She fainted. Her women opened the shutters to give her air. She did not feel any better. She left the room.

Out of prudence, the governor had decided that their departure should take place very early in the morning. Anna's women dressed her by candlelight. Then they went downstairs with the chests. Left alone, Anna went out onto the balcony to look at Naples and the gulf in the flat paleness of dawn.

It was a day in mid-September. As she leaned on the balustrade, Anna looked below her for each of the places, like stations on a road she would never again travel, where her life had halted for a moment. The slope of a hill on her right hid from her the island of Ischia, where two children had once spelled out together a page of the *Symposium*. On her left, the road to Salerno disappeared into the distance. Near the port, she recognized the little church of San Giovanni a Mare where she had been with Miguel for the last time, and, rising above the tiers of terraced roofs, the campanile of San Domenico degli Aragonese. When her women came back up, they discovered their mistress lying on the stripped great bed, prostrate beneath the weight of memory.

A carriage was waiting in the court of honor. Docilely, she took her place in this vehicle in which her father was already seated. In front of the entrance, the servants of the new governor, lugging furniture and utensils, were arguing with the valets who were departing. The equipage got underway. As they were crossing the city, virtually deserted at that hour, Anna asked that they stop for a moment in front of San Domenico, whose doors had just been opened. Don Alvaro did not object.

Minutes passed. The Marqués became impatient. At his command, her women went into the church to beg Donna Anna to come out. Soon, she reappeared.

She had lowered her veil. She took her seat again without a word, hard, indifferent, impassive, as if she had left in that chapel her heart as an ex-voto.

Donna Anna had composed the customary epitaph for the tomb. There, written on the plinth, it said:

LVCTV MEO VIVIT

The name and titles followed, in Spanish. Then, on the base:

ANNA DE LA CERNA Y LOS HERREROS

SOROR

CAMPANIAE CAMPOS PRO BATAVORVM CEDANS

HOC POSVIT MONVMENTVM

AETERNVM AETERNI DOLORIS

AMORISQVE

The Infanta, in Flanders, was obliged to M. de Wirquin, the colonel commandant of a troop levied on her lands near Arras, for having lately disbursed out of his own funds the pay of her soldiers, which had been in arrears for a long time; and she knew that her officers appreciated his brute courage. Yet this Frenchman, who forced himself to speak court Spanish, rather the way deceptive lace ornament is sometimes worn over armor, appeared to be one of those people born with a double face who in the twinkling of an eye could desert to the other side. And the fact was, no loyalty whatsoever attached Egmont de Wirquin to those eloquent Italians or those Spanish braggarts —gilded beggars, bastards sometimes—whose blood, according to him, was not remotely worth his own. One day he would know how to avenge himself with a clever insult on those who had made him feel that his title of nobility had been established only the day before yesterday; and if fate waited too long or the political breeze should blow from another quarter, he could always pass over to the French side.

In Brabant, the night before they were to be received

by the Infanta, while riding in the coach which carried
them back to camp, the Duke of Parma sketched out
the situation for his subordinate. The seven provinces
of the North were, to speak the truth, definitively lost;
Spain, hardly recovered from the squall which had carried
off her ships, could no longer pretend to patrol those long
coasts, whose dunes covered so many dead. In the interior,
to be sure, loyalty would flower again in the good towns.
He admitted, however, that they were having trouble re-
paying the cost of supplies owed to the rich bourgeois of
Arras, the merchants of cloth and wine, to whom M. de
Wirquin was related through his mother. A loan made to
the royal cause was, he added, an honor as well as an in-
vestment in the future: the amount would be reimbursed
at the next return of the galleons. The colonel commandant
smiled without responding.

Then the astute Italian casually observed that a marriage with one of the young beauties lately arrived from
Spain whom the Infanta, for political reasons, intended to
marry off in Flanders would assure a wellborn man without friends at court a chance to advance himself with the
Archduke and his spouse. Not much tempted by the conjugal state, M. de Wirquin was nonetheless attracted by the
idea of a brilliant marriage. He said merely that he would
see.

Herself married late, garbed in clothes of a monastic
austerity, the Infanta would readily have confined her
meninas within the penumbra of the Church; nevertheless,
she objected neither to the finery appropriate to their rank
nor to their authorized amusements nor to the homage paid
them by gallants carefully chosen with a view to good
matches which would consolidate her politics of concilia-
tion. Perhaps she was even envious of those eyes brimming
with laughter or childish tears, which were not haunted

by the vision of armies, fleets, and forts. That particular day, sitting at the end of a rainy afternoon beside the imposing fireplace, she cast a melancholy gaze on her retinue, wondering which of them to sacrifice. Words of devotion to the royal cause and of submission to the will of heaven fell from her lips. The young girls recoiled from her scrutinizing gaze: those who had lovers feared they would be obliged to abandon them, and Pilar, Mariana, and Soledad prayed they would not be chosen.

But the Infanta turned to the newest arrival among her maids of honor. Anna de la Cerna, twenty-five years old, was also the oldest of them. She had dressed in mourning since the death of her brother, killed four years ago in the service of the King, and the sumptuousness of the fabrics gave a kind of ostentation to her grief.

"I have addressed myself to your father on the subject of this marriage," said the Infanta. "He gives you the choice between this arrangement and the convent."

They assumed she would choose the cloister. She astonished her companions by replying, almost in a whisper: "I have little taste for marriage, Madame, but neither do I feel ready to give myself to God."

The arrival of the caballero was announced. The Infanta rose to go into the next room. Anna de la Cerna was to follow her. M. de Wirquin, who really had an eye only for plump Flemish beauties, was nonetheless attracted by this girl whose black robes made her even paler and thinner. He was moved by Anna de la Cerna as by a battle standard.

Then, too, it was rumored that she would inherit from her father immense estates in Italy. As if he already possessed such vast riches, as distant as they were fabulous, he wrote to his mother, instructing her to refurbish their castle of Baillicour.

The Marqués de la Cerna, recently made a member of the Privy Council, encountered his daughter by chance at the Infanta's court several days after the engagement. He was manifestly in one of his moods of humility during which his rationality was impaired. He said to her: "I have forgiven you."

She realized that he had not forgiven her.

Anna's nuptial Mass was celebrated on the seventh of August, 1600, in Brussels, at the church of Sablon, in the presence of the Infanta. At the moment of the Offertory, Anna fainted, which was attributed to the heat, the great crush of the crowd, and her voluminous robes of cloth-of-silver, which smothered her. Don Alvaro, standing next to the choir during the long ceremony, maintained an imperturbable calm, which was admired even by his detractors; two Calvinists determined to assassinate him had just been apprehended, and his entourage could not restrain themselves from turning to look over their shoulders at the slightest noise.

Don Alvaro, also, was looking over his shoulder; for that day he never stopped reviewing his past. This man, who could not recall ever having loved any living creature body and soul, thought a good deal about his son now that he had taken his place among his host of ghosts. He felt he was nearly losing his mind; he had taken to falling into mysterious fits of distraction which carried him to the very frontiers of that burning but colorless, formless country in which, of all our deeds, only our remorse survives. Not daring to look Miguel's sin in the face, perhaps because he feared it might not cause him sufficient horror, he nevertheless felt a sort of envy when confronted with a passion which had swept away everything before it, even the fear of sin. Love had spared Miguel the dread of being, like his father, all alone in a universe emptied of everything that is not God. Above all, he envied him his having already been judged. Anna's marriage cut the final cord, however tenuous, which attached him to his living line; ambition was nothing more than a bait which no longer deceived him; the demands of the flesh grew quiet with age; and that sad triumph obliged him to turn to his soul. Worried but exhausted, the Marqués felt the moment had come to give himself over to that terrible great hand, which would perhaps be merciful once he had ceased to struggle.

Several months later, he participated for the last time in the deliberations of the Infanta's Privy Council. His resignation was accepted without any ado. That pained him: he had hoped that the world would argue a little more with God over him.

Egmont de Wirquin took his wife to his estate in Picardy. In the presence of this stranger who thought he possessed Anna (as though one possesses a woman so long as one is ignorant of her reasons for weeping), the Marqués felt bound to his daughter by a mute complicity, despite the resentment he continued to hold against her. Still, their farewell was without emotion; in spite of himself, Don Alvaro hated her for having survived; Anna herself regretted that she was still alive. Resigned to submit to a husband whom, at least, she had no fear of loving, she was glad that her face, her arms, and her shrunken breasts were so different from those that hands now fallen into dust had once caressed.

His concerns over war and money kept M. de Wirquin from paying much attention to her. Too disdainful of women to look for any motives in their caprices, he never even wondered at the fact that, during Holy Week, Anna spent her nights in prayer.

In Naples, on a certain evening in July, 1602, a poorly dressed man knocked at the gate of the Certosa di San Martino. A grilled judas window was cautiously opened, and the monastic porter at first refused entrance to the stranger because of the lateness of the hour. But then, surprised by a tone of command he was not accustomed to from that sort of beggar, the monk unlocked the gate and let the stranger in. On the threshold, the man turned around. It was the moment when the ruddy sun slips behind the Camaldoli. Without a word, the man stared out over the pale sea, the imposing façade of Sant'Elmo gilded by the sunset, and, beyond the battlements that blocked his view of the port, the swelling sail of a galliot leaving the roadstead. Then, with a brusque shrug of his shoulders, he pulled his hat down over his eyes and followed his guide down a long corridor. On his way through the church, which was new and richly decorated, he knelt for a long moment, but he observed that the monk never took his eyes off him, as if he feared he was dealing with a thief. Finally, they both entered the parlor attached to the sacristy. The

monk then closed the door on the stranger, turned the key
with a metallic scraping sound, and went to tell the prior.

The stranger, lost in thought as if in prayer, waited
for an indeterminate time. The same scraping sound was
heard once more, and the prior of San Martino, Don Ambrosio Caraffa, appeared. The two monks who accompanied
him stopped just inside the doorway. Each of them carried a taper. Their pale flames were reflected in the wood
paneling.

He was an obese man, quite aged, with a benevolent,
calm face. The other man took off his hat, unfastened his
cape, and knelt without speaking. As he lowered his head,
his rough, gray beard rubbed across the velvet of his jerkin.
From out of his emaciated face, which was nothing more
than a network of muscles, his eyes looked directly before
him, straight through the prior, as if he were trying not to
see this monk to whom he had come to ask for something.

"Father," he said, "I am old. Life has only death to offer
me now, and I hope it will be better than life has been. I
beg you to accept me amongst you as the humblest and
poorest of your friars."

The prior stared silently at this haughty suppliant. The
man who spoke had no jewelry, no ruff, no gold braid;
yet about his neck, whether out of negligence or some last
vanity, the Spanish Order of the Golden Fleece still hung.
Reminded by the prior's stare, the stranger reached up
and took it off.

"You are of noble lineage," said the prior.

The man answered: "I have forgot all that."

The prior shook his head. "You are wealthy."

"I have given everything away," replied the man.

At that moment, a long-drawn-out cry rose, hung suspended in the air, and then descended. It was the cry of
the sentinels, the sound of the changing of the guard at

Castel Sant'Elmo, and the prior saw the stranger shudder
to hear this unexpected echo from the world. Don Ambrosio
Caraffa had, some moments back, already recognized Don
Alvaro.

"You are the Marqués de la Cerna," he said.

Don Alvaro humbly replied: "I was."

"You are the Marqués de la Cerna," repeated the prior.
"If it were known you were in Naples, many people whose
existence you are probably unaware of would have come
to welcome you with a dagger. Ten years ago, I would
have done the same. But the blow you gave me took me
out of the world. You in turn now wish to die to the world.
Ghosts do not kill each other in this place of peace."

When Don Alvaro had got up, he added: "Don Alvaro,
here you are my guest, as you were when I used to receive
you in my arbor at La Cascatella."

And a delicate patrician smile, half lost in the folds of
fat, passed over the face of the Carthusian. Don Alvaro's
face became even sadder. The prior noticed it.

"I was wrong to call up the past," he said. "Here you
are the guest only of God."

Then Don Alvaro turned to stare at something in the
shadows. A bit of the old terror came back to him, with
its horror of the yawning abyss. But the walls of the monastery protected him from the void, and, behind them,
other walls even more solid, which the Church placed
around him. And Don Alvaro knew that the gates of hell
would not prevail against them.

Henceforth, his life was nothing but penitence.

Don Ambrosio Caraffa retained, in all Cistercian simplicity, that taste for art which had so distinguished him
in secular life. At his expense, the cloisters were rebuilt
in strict conformity with the Vitruvian order, and with a
subtle mixture of Christian piety and refined Epicurean-

ism, each pilaster bore a delicately sculpted death's-head. The prior's fat hands carefully confirmed the polish of the stone. This patrician, for whom religion was perhaps merely the crown of human wisdom, found God in the veins of beautiful marble just as he found Him in reading the *Charmides.* Without breaking the rule of silence, when some flower in his parterres seemed to him especially beautiful he managed to point it out with a smile.

Don Alvaro would think then of the underground struggle in which the roots were engaged and of that warmth of sap which makes a receptacle of lust out of each corolla. The unfinished construction work, whose appearance, as if to discourage the foreman, imitates in anticipation the ruin it will one day become, reminded him that every builder, in the end, constructs only something that will collapse. He still had an aching feeling, as if from a fever, from his tired ambitions and that astonishment produced after a loud noise by the deafening silence. The arches of the cloisters, where the noon sun, in duplicating each arcade on the opposite wall, gave every stone column a pendant in the form of a column of shadow, alternated black and white like a double file of monks. Don Ambrosio and Don Alvaro would salute each other as they passed. The one, reciting to himself the verses of a poet of Shiraz that an ambassador from the Sultan to the Papal Court had once explicated for him, would rediscover in each anemone the fresh youth of Liberio. The dry earth in which from time to time a grave was dug recalled Don Miguel to the other. Thus, each of them read differently the book of creation, which can be deciphered in two senses; and both senses are valid, since no one yet knows whether everything lives only to die or dies only to live.

From then on, the story of Anna has the monotony of a long-endured trial. M. de Wirquin had early abandoned the side of Spain to turn to France, which increased the disdain Anna felt for him. Many times their lands were ravaged by warfare; they had to safeguard as best they could their peasants, cattle, and chattels, but these common concerns did not bring them any closer together. On his side, Anna's husband did not forgive her father for having dissipated his fortune in pious foundations; the almost fabulous wealth for which he had, at least in part, entered into that match had turned out to be nothing but a mirage. Between Anna and himself, courtesy took the place of affection, an emotion which he did not in any case deem necessary in relations with a woman. At first, Anna had endured his nocturnal attentions with revulsion, but then sometimes pleasure had suffused them despite herself, but pleasure restricted to a lower, narrow part of her body and not agitating her entire being. She was subsequently grateful to him for taking mistresses who kept him away from her.

Several pregnancies, borne with resignation, left her,

above all, with the memory of prolonged nausea. She
loved her children, however, but with an animal love
which diminished as soon as they ceased to need her. Two
boys died in infancy. She especially missed the younger,
whose baby features reminded her of Miguel, but eventually this pain, too, passed. The oldest of her sons survived to become a soldier and courtier, to fight with the
creditors his father had left him, and to be killed in a duel
resulting from some obscure affair of honor. Her daughter became a nun at Douai. Several months after the death
of M. de Wirquin, one of his friends who was escorting
Anna from Arras to Paris, where her son was, took advantage of a chance overnight stop to lay siege to the still
beautiful widow; too tired to struggle, or possibly urged on
by her own flesh, Anna received him with neither more
nor less emotion than she had known in the conjugal bed.
There was no aftermath to this incident; the gallant left
for Germany to join his regiment. And, in truth, none of
that mattered. During Anna's rare visits to the Louvre,
the Queen became infatuated with this Spaniard of high
lineage, with whom she took pleasure in speaking her
native language. But the widow of Egmont de Wirquin
refused a position as her lady-in-waiting. French pomp
and Flemish luxury, under those leaden skies, were as
nothing compared to the memory of the sunlit splendors
of Naples.

With the years and the isolation and the fatigue, a sort
of stupor fell upon her. She was denied the consolation of
tears and wasted away in aridity as if in the middle of a
parched desert. At certain moments, delicate fragments of
the past inexplicably inserted themselves into the present,
without her knowing whence they had come: some gesture
of Donna Valentina's, the entwinement of a vine around
the pulley of an ancient well in the courtyard at Agropoli,

one of Don Miguel's gloves left on a table, still warm from
his hand. It seemed to her at such times as if a warm
breeze were blowing; she would almost swoon from it.
But then, for long months, she would lack air. The Office
of the Dead, recited every night for almost forty years,
suddenly lost all its meaning from having been said too
often. Sometimes the face of her beloved would appear
to her in dreams, precise to the smallest detail of the
down on his upper lip; the rest of the time he lay in her
memory as decomposed as he did in his tomb. And at
times it seemed to her that Miguel had never existed except
in her mind, at other times that she was, in some almost
sacrilegious way, forcing a dead person to go on living.
As others whip themselves to rekindle their senses, Anna
flagellated herself with her thoughts to revive her mourning, but her worn-out grief was nothing more than lassi-
tude. Her battered heart refused to bleed.

As she approached sixty, she left the estate to her son
and installed herself as a pensioner in the convent at Douai
where her daughter had taken the veil. Other ladies of the
nobility lived out the end of their lives there. Shortly after
Anna's arrival, a chamber was made ready for a certain
Madame de Borsèle, one of the mistresses for whom Egmont de Wirquin had ruined himself. What time these
ladies did not give to the Holy Offices was passed in needlework, in reading aloud letters received from their children,
in light repasts or elegant little suppers which they offered
one another. Their conversations turned on the fashions
of their youth, the respective merits of their dead husbands
or current confessors, the lovers they boasted of having
had or of not having had. But they always returned, with
a repugnant, almost grotesque insistence, to their visible
or hidden bodily ills. It almost seemed as though thus to
display their infirmities became for them a new form of
lewd indecency. A touch of deafness prevented Donna

Anna from hearing their chatter and allowed her to stay out of it. Each of them had her maid, but these girls would turn out to be negligent or else, for one reason or another, would be dismissed, and the lay sisters could not always attend adequately to the pensioners. Madame de Borsèle was obese and practically a cripple; Anna would sometimes help her comb her hair, and the former beauty would clap her hands when a mirror was lifted to her face. Or else she would whimper pitifully because someone had forgot to put her comfit dish within her reach. Anna would then get up from her chair, something she could no longer do without difficulty, find the comfit dish, and leave Madame de Borsèle to stuff her mouth with sweetmeats. Once, an aged pensioner coming back from the refectory vomited in the corridor. No servant was about at the moment, so Anna cleaned up the floor.

The nuns admired her meekness toward her old and scandalous rival, her austerity, her humility, and her patience. But none of it was meekness, austerity, humility, or patience as they understood those things. Anna was, quite simply, elsewhere.

She went back to reading the mystics: Luis de León, Juan de la Cruz, the holy Mother Teresa—the same ones read to her long ago in the sun-drenched Neapolitan afternoons by a young cavalier dressed all in black. The book lay open under the casement; Anna, sitting in the pale autumn sunlight, would let her eyes fall upon a line from time to time. She did not seek to follow the sense, but those great ardent phrases formed part of the amorous, dolorous music which had accompanied her life. Images from former times shone anew in their immutable youth, as if Donna Anna, in her imperceptible descent, had begun to reach the place where all things come together. Donna Valentina was not far away; Don Miguel shone forth in the refulgence of his twentieth year and was very near. An Anna in her twenties burned and lived, she too unchanged, within the body of this aged, worn-out woman. Time had thrown down its barriers and broken its bars. Five days and five nights of violent happiness filled with their echoes and reflections every corner of eternity.

Her death agony, however, was long and painful. She forgot her French; the chaplain, who flattered himself that he knew a few words of Spanish and a little Italian out of books, came occasionally to exhort her in one of those two languages. But the dying woman scarcely heard or understood him. The priest continued, even though she was no longer there, to present her with a crucifix. At the end, Anna's ravaged visage became slack, and she slowly closed her eyes. They heard her murmur: *"Mi amado . . ."*

They thought she was speaking to God. Perhaps she was.

POSTFACES

TRANSLATOR'S
NOTE

The first novella in the present collection, the long short story or short novel, "An Obscure Man," and the brief fantasy, "A Lovely Morning," divide into two parts a pallid novella of 1935, "After Rembrandt," which a few years earlier in its unpublished form was entitled "Nathanaël." Read and reread a number of times in 1979, this rather unfocused text, one of my first works, written when I was about twenty and scarcely revised since then, proved to be completely unusable. Not one line of it survives, yet it nonetheless contained within itself seeds which finally, after many seasons, germinated.

My first thoughts about the character of Nathanaël were practically contemporaneous with those about the character of Zeno: very early on, and with a precociousness that surprises even me, I had dreamed of two men whom I vaguely imagined against a background of the Low Countries long ago: the one avidly bent on the pursuit of knowledge, covetous of everything life had to teach if not to give him, suffused with all the cultures and philosophies of his time and rejecting them in order painfully to create his own; the other, who in a sense lets life flow over him, persisting yet at the same time apathetic to the point of passivity, virtually uneducated yet endowed with an ingenuous soul and a judicious mind which turn him away, almost instinctively, from what is false and vain, who dies young without feeling sorry for himself or being very surprised, much as he had lived.

In the early version written in my twentieth year, I had made Nathanaël the son of a carpenter, somewhat in allusion to Him who proclaimed Himself the Son of Man. That notion no longer exists in "An Obscure Man," or, if it does, only in a very diffused way and in the fairly conventional sense that every man is a Christ. From the beginning I placed Nathanaël in Holland, a country at least certain regions of which I knew very early in my life and which all of us have visited through its painters. But what was ill-defined and false in that early story was so for very simple reasons: I had chosen to make Nathanaël a workingman without knowing anything about the life of a workingman either in my own time or in times past. I was almost completely ignorant of urban misery; I was too inexperienced in the big compromises and little daily defeats of every person's existence. As has remained the case in the present story, I imagined that Nathanaël, already stricken with a pulmonary illness, finds some sedentary work in an Amsterdam bookseller's, but I hadn't taken the trouble to figure out where the knowledge necessary to a proofreader might have come from. As is still the case today, I caused him to marry a Jewess from a tavern, but that earlier portrait of a prostitute sketched out by a girl who scarcely knew anything about women was at best a *profil perdu*: the element of uniqueness which distinguishes every living creature and which love immediately discloses to the eyes of the lover was lacking in her. At the end, after a long, dreary walk through the streets of Amsterdam, Nathanaël, exhausted, died of a convenient pleurisy in a hospital, without one's sufficiently sensing either the anguish or the disintegration of the body. All that was painted gray on gray, as it often is with a life seen from without and never is with a life seen from within.

And yet this character continued to live in some shadowy corner of my being. In 1957, while living on l'Île des Monts-Déserts (I prefer to use this name, which Champlain put on his map, rather than the more recent one, Mount Desert Island), I accepted, as I often did in those days, the offer of a short lecture tour—an easy way to deduct some of the expenses of a trip. The tour was to take me to three Canadian cities, Quebec, Montreal, and Ottawa, and my audience would be drawn from universities and French clubs. At that time, the easiest way for me was to go to a railway station some distance from my village in Maine and board the only New York-to-Montreal train which still carried passengers. It was already the period when trains were joining dinosaurs in the attics of time, while waiting for automobiles to join them sooner or later in turn: the railways of Maine were maintained only for cargoes of tree trunks destined to become pulp paper. That particular train, equipped with only one Pullman car, stopped at that station at 2 a.m.; it still does. At around ten in the evening, the last bus deposited me and Grace Frick, who was traveling with me, at an empty, locked station: the waiting room didn't open until 1:45. We took refuge in the local tavern. The place, a sort of roadhouse, was boiling hot and filled with smoke. While Grace made do with a table and a book, which she read by the light of a weak bulb, I requested a bedroom for those few hours. I was given one on the second floor. Narrow, bare, decorated with garish wallpaper, the little room had only a bed and one chair and was obviously intended for traveling salesmen stuck in this area for some reason.

The cold and my neuralgia kept me from sleeping; but for two hours an extraordinary thing happened: I saw pass before my eyes, suddenly issuing out of nowhere in rapid acceleration like the frames of a film, episodes in the life of Nathanaël, whom I hadn't even thought of for twenty years.

I exaggerate somewhat, for there is one exception: two or three years earlier I had read a biography of Samuel Pepys, that Englishman who had a passion for chamber music, for a well-ordered domestic life, and for brief sexual liaisons. He was not only, as had long been known, an astute chronicler of London in the seventeenth century, not only, as had been known since the suppressed parts of his journal had been published, a precursor in the matter of complete sexual candor, but also—on working days, so to speak—a highly successful Secretary of the Admiralty. In reading that biography, I learned that in his day Dutch carpenters worked in the British arsenals. That fact reminded me of my young workingman from Amsterdam, and I told myself that that sort of beginning would fit well into his life. Had these thoughts silently left in me some humus of images or directed toward me the flotsam of adventures? Whatever the case, for two hours, in the reflections of an arc lamp on the wall of my room, I saw a sixteen-year-old Nathanaël whom I did not yet know pass before my eyes. He had a weak leg and had been placed as an apprentice with a schoolmaster since the scaffolding and labor of the dry dock were not for him. Forced to flee after a brawl, he hid in the hold of a three-master leaving for the Antilles; I followed his wanderings from Jamaica to Barbados, and from there northward aboard a British privateer which was patrolling the coasts of Maine, which had only recently been opened to European greed; I imagined him involved in a true episode, which is in fact the only "historical" part of my story, the attack by this English pirate ship on a group of French Jesuits newly disembarked on l'Île des Monts-Déserts, which at that time truly deserved its name. That encounter took place in 1621; my novella, intentionally quite vague about dates (Nathanaël does without them), displaces it by several years. A little later, and a little farther away, I saw him stranded on the "Île Perdue" (which can be located wherever one wishes, without too much precision, in the far north of Maine or on the present Canadian border between Great Wass Island and Campobello), then returning to Europe, I didn't quite know how yet, and, thanks to the little learning he had previously acquired at the schoolmaster's, finding a job as proofreader with an avaricious uncle who was a bookseller in Amsterdam and who had already figured in the earlier version.

He still married a young Jewess named Saraï, but now she was as much a thief as a prostitute. The dreary walk in the snow still took place, but Nathanaël died less quickly. Released from the hospital, he became a footman who came somewhat into contact with the world of the rich, of elegance, and of the arts, which he judged as a man who had known the obverse of these things. It appeared that he then went to die on one of the islands off the Frisian coast, I didn't at that time really know which nor in what circumstances. At that moment, they came to tell me the train was arriving.

The series of good, bad, or indifferent lectures, then a serious illness which kept me almost three weeks in Montreal, other work, and finally a number of difficult years caused me to abandon completely the idea of setting down my visions from that one night in a remote village of Maine. I told myself, as I often have in similar situations, that if anything in them was really important it would reappear. I wrote *L'Oeuvre au noir* (in English, *The Abyss*), *Souvenirs pieux*, *Archives du Nord*, some essays, several translations; but Nathanaël himself retreated into his obscure corner. He finally emerged from it in 1980, a quarter century later.

The present text of "An Obscure Man" dates completely from those years 1979 to 1981—for me so full of events, changes, and voyages. To the images I had seen go by twenty-two years before, others quickly added themselves, born out of those earlier ones. With every book which has arrived at the point where it has only to be written down, such a moment of proliferation always occurs. New characters encountered by accident in the byways of some episode, scenes hidden behind others like stage flats: young Foy, her aged parents, her little idiot brother; Mevrouw Loubah and her rather questionable, rather disreputable house; the dissipated Hellenist who is always broke; the burgomaster van Herzog's housekeeper with the face of Doom, who leads Nathanaël by anfractuous routes to the island where he ends his days; the denizens of the workshop and those of the paneled salons; the story of the dog rescued from the jaws of the tiger, which I found while going through notes on old gazettes of the eighteenth century; the dull sound of waves building and rebuilding the dunes, the flapping of thousands of wings which I had recently gone to hear once more on one of the Frisian Islands; the pocket of sandy moorland largely sheltered from the wind where I lay down under the arbutuses looking for the place where Nathanaël might die as comfortably as possible. Every literary work is fashioned thus out of a mixture of vision, memory, and act, of ideas and information received in the course of a lifetime from conversations or books, and the shavings of our own existence.

The main difficulty of "An Obscure Man" was to present an almost uneducated individual silently formulating his thoughts about the world around him and, at certain very rare moments, attempting, with omissions and hesitations analogous to the stutterings of a stammerer, to communicate to someone else at least a portion of them. Nathanaël is one of those people who think almost without the mediation of words. That is to say, he is practically devoid of that vocabulary which is both customary and exhausted, as worn down as overused coins, with which we exchange what we take to be ideas, what we think we believe and what we believe we think. Yet in order to write this story it was necessary to transcribe his almost formless meditation. I'm not unaware that I cheated by giving Nathanaël his little learning acquired from the village schoolmaster, thus providing him with the opportunity not only of getting an ill-paid job with his uncle, Elie Adriansen, but also of connecting and assimilating certain notions and concepts: those few bits of Latin, ancient history, and geography serve as buoys for him, despite himself, in the world of ebb and flow which is his. He is not as completely ignorant nor as unencumbered as I should have wished. Yet he nevertheless remains as independent as possible of all inculcated opinion, a virtual autodidact who is not in the least simple yet is unburdened in the extreme, instinctively wary of what the books he leafs through, the music he happens to hear, and the paintings on which his eye occasionally falls add to the nakedness of things, indifferent to the important events in the newspapers, unprejudiced about whatever touches on the life of the senses but equally lacking the excitement or the factitious obsessions which result from constraint or from an acquired eroticism, taking science and philosophy for what they are and especially for what the scientists and philosophers he meets are, and looking at the world about him with an eye as unclouded as it is incapable of pride. There is nothing more to say about Nathanaël.

A LOVELY MORNING

"A Lovely Morning" takes as its point of departure the final episode of the early novella I had entitled "Nathanaël." I had conferred a son, real or supposed, on my protagonist, given him by Saraï; the child, brought up by his mother in the alleyways of the Jewish quarter, took a job when he was about thirteen with a company of English players on tour. Similar companies at that time made such tours to the princely houses of Germany or of the Scandinavian countries, whose lords had frequented the court at Whitehall or married English princesses eager for the latest novelties from London. At the last minute, the company was obliged to replace a young leading lady, who, as we know, was always a little boy or an adolescent lad dressed as a girl.

In the first draft, made when I was twenty, I hadn't bothered to ask myself how this boy from the streets of Amsterdam knew enough English to appear in a play by Ford or by Shakespeare: I am persuaded that the criticism someone made of that lapse, quite as much as my own desire to paint a larger canvas, was the motivation, at the time I rewrote "An Obscure Man," for the account of Nathanaël's early years in Greenwich, on the one hand, and, on the other, for the allusions to Saraï's success in the brothels of London; from that point on, the Dutch decor had an English backdrop. Nor did the character of the old actor from London staying at Mevrouw Loubah's and giving the boy some lessons in elocution figure in the earlier text.

Other details were, naturally, omitted, added, or changed, until not one line remains either from the earli-

est sketch or from those revised pages concerning the boy
in the version of 1935. The essential point, in the present
story, is that little Lazarus, sufficiently acquainted with a
few Elizabethan or Jacobean dramas which were already
out-of-date but which he knew from the torn quartos of
the old actor, lives in anticipation not only his own life
but the life of every man: successively girl and boy, youth
and old man, murdered child and murderous villain, king
and beggar, the prince garbed in black and his fool in
motley. Everything which is worth being lived out is already experienced at the moment when he glides through
a rainy dawn, along with the rest of the actors dressed up,
like him, in their stage finery, under the canvas cover of
a cariole which is taking them to the gardens of Monsieur
de Bréderode to play *As You Like It.* Just as he did in the
early version, the actor charged with the role of Death in
a reprise of a medieval farce takes the reins, his white
sheet impervious to any rainstorm. This detail, taken from
a similar episode in Cervantes, provided the title for this
collection as it stood in 1935: *Death Drives the Cart.* Endowed with a symbolism I could hardly resist putting
there, it seems to me today too oversimplified to serve as
a title. Death does drive the cart, but so, too, does life.

Cintra
2–5 March 1981
Paris
29 October 1981

"Anna, soror . . ." is an early work, but one of those
which continue to remain important and precious to its
author. These hundred or so pages originally were part of
a vast, shapeless novel, *Crosscurrents* (of which I have
spoken elsewhere), which was sketched out between my

eighteenth and twenty-third year and which contained the seeds of a good part of my later production.

After I had abandoned this "grand design," which would have resulted in more of a *roman-océan* than a *roman-fleuve*, the fortuities of life dictated quite another work to me—*Alexis*, whose chief merit was probably its extreme brevity. But a few years later, having taken up a "literary career," as it were, it occurred to me to rescue at least some parts of that earlier, abandoned work. Thus it was that the story called "Anna, soror . . ." appeared in 1935 in the collection of three novellas entitled *Death Drives the Cart* (an episode from one of the rescued fragments provided the title). To give them at least the appearance of some unity, I chose to call them respectively "After Dürer," "After El Greco," and "After Rembrandt," without realizing that these titles were inevitably bound to smell of the museum and ran the risk of interposing themselves between the reader and these often clumsy but spontaneous and almost obsessive earlier texts.

The original French title* of the present collection, *Comme l'eau qui coule*, is somewhat similar to *Crosscurrents (Remous)* but substitutes for an image of the surges and undertows of the ocean that of the sometimes muddy, sometimes clear, stream or rushing river which is life. (After considering several dozen possible and more or less literal translations of my original title, all of which ultimately dissatisfied me, I have decided to substitute the present English title.) "After Dürer," which was com-

---

* These three stories were first published together in 1982 under the title *Comme l'eau qui coule* (Gallimard, collection Blanche), and the same title is used in the Bibliothèque de la Pléiade volume, *Oeuvres romanesques*, of the same year. Now, however, Gallimard publishes these three stories in two separate volumes: *Anna, soror . . .* (1981) and *Un homme obscur, Une belle matinée* (1985). [W.K.]

pletely absorbed into *The Abyss*, is obviously no longer
present; "After Rembrandt," quite unworthy of that noble
patronage in its present form, has been divided into the two
novellas of which I have spoken already. As for "Anna,
soror . . . ," the reference to El Greco was meant merely
as an allusion to the nervous, agitated style of that great
artist; yet its Neapolitan ambience and its sensuous passion make me think today rather of Caravaggio—should
one still feel obliged to assign to this violent story the name
of a painter. The present title is taken from the two pre-
dominant words of the epitaph carved on Miguel's tomb
at Anna's command, and they say everything that matters.

In contrast to the two novellas which precede it, "Anna,
soror . . ." reproduces almost integrally the text of 1935,
which is in turn virtually identical to the story written in
1925 by a young woman of twenty-one. Nevertheless, a
number of purely stylistic changes, and perhaps a dozen
more substantial ones, have been made for the republica-
tion of this story now. I shall discuss several of them later
on. But if I insist on the fact that these pages are really
essentially unchanged, it is because I perceive in that fact
one additional indication, among a good deal of other
evidence which has presented itself to me bit by bit, of the
relativity of time. I feel as completely at home with this
story as if the idea for it had come to me this morning.

Its subject is the love between brother and sister*—that

* The story of the incest committed by Amnon and Thamar, which
so obsesses Miguel, will be found by readers of Protestant Bibles in
English at II Samuel 13, even though the text of *Anna, soror . . .*
refers to the Book of Kings. In the Septuagint, what English Bibles
call I & II Samuel and I & II Kings were all called Books of Kings,
and this formula was followed by St. Jerome in his translation of the
Vulgate Bible. However, in a Hebrew Bible published in Venice in
1516, the Jewish printer introduced the title of Samuel for the first
two books, and this nomenclature has been followed by Protestant
English translators from the time of the Geneva Bible (1560). [W.K.]

is, that form of sin which has most often inspired poets who have attempted to deal with a *voluntary* act of incest.* In attempting to take account of at least some of the Western, Christian authors who have treated this subject, I first came upon the extraordinary *'Tis Pity She's a Whore*† by the great Jacobean dramatist John Ford. This frenzied play, in which human baseness, atrocity, and folly serve as a foil to two incestuous people with pure hearts, contains one of the most beautiful love scenes in all theater, that where Giovanni and Annabella, about to surrender to their passion, kneel before each other. "You are my brother, Giovanni. —And you my sister, Annabella."

From that work, we may proceed directly to Byron's fuliginous *Manfred*. That rather confused play, whose hero bears the name of an excommunicated German prince of the Middle Ages, takes place in an indeterminate alpine landscape: it was, in fact, in Switzerland that Byron composed this text which simultaneously veils and unveils his scandalous affair with his half sister Augusta—an affair which had just caused the gates of England to be definitively closed behind him. This Romantic reprobate is haunted by the ghost of his sister Astarte, whose death he

---

* Incest between father and daughter or mother and son is rarely depicted as *voluntary*, at least on both sides. Completely unconscious in *Oedipus Tyrannus*, it is conscious only for one of the partners in the story Ovid tells of Myrrha, where the daughter gives herself in disguise. It appears that the notion of an abuse of authority, or of physical or moral coercion, counts for a great deal in what offends people in this version of the subject.

† One should be on one's guard, however: the word *whore* in the sixteenth century signified not only a prostitute but any woman accused of a carnal sin. *'Tis Pity She's a Sinner* would perhaps be a more accurate title, but it would lack the necessary vernacular tone. When Maeterlinck translated this play, he made do with the name of one of the characters for a title: *Annabella*.

has brought about, but the author leaves us almost completely in the dark about the causes of that mysterious disaster. Curiously, it would appear that the name Astarte, unusual in this medieval Swiss setting, was taken from Montesquieu's story in the *Lettres persanes*, "Histoire d'Aphéridon et d'Astarté," an affecting narrative which at first glance seems incongruous in that web of mordant satires spiced with Levantine exoticism, complete with blood and rahat lakoum. Aphéridon and Astarté, a young Parsi couple whose religion permits such unions, die of persecution in a Moslem milieu where incest is an abomination. With this touching, somewhat extraneous chapter, Montesquieu seems to display, as he does elsewhere with his tone of raillery, an anti-dogmatism regarding morals approved of in one place and disapproved of in another— an anti-dogmatism which Montaigne, Pascal, and Voltaire, each in his own way, had endorsed or would presently. One can hardly speak of these two young Parsis, who live and die within the limits of their own laws, as being in revolt: it is their author who causes us to feel that innocence and crime are relative concepts. With Ford, on the contrary, it was Giovanni himself who insolently attacked the proscriptions which forbade incest, and with Byron it was Manfred who, charged with a crime which in fact remains unspecified, derives his Luciferian pride from being a transgressor.

Finally, the French reader cannot forget *René*, in which Chateaubriand, unquestionably thinking of his sister Lucile, takes as his central *donnée* Amélie's incestuous love and her retreat into a nunnery. Goethe also, in *Wilhelm Meister*, romantically employs the theme of incest.

Much more recently, the very beautiful novella of Thomas Mann, *Wälsungenblut*, depends on two themes that occur frequently in all depictions of fraternal incest:

one is the perfect harmony between two beings united by a kind of birthright; the other is the almost vertiginous lure of defying custom.* A young Jewish brother and sister of singular beauty and refinement, from a wealthy family in pre-1935 Berlin, make love while intoxicated by Wagner's opera depicting the incestuous love affair of Siegmund and Sieglinde. The Jewish Sieglinde is engaged to a Protestant Prussian officer, and her brother-lover's first words after they have had intercourse are, cynically, "He ought to be grateful to us." The pleasure in flouting beforehand a marriage that the family considers a *social* advancement; the intellectual pride of the transgressor. We are back, under the guise of an ironic gibe, at Ford's Giovanni arrogantly announcing to the priest who is his tutor that he has decided to commit incest and, later, snatching his sister, by means of death, away from a deceived and hated husband.†

---

* If the importance a theme has for an author can be judged by the frequency with which it is employed, one may perhaps speak of an obsession with incest in Byron and Mann. Byron's *The Bride of Abydos* is a pallid work in which everything is resolved by means of the discovery of a mistaken kinship; *Cain*, whose subject is the union of the sons and daughters of Adam, contains stronger allusions to the same subject. As for Mann, the novel of his old age, *Der Erwählte*, which contains one of the most daring scenes of fraternal incest (its eroticism is veiled for the German reader by the fact that the lovers speak in Old French), is complicated by the introduction of an Oedipal union with the mother. Fairly numerous allusions to the subject are found elsewhere in Mann. Finally, one ought to analyze, as a story of the same type, the extraordinary anonymous novel which appeared in England in 1956, *Madame Solario*, which, although a best-seller, has never been closely studied. However, the extreme complexity of the psychological themes which are interwoven in this story makes it difficult to isolate that of incest.

† The date of Ford's play is highly uncertain; scholars have argued for various dates from 1615 to 1633. It seems very probable, however, that it was inspired, at least in part, by a tragic French *cause célèbre*,

Beyond these masterpieces, I can scarcely find anything
other than Roger Martin du Gard's *Confidence africaine*,
itself a masterpiece, but with which we move from poetry
to sociological insight. It is their nocturnal proximity and
the necessity of sharing a bed lamp in order to read which
throw this North African boy and girl into each other's
arms, and their sensual turmoil ends when the sister es-
pouses, as planned, a neighborhood bookseller, and the
brother, having departed for his regiment, begins to make
love to other girls. Later, we see the former beloved, worn
out and disgruntled, taking care of a tubercular son who
is the wretched result of this passionate episode. Gide
rightly reproached Martin du Gard for this facilely conventional ending: however detrimental habitual and exclusively consanguineous unions may *ultimately* be, they
can also (and no breeder is unaware of it) concentrate in
their offspring the best qualities of their line: they do not
necessarily produce infirmities or illness immediately.
Martin du Gard protected his story with a moralizing
conclusion. But Gide is no more in the right when he

---

the execution of an incestuous brother and sister, Julien and Marguerite de Ravalet, in 1603. Ford appears to have used one of the
contemporary French tales based on this episode, that of François de
Rosset entitled "Des Amours Incestueuses d'vn Frère et d'vne Soeur,"
published in his *Les Histoires Tragiques de Nostre Temps* (Paris,
1615). Ford's play is set, as was customary, in a stage Italy, but the
forced marriage with an older man who is deceived and detested, the
rage of the jealous husband, who beats his wife and drags her on the
ground by her long hair to make her confess the name of her lover,
the presence of a pious ecclesiastic who is the tutor (and, in the French
version, the uncle) of the young man are found in both works. Elizabethan playwrights rarely invented their romantic subjects but took
them either from Italian *novelle* or from contemporary incidents. It
would be a moving fact if *'Tis Pity She's a Whore*, like Chapman's
Bussy d'Amboise, were connected with an authentic French incident,
even if through the medium of a cheap French novelette of the time.

adopts, with a perhaps excessive enthusiasm, the mythic approach which endows the child of incest with prodigious qualities, as in the case of Siegfried, the son of that Sieg-mund and Sieglinde whose story had served as a model for the lovers of *Wälsungenblut*.*

Except for *Confidence africaine*, whose tacit intention seems to be to show how banal those situations thought to be unusual and rigorously forbidden really are, two themes are therefore dominant in these depictions of incest: the union of two exceptional people joined by blood, isolated by the very fact of their special qualities, and the bewil-derment of the spirit and the senses in breaking the law. The first theme is encountered in "Anna, soror . . . ," where two children live in a comparative isolation which becomes total after the death of their mother; the second is absent. No spiritual revolt touches his brother and sister, who are suffused to their very marrow with the rather rapturous piety of the Counter-Reformation. Their love grows amidst grief-stricken Pietàs, Marys-of-the-Seven-Sorrows, saints "chanting through the mouths of their wounds," in the depths of dark, gilded churches which constitute for them the domestic decor of their childhood and a supreme asylum. Their passion is too powerful not to be acted upon, yet, despite the long inner conflict which precedes their fall, is immediately felt to be an ineffable happiness, so that no remorse penetrates them. Miguel alone recognizes that such joy is possible only on condi-tion that its price be paid. His practically voluntary death aboard one of the King's galleys becomes the ransom, deter-mined in advance, which permits him to experience, while

* For this debate, see the *Correspondance d'André Gide et de Roger Martin du Gard*, vol. 1 (1913–34), letters 316–18, 322, 327–31, 341— and the *Annexe* to letter 329—from 31 January to 14 July 1931 (Gal-limard, 1968).

attending Mass on Easter Monday, an exaltation stripped of repentance. Nor is it remorse which will cause Anna anguish for the rest of her life, but rather her inconsolable grief. Even in old age, she continues without difficulty to harmonize her unrepentant love for Miguel and her belief in God.

The portrait of Valentina is painted in other colors. This woman, bathed in a mysticism that is more Platonic than Christian, has an influence on her passionate children she is unaware of; she lets something of her own peace flow into their tempest. In what I pretentiously allow myself to call my *oeuvre*, this serene Valentina seems to me an initial sketch of the perfect woman I have often dreamed of—at once loving and detached, passive out of wisdom rather than out of weakness—and whom I later endeavored to portray in the Monique of *Alexis*, in the Plotina of *Memoirs of Hadrian*, and, seen from a greater distance, in that Lady of Frösö who, in *The Abyss*, bestows a week of safe haven on Zeno. If I take the trouble to list them here, that is because, in a number of books in which I have sometimes been reproached for neglecting women, I have put into these women a good part of my ideal of humanity.

It would appear (and I use this formula of uncertainty because I believe that the motivations of his characters should often remain unclear to the author himself: their liberty is at that price) that from the beginning Valentina perceives the love her two children have for each other without doing anything to extinguish it, knowing it is inextinguishable. "Whatever happens, never come to hate each other." Her final admonition warns them against the mortal sin of passion pushed to its extreme, where it so quickly turns back on itself and transforms itself into hatred, bitterness, or (what is worse) annoyed indifference. The happiness they achieve and the sorrow they accept save them from that disaster: Miguel escapes by means of his premature death, Anna by means of her enduring constancy. Society's idea of the forbidden and Christianity's idea of sin both melt away in this flame which burns all her life.

"Anna, soror . . ." was written in several weeks in the spring of 1925, during a visit to Naples and immediately upon the return from that visit: that perhaps explains why the love affair of the brother and sister takes place and reaches its climax during Holy Week. Even more than by the antiquities in its museum or the frescoes of the Villa of the Mysteries at Pompeii (which it has been my fate to love from one end of my life to the other), I was spellbound in Naples by the grinding poverty and liveliness of the popular quarters, and by the austere beauty or faded splendor of the churches, some of which have since been badly damaged or completely destroyed by the bombings of 1944—like the little church of San Giovanni a Mare, where I depict Anna opening the coffin of Miguel. I visited Castel Sant'Elmo, where I cause my characters to live, and the Certosa next door, where I imagine Don Alvaro finishing his life. I had passed through a few of the small, desolate villages of the Basilicata, in one of which I situated the semi-seigneurial, semi-rustic building where Valentina and her children come for the grape harvest; and the ruins seen by Miguel as if in a dream are unquestionably those of Paestum. Never was a novel's creation more directly inspired by the locales in which it is placed.

With "Anna, soror . . ." I tasted for the first time the ultimate privilege of the novelist, that of losing himself completely in his characters, or of letting himself be possessed by them. Throughout those few weeks, even while continuing to make the habitual gestures and to carry on the habitual relationships of existence, I lived uninterruptedly within those two bodies and those two souls, slipping from Anna into Miguel and from Miguel into Anna with that indifference to sex which is, I believe, that of all creators in the presence of their creations,* and which silences with shame those who express astonishment that a man could excel in depicting a woman's emotions—the Juliet of Shakespeare, the Roxane or Phèdre of Racine, the Natasha or Anna Karenina of Tolstoy (indeed, through prolonged acceptance of the fact, the reading public isn't even surprised by it anymore)—or the rarer paradox that a woman could create a man in all his essential masculinity, whether the Genji of Lady Murasaki, the Rochester of *Jane Eyre*, or the Gösta Berling of Selma Lagerlöf. Such involvement also erases other differences. I was twenty-one, precisely the age at which Anna has her passionate affair, yet I entered into a worn-out, aged Anna or into a declining Don Alvaro without the slightest difficulty. At that time my sexual experience remained fairly limited; that of real passion lay just around the corner; but nonetheless the love of Anna and Miguel burned within me. Such a phenomenon is no doubt very simple: everything has already been lived and relived a thousand times by those who have disappeared but whom we carry in the very fibers of our being, just as we also carry in us the thousands of beings who will one day live after us. The only question which incessantly poses itself is why, of all these innumerable particles floating in each of us, cer-

---

* One might cite here the experience Flaubert recounts to Louise Colet in a letter written at the time of the composition of *Madame Bovary*: "Today, for example, both a man and a woman, a lover and a mistress at the same time, I rode on horseback through a forest beneath the yellow leaves of an autumn afternoon, and I was the horses, the leaves, the wind, the words they spoke, and the red sun which closed their eyelids brimming with love." (*Correspondance de Gustave Flaubert*, letter to Louise Colet of 23 December 1853, Bibliothèque de la Pléiade, vol. II, p. 483.)

tain ones come to the surface rather than others. Freer then from emotions and personal cares, perhaps I was readier than I am today to let myself dissolve completely into those characters I was inventing or thought I was inventing.

On the other hand, having early on ceased all religious observance and retaining merely the imprint (certainly a very strong imprint) of the legends, the ceremonies, and the imagery of Catholicism, it was easy for me to assume the religious fervor of these two children of the Counter-Reformation. As a little girl, I had kissed the feet of painted plaster Christs in village churches; and it mattered little that they were not like the splendid terra-cotta cadaver of the church of Monteoliveto before which Anna prostrates herself. The scene where the brother and sister, just about to consummate their union, look out from their balcony in Castel Sant'Elmo at the sky "aglow with wounds" on the night of Good Friday shows (even if some people consider it sacrilegious) to what extent Christian emotions persisted within me—even though I was at that time, out of an inevitable recoil from an ambience whose insufficiencies and weaknesses are only too apparent, in full reaction against Christian dogmas and interdicts.

But why this choice of incest for a theme? To begin with, let us brush aside the hypotheses of those simple-minded people who always imagine that every work comes out of some personal experience. I have recounted elsewhere how the circumstances of life gave me only a half brother, nineteen years older than I, whose presence, sometimes peevish, sometimes morose, but luckily only intermittent, was an unpleasant part of my childhood. In any case, by the time I was writing "Anna, soror . . ." I had not seen this rather unlikable brother for some dozen years. Nevertheless, I do not deny, if only out of simple courtesy to the hypothesizers, that imaginary situations which are in some way the opposite of real situations can occur in a novelist's mind: in my case, however, the precise opposite would not have been a young incestuous brother but a friendly older brother.

Yet, despite that, the fact that Anna's brother is named Miguel, and that from generation to generation the oldest sons in my family were called Michel, tends to prove that I couldn't imagine the hero of this story with anything but the name that all the sisters on my father's side called their brothers. But it's also possible that these two syllables seemed suitable to me for their easily recognizable Spanish sound, lacking the excessive Hispanicism of names like Guzmán, Alvar, or Alonzo or the seductive odor that always surrounds the name of Juan. One must never build too much on that type of explanation.

Myth, legend, the dark byways of dreams, sociological statistics, and various facts prove that incest exists as an omnipresent potentiality in human emotions, attractive to some, revolting to others. Perhaps one could even say that for poets it quickly became the symbol of all sexual passions, which become more violent the more they are restrained, punished, and concealed. The fact is, belonging to two enemy clans, as Romeo and Juliet do, is rarely felt to be an obstacle in our culture; in addition, the commonplace of adultery has lost much of its glamour as the result of the ease of divorce; the love between two people of the same sex has at least partly emerged from secrecy. Only incest remains inadmissible and practically impossible to prove even when we strongly suspect it. It is against the steepest cliffs that the wave breaks with the greatest crash.

I should like to say a bit more about the few corrections that have been made in this text, if only to answer in advance those who suppose I pass my time obsessively redoing or changing everything, or else to forestall the opinion which would consider "Anna, soror . . ." merely a youthful work published as it was. The changes made in 1935 to the text of 1925 were grammatical, syntactical, or stylistic. The initial "Anna" still dated from a period when, struggling with a huge fresco doomed to remain unfinished, I wrote rapidly without any attention to composition or style, drawing directly from whatever springs were within me. It was only later, after *Alexis*, that I set myself to study the strict discipline of French narrative; it was even later, around 1932, that I devoted myself to exploring the possibilities of embedding poetic techniques in prose—and sometimes contorting them. The text of 1935 bears the marks of these various methods: as if by putting them in a vise, I had tightened up certain sentences so much that they ran the risk of exploding; here and there, a clumsy attempt at stylization stiffened the attitudes of the characters. Virtually all my corrections in 1980 consisted in loosening up certain passages. In the earlier text, a prologue of several pages showed Anna in Flanders, grief-stricken at twenty-five, married by an order from on high to a Frenchman in the service of Spain. This burdensome prologue was appropriate to *Crosscurrents*, which was situated, insofar as it was situated anywhere, in the Low Countries. Here the passage, considerably shortened, has been relocated to its proper chronological place, preceding Anna's late maturity and old age. The scene or two in which the snake girl encountered by Miguel in the desolate countryside near Agropoli figures have been more retouched and pruned than others; as I reread them from the distance of some years, these too evidently oneiric episodes seemed to me to have something of the affectation of those dream scenes in early tragedies. I've kept only those appearances of the snake girl which were necessary to underscore the feverish state of Miguel. At the same time, a few brief additions reveal my attempt to achieve a *local* reality—that is, one strictly tied to a place and a time, which is the sole reality that seems to me completely authentic. I learned about the violent acts and the debauches of monks in some of the monasteries of southern Italy only much later, at the time when, for *The Abyss*, I was studying such cases of masked or overt rebellion in monasteries at the end of the sixteenth century; here they serve to indicate more fully the wildness of the place where Valentina dies and where the two children begin to be fearfully aware of their love for each other.

Finally, two very brief additions should be mentioned, because they reveal a modification in the author's conception of life. In the earlier story of 1925, which was published only ten years later, the feverish exaltation of Don Miguel once the incest has been committed was immediately followed by his embarkation with no hope or intention of returning; now, a calm which immobilizes the galley allows him to return to Castel Sant'Elmo and gives the lovers two more days and nights. It is not in order to prolong their tragic happiness for a few moments that I have given them this additional time but rather in order to remove from the story what may have been too contrived, allowing them this drifting which life possesses to its very end. That which was felt by Miguel and Anna to be a final separation turns out not to be one after all, since they are unexpectedly given a two-day reprieve. The silk scarf which Miguel ties to the shutters of Anna's room to warn them when the wind rises is the symbol of this fluctuation. Since their first, solemn farewell was only a delusion, it is possible that their second will be too.

In the same way, the account of the long years spent by Anna with a husband she did not choose, followed by the widow's mourning which conceals her true mourning, has been slightly altered. I wanted to present a husband and wife who did not love each other yet had no reason to hate each other, bound to one another despite everything by the daily concerns of life and even to a certain extent by their physical relations, whether it was because a faithful, proud lover acceded to them with shame or (and the one does not exclude the other) because her sensual desires overcame her, giving her the brief and deceptive pleasure of knowing once again, if only for a second, the sensation of being desired. I have added a passage in which Anna, now widowed, lets herself be possessed one night during a journey by a virtually unknown man she quickly forgets; but this brief, almost passive, carnal episode only further emphasizes, in my eyes, her immutably faithful heart. That incident is intended to be a reminder of how strange each existence is, where everything floats past like an ever-flowing stream and only those things which matter, instead of sinking to the depths, rise to the surface and finally reach, together with us, the sea.

Taroudant, Morocco
5–11 March 1981

It is an honor to acknowledge once again my deep obligation to Madame Yourcenar for her generous collaboration and encouragement. With unfailing patience and sensitivity, she has gone over several versions of this translation, saving me from occasional schoolboy errors and helping me to make the English a little less distant than it otherwise would have been from the subtle artistry and contrasting prose styles of her original French. An accomplished translator herself, she is the ideal collaborator; she is also among the most faithful and understanding of friends.

This translation was undertaken purely as an act of homage and affection; yet from the very outset it somehow became, unforeseeably, an affecting personal experience as well. For example, the world of Naples and the Basilicata in which Anna and Miguel act out their destiny is a world with which I once had, a quarter century ago, a close relationship, and my undiminished memory of its landscape, of its splendors and miseries, and of its idiosyncratic palimpsest of history and passion often assailed me with Proustian reverberations as I attempted to render the baroque intensity of that tale. So also, the world of the Shakespearean theater into which the young boy Lazarus is drawn happens to constitute one of the literary subjects that have dominated my professional work at Harvard in recent years. Both of these stories existed in early versions long before I knew their author; but by the time the life of Nathanaël was being written, its chronicler had already become an esteemed friend, and she and I would sometimes discuss aspects of his character and personality as they were being developed; later, on a visit to the Rijksmuseum one October morning in 1983, it seemed to us as if we had come upon the man himself in a recently acquired, very early (*c.* 1629) Rembrandt self-portrait. Such factors, and others too personal to record here, gradually transformed this undertaking from a labor of love into a gift of grace.

At my request, two other friends, Sheila La Farge and Jess Taylor, kindly read and annotated a first draft of this translation. Their incisive, helpful suggestions have been gratefully, if silently, incorporated, and I should like to register here my loving thanks to them both. Jane Bobko, most astute and vigilant of editors, has also made significant contributions to the text of this translation, for which both Madame Yourcenar and I are greatly appreciative. The continuing debt I have to Walter Hughes was substantially augmented during the composition of this English version, and I thank him for his patient fidelity. But, most of all, I am grateful to Davey and Miranda for their good-humored tolerance of the professor's absent-mindedness whenever he rode off into lexical mists on his quest for that elusive quarry, the *verbum ipsissimum.*

Finally, Daniel and Prudence Steiner have, for decades now, unceasingly sustained my endeavors, shared my joys and sorrows, and enriched my life: the inexhaustible bounty of their devoted friendship has itself been *comme l'eau qui coule*. This translation is dedicated to them, with enduring love and gratitude, on the twenty-fifth anniversary of their marriage.

W.K.

Cambridge, Massachusetts
12 June 1985